More Than Anything

A Magnolia Beach Novel

Kimberly Lang

BERKLEY SENSATION
New York

BERKLEY SENSATION
Published by Berkley
An imprint of Penguin Random House LLC
375 Hudson Street, New York, New York 10014

Copyright © 2016 by Kimberly Kerr
Penguin Random House supports copyright. Copyright fuels creativity, encourages
diverse voices, promotes free speech, and creates a vibrant culture. Thank you for buying
an authorized edition of this book and for complying with copyright laws by not
reproducing, scanning, or distributing any part of it in any form without permission.
You are supporting writers and allowing Penguin Random House to continue to
publish books for every reader.

BERKLEY and BERKLEY SENSATION are registered trademarks and the B colophon
is a trademark of Penguin Random House LLC.

ISBN: 9780451471055

First edition: December 2016

Printed in the United States of America
1   3   5   7   9   10   8   6   4   2

Cover art by Ross Jones
Cover design by Emily Osborne

Song lyrics © 2011 Polhemusic Publishing.

*To my Amazing Child, who is no longer a child,
but is still amazing in every way.*

Author's Note:

I want to thank the amazingly talented Chapman James, who loaned me both his name and the lyrics to "My Soul's in Alabama" for this book. The song was running through my mind as I wrote, and I knew it would be perfect for Shelby and Declan. Visit my website or www.cdbaby.com/cd/chapmanjames2 to listen for yourself.

I also want to thank Kira Sinclair for her time and brilliant ideas (even though she was on vacation) and Dr. Shelley Visconte for sharing her knowledge of ADHD and dyslexia.

And in case you're wondering, the poem Declan recites to Shelby is John Donne's "Elegy XIX: To His Mistress Going to Bed." There are also quotes from JRR Tolkien, Shakespeare's Sonnet 18, and Jane Austen, because, yes, I am *that* big of a nerd.

Chapter 1

Phone calls after midnight never brought good news. Shelby Tanner knew that, which made being woken out of a sound sleep and a really good dream even worse. She groped for her phone on the nightstand, but it was dark and silent. She stared at it blankly until she heard another ring, then rolled out of bed cursing and ran downstairs to the office to answer the main line.

"Marina. This is Shelby." *And this better be important.* She blinked and rubbed her eyes to clear them as she turned on the big desk lamp and peered at the caller ID. It wasn't a local number, and she didn't recognize the area code.

"This is Declan Hyde and I need some assistance. I'm . . . um . . . Well, I seem to be . . . floating. Out on the water."

This guy sounded a little too old to be making crank calls, but not everyone outgrew their adolescence. "It's the middle of the night, and I'm really not in the mood for pranks, so—"

"This is not a prank," the man said quickly. "I'm supposed to be at the dock, yet I'm . . . not." There was a frustrated sigh. "I've been staying on a boat in slip seven. I woke up a few minutes ago, and I'm not in slip seven anymore."

That got her attention. Balancing the phone on her shoulder, she raised the blinds on the window and looked out, scanning the boats below. Sure enough, slip seven was empty. The *Lady Jane* hadn't moved from that spot in more than six weeks, so the absence was glaring. She didn't see the *Lady Jane* anywhere. "Well, where *are* you?"

"As I said, I seem to be adrift."

Okay, now I'm awake. While the man seemed to be frustrated, he did not sound afraid or freaked out, so that was good. Whatever had happened to the *Lady Jane*—and she'd riddle that out later—it couldn't have been more than a few hours ago, so there was a good chance he wouldn't be more than a couple of miles offshore, max. That was good news; it would make the search easier.

But she could tell by the way he talked that he wasn't a very experienced sailor—which wasn't all that uncommon in Magnolia Beach. They had a lot of tourists come to town with an overestimation of their skills, and a dark night and unfamiliar waters could lead to disaster easily, even close to land. Adrenaline rushed through her. "Don't hang up. I'm going to get the Coast Guard on the radio—"

"I was assuming you could just come get me."

"What?"

"It shouldn't take you long," he said in the most ridiculously reasonable-sounding voice she'd ever heard. "I mean, I can almost make you out in the window, so I've not made it all that far out yet."

She nearly dropped the phone. "You can *see* me?"

"Well, not clearly, no. But I assume that's you. The

light in that building did come on about the time you answered."

She'd only looked to see that the *Lady Jane* was actually out of her slip. This time, Shelby looked out toward the bay. A cloudy sky shrouded everything beyond the marina's entrance in darkness, but sure enough, there were lights bobbing just beyond. It would be unbelievable without confirmation. "Can you flash your lights for me?"

"Um, sure. Hang on."

Suspicions growing and her irritation barely held in check, she drummed her fingers against the windowsill as she waited. A moment later, those lights in the not-very-far-at-all distance flashed off and back on again.

"Do you see me now?"

"Oh, I see you." That probably sounded snarky, but *jeez*. Thank goodness she hadn't called the Coast Guard. She'd have never heard the end of it. Reminding herself that Mr. Declan Hyde was a paying customer and shouting at him would not be good for business, she took a deep breath to steady her voice. "Sir, is there something wrong with your boat?"

"No, not that I know of."

"Then why don't you just come back?" she said carefully.

He laughed. He actually laughed, causing Shelby's hand to curl into a fist. "That would make sense, except I don't know how. I've never driven a boat before. I wouldn't know where to begin."

The number of wrong things in those few sentences made Shelby's head hurt. He'd been living on that boat for six freakin' weeks. That boat cost more than some people's houses.

And he didn't know how to operate it.

Who the hell lives on a boat when they don't know how—

She took a deep breath to calm herself. Even if she walked him through, step by step, he'd probably ram the thing into something on his way back. Maneuvering space was limited in the marina, and there was no telling how much damage he could do—both to the *Lady Jane* and every other boat in the place. And not to mention, it would be illegal if he didn't have a boating license. It would just be quicker, safer, and involve fewer insurance claims to just go get him.

Oh Lord, deliver me from idiots.

"Miss? Are you still there?"

She sighed. "Yes. I'm on my way. Just sit tight." *And try not to fall overboard.*

Grumbling, Shelby headed back up the stairs to her tiny apartment. It had just been a storage room until she'd converted it three years ago—shortly after she'd pretty much taken over the day-to-day running of the marina. Her parents hadn't liked the idea at all, claiming worries about her safety being there alone at night, but Magnolia Beach wasn't exactly a hot spot of crime— or anything else for that matter.

She'd always wanted to live near the water, but since Magnolia Beach was a tourist location, all the waterfront property was either too expensive for her to purchase or designed for tourists to rent. Living here at the marina was both convenient and cheap, allowing her to save money for later. The apartment was small, but cozy, and thanks to her cousin Ryan's handyman skills, comfortable and perfect for her needs—which weren't all that many.

A glance at the clock told her it was close to three, and that only made her grumpier as she pulled on shorts and a sweatshirt and slipped into her shoes. She took a minute to pull her hair back and braid the ponytail to keep it out of her face—Mr. Hyde wasn't going to drift out to sea or anything in that extra minute. Hell, he was still in the No Wake area, for goodness' sake—then she grabbed the keys to the dinghy and stomped down the stairs. There was even an eighty percent chance that he'd end up on the sandbar in another hour or so, where he could safely wait until a reasonable hour to be fetched back. But she couldn't ignore that twenty percent chance he wouldn't.

Cupid woofed at her questioningly as she got off her doggie bed and followed Shelby outside. Shelby patted the shaggy head. "I know. It's crazy to be up at this hour."

Crazy or not, it was a beautiful night. The clouds blocked the stars, but they also kept the temperature from dropping too much, making the October air a little warmer than usual. Everything was quiet, only the wind making the rigging on the sailboats sing, and mostly still except for the gentle movement of the boats. And while she would much rather be asleep in her bed, at least going out wasn't going to suck.

Cupid sat on the wooden dock, a little miffed she wasn't going as well, as Shelby untied the dinghy and started the small motor, which in the quiet sounded unnaturally loud.

It wasn't like this was the first time she'd had to go help a tourist out of a jam. It just came with the territory, and normally she didn't mind. People came to Magnolia Beach to enjoy the water that surrounded the town on three sides—Mobile Bay to the east, Heron Bay to the south, and Heron Bayou to the west. It was a quiet, almost stereotypical small town, just like they'd seen on TV, and very family-friendly, perfect for water-centric vacations.

She was quite used to people with more enthusiasm

for boats than skill at operating them, but never in her life had she heard of someone living on a boat when he had no idea what to do with it. Aside from being just *wrong*, it didn't seem safe, either. It simply hadn't occurred to her to check that the inhabitant of the boat would possess that minimum level of skill.

The *Lady Jane* belonged to Mr. Farley's cousin's nephew—or something like that—and was normally docked in a marina over near Laguna Beach. But that marina didn't allow live-aboards, so Mr. Farley had asked whether the *Lady Jane* could dock at their marina for a few months. Had it been summer, Shelby would have had to turn down the request, but she'd figured it would be okay this time of year. It wasn't something they allowed often, as live-aboards often turned out to be sketchy and dubious situations, but Mr. Farley had given his personal guarantee that Declan Hyde wouldn't be a problem.

And until right now, he hadn't been.

A college-age kid had brought the *Lady Jane* in and got everything settled, and at some point shortly after, the occupant had arrived and the kid had left. She'd been in Hattiesburg at her cousins' for a couple of weeks, so her father had been the one to get Declan settled in. By the time she'd gotten back from Mississippi, their new resident had established himself as a bit of a ghost—to the extent that Shelby often forgot he was even there. She'd see lights on at night, and his car would disappear from the parking lot on occasion, but aside from servicing the water and waste tanks, he might as well *not* be living aboard for all the extra effort it had caused her.

It was odd, sure, but not odd enough to even ping on her radar as concerning. This was Magnolia Beach; they had plenty of odd ducks in town. And most of *them* were far more interesting than some Yankee—the SUV in the parking lot had Illinois tags—who was probably just suffering through a Jimmy Buffet–inspired midlife crisis.

The *Lady Jane* was starting to take shape in the dark in front of her. It really was a damn nice boat, the kind a lot of people only dreamed of owning one day. Built for serviceable, but not overly luxurious, comfort, it was easily big enough for one person to live aboard reasonably comfortably for an extended but limited time, as it was really designed more for weekend excursions and deep-sea fishing.

The hermit in question came into view, standing near the rail of the cockpit. In the dark and from this distance, it was hard to tell much beyond that he was tall and broad-shouldered. She cut the engine on the dinghy and let it glide the last little bit, sliding easily alongside the bigger boat until she could catch hold.

It only took a second to secure her dinghy to the *Lady Jane*, then she was climbing aboard, ignoring the hand extended to help her.

"I'm very glad to see you."

Her earlier assumption was proven wrong immediately. Declan Hyde was not some middle-aged former salesman in an existential crisis. In fact, he probably wasn't much older than she was, maybe in his early thirties or so. It was hard to tell due to the darkness and the wild, overgrown, "I've been living on the sea" hair and beard combo he sported. He was wearing jeans with the knees ripped out and a T-shirt that once upon a time might have been blue.

"I'm Declan Hyde," he continued, offering his hand again. "Welcome aboard."

"Shelby Tanner," she replied, returning the handshake briefly while biting back the urge to say something she knew she'd probably regret later. He seemed about to say something else, but she knew she would not be able to manage polite chitchat right now. Not under these circumstances. "The keys?"

Declan nodded and opened the door to the cabin, giving her a glimpse inside. Papers and books were scattered around, and a laptop graced the center of the mess. A writer, then. She'd seen that before, too.

Please don't tell me about your book.

She accepted the keys and tried to start the boat, but the engine wouldn't turn over. "Great," she muttered, praying for patience.

"It looks like I would have had to call you, regardless." The voice came from right behind her, causing her to jump. He'd followed her up and was now eyeing the controls with a shake of his head. "I certainly don't know anything about engine repair."

Of course you don't. He seemed to find this slightly amusing, but Shelby was unable to share in the humor. "Well, it's a good thing I do. There's a small toolbox under the seat in the dinghy. Would you mind?"

Declan went to get her tools as she assessed the situation. There was a flashlight stowed inside the engine door, and she held it between her cheek and her shoulder as she checked the most obvious culprits, hoping it would be something easy.

"Maybe we should call the Coast Guard," Declan said, returning with her tools and setting them beside her.

"I don't think that will be necessary." She'd have to be on fire or sinking before she'd call the Guard. She knew every one of those guys, and she'd never be able to hold her head up again if they had to come get her for anything less than a bona fide maritime disaster. And probably not even then.

"Should we drop the anchor or something? We're still drifting."

The fact he hadn't dropped anchor already meant he probably didn't know how. "I promise we won't drift far. We're fine."

He squatted beside her. "Can I hold the flashlight for you?" he offered. She must have looked at him funny because he added, "At least that way I won't seem completely useless in this time of need."

Declan's self-deprecating smile told her he saw both the ridiculous in the situation and his part in it, and that finally helped tamp down her irritation. "It's hardly desperate times." But she put it in his hand anyway and adjusted him so it would point where she needed it.

As if he knew she was not in the mood, Declan didn't try to make conversation while she worked. Thankfully, the problem was easy to find—and would be easy to fix. "It's just a bad wire. Won't take me but a minute," she told him.

Declan was quite large and the space was not, so his head was right over her shoulder. Contrary to what his hair and clothing said, he wasn't doing the unwashed hippie thing. He actually smelled nice, kind of woodsy. "You're very capable," he said after a minute or two of watching her.

She snorted. "We are a full-service marina."

"I think this situation is a little above and beyond the usual offered services."

He sounded sincere, which took the edge off. *A little.* "It's a first, that's for sure."

"I'm sorry I had to wake you up. I honestly have no idea how the boat got loose. I worked until after midnight, then went to bed. I don't know what woke me up, but I realized it was a lot darker than normal and there was a lot more movement. I was rather surprised to find myself out here."

It would be disconcerting, to say the least. "Well, I'll tell you all about it later."

"You know how this happened?" He sounded surprised.

"I have my theories, but I also have video surveillance of the entire marina. It won't be hard to find out." She reached for the electrical tape, thumping Declan in the chest with her elbow in the process. He grunted. "Sorry. I'm not used to working with an assistant."

It wasn't the cleanest of repairs, but it wasn't terribly bad, either, for three-something in the morning. Declan moved aside as she stood and tried again to start the boat. This time, the engine came to life easily.

"I'm impressed."

He was obviously easily impressed then, but since it wasn't often that she was able to impress people, she took the ego boost happily. "It's holding together with tape and a prayer, but it'll get us back to shore. I'll fix it properly tomorrow—I mean, later today."

"There's no real rush. I don't exactly have plans to take her out or anything."

The smile on his face told her he thought he was being funny, but she didn't see the humor this time either. She stowed the flashlight and closed the engine door. "It's a safety hazard, though. Any particular time you'd prefer I come?"

He finally took the hint and quit trying to be cute about it. "At your convenience."

That would be a nice change. Yawning widely, she turned the boat toward shore.

* * *

Shelby Tanner was not happy with him, that much was very clear. Declan couldn't exactly blame her, though. No one liked being dragged out of bed in the small hours of the morning, but what else could he have done? Thomas had loaned him the *Lady Jane* with a laugh simply because he *didn't* know anything about boats. He'd have plenty of time to study and catch up on all those books he said he wanted to read and all the movies he'd missed—and he'd get to catch up on all the sleep he'd lost in the last few years, too.

And, Thomas had added, he needed to start finding his sea legs. Miami was a boat culture. A few months in Magnolia Beach would be an easy introduction.

Shelby, though, obviously knew a hell of a lot about boats. It was to be expected, of course, since she worked at the marina, but there was an ease and confidence to her movements that told him this was second nature to her. Even the matter-of-fact way she'd fixed the problem with the engine spoke to a level of competence unusual in someone so young.

And she was young—maybe early or mid-twenties—which seemed very young to be in charge, yet she was the one answering the marina's phone in the middle of the night. She must have some level of responsibility. *Interesting.*

The same ease with which she handled the boat was almost a rebuke to his lack of skills. It wasn't a slap to his ego or anything—he was well aware of his skill set and had no need to get into a pissing contest over it—and he could see her side of things. In a broader sense, yes, someone living on a boat should at least know how to start the engine.

And he'd had every intention of learning.

He just hadn't found the time, yet. The movies and
books and sleep—and the amazing antebellum architecture in this part of the country—had proven far more
attractive.

She would have still had to come and get him—the
engine *had* been broken, after all—but the event wouldn't
have had that farcical overlay, adding insult to injury.

It wasn't going to be a long trip back to shore—he
hadn't drifted that far—but he wasn't sure what he
should do during that time. He had nothing to offer in
the way of helping—not that Shelby seemed to need
it—but it seemed rude to go below into the cabin as if
Shelby were some kind of chauffeur. At the same time,
it seemed rude to stand here and hover like he needed
to supervise her.

He settled for leaning back against the console, out
of the way but still nearby, and scanning the shoreline.
Magnolia Beach was a poor substitute for Miami. It was
just a tiny Southern town, smaller than even one of
Miami's minor suburbs, and without any of the culture
or excitement. Yes, both towns were on the water, but
he wasn't sure this interlude was going to transition him
from life in Chicago to life in Miami in any meaning-
ful way.

But he couldn't take possession of his apartment in
Miami until January second, and Suzanne had been
very clear that he couldn't continue to live in their apartment in Chicago. He had too much pride to couch surf
at his friends' places for the next couple of months, and
with winter setting in, leaving Chicago seemed to be a
good idea anyway. Even a born-and-bred Midwesterner
could be sick of snow.

So one drunken night, two weeks after he'd lost his
job and Suzanne had kicked him out, he'd let Thomas

convince him that living on his family's boat in Back-water, Alabama, was an excellent idea. To someone who hadn't had an actual vacation in more than five years, four months on a boat had sounded like paradise.

And while the last six weeks had been restorative, he wasn't sure he would make it all the way through December.

Shelby wasn't one for small talk, it seemed—whether it was her personality or the fact she was peeved at being pulled out of bed, he didn't know. If it was her personality, that trait put her in the minority of people he'd met down here. He'd never had so many small-talk conversations with strangers in his entire life as he'd had recently. But even if that was her preference, he felt he needed to say *something*. He settled for, "How long have you worked at the marina?"

"My whole life," she answered. "My parents own it."

That explained her familiarity not only with boats, but also with the dock area, as she maneuvered around buoys and navigated without so much as crinkling her forehead with the effort. So while he doubted she needed full concentration to work, he took her lapse back into silence as a hint.

After killing the engine, Shelby quickly jumped to the dock and the *Lady Jane* slid back into her spot with a gentle bump. Within moments, the boat was secured in place and Shelby was plugging it back into the main power, bringing the lights on the boat back to full strength. The whole adventure had taken less than an hour from start to finish. A mere "thanks" didn't seem like enough, but Shelby merely shrugged when he said so.

"You're safely back, and that's what matters. We'll sort everything else out in daylight. Try to get some sleep." Then, without even waiting for him to respond, she was untying her little dinghy from the *Lady Jane* and puttering over to the main dock, where the large shaggy dog that roamed the property came out to meet her.

Shelby stopped to pet it briefly, then the dog followed her back to the main building. A moment later, the light downstairs went out.

No other lights came on, meaning Shelby was doing exactly what she'd told him to do: getting some sleep. But he was awake now, the adrenaline in his system not quite flushed out yet. Back in the cabin, he shot a long look at the bed visible through the open bedroom door and sighed.

Another episode of Breaking Bad, *coming right up.* It wasn't like he *had* to get up in the morning or anything.

He opened his laptop and took it over to the couch.

Out of habit, he opened his e-mail client first, but only a few e-mails had landed in his in-box since he'd last checked a little before midnight. Most of it was spam, so he started tagging it for deletion.

One subject line caught his attention, though:

NO BETTER WAY TO SAY "THANK YOU!"
THEN WITH FLOWER'S!!

Unnecessary exclamation points and poor grammar notwithstanding, the message did ping his conscience. Hadn't he just been thinking that a simple "thanks" wasn't really adequate enough for Shelby's assistance tonight? Flowers would be a nice gesture, and might help smooth over her irritation with him. Hell, it had always worked with Suzanne. If he irritated her and *didn't* send flowers, he'd be asking for the silent treatment.

Suzanne had required large flower arrangements, sized in relation to the magnitude of the transgression committed. Waking her up in the middle of the night to come get him? He snorted. He didn't know if they made arrangements *that* large.

A small bouquet for Shelby, though, should be enough; just a token of his appreciation for going above and beyond in customer service.

It took less than ten minutes to find a local florist with an online order function and arrange for delivery to the marina office tomorrow—or later today, actually.

Oddly pleased with himself, he shut down the computer, grabbed a bottle of water out of the fridge, and stepped out onto the deck of the *Lady Jane* to stretch. This wasn't a small boat, but he was a tall guy, and there was something weird about always brushing the ceiling when stretched full-length. The sky was still completely dark, and sunrise was probably another hour or more away. It was quiet and peaceful out here, though, and the view would be beautiful as the sun came up.

When was the last time he'd watched the sun rise?

So instead of staying inside with his laptop, he sat on one of the benches, propped his feet up on the rail, and relaxed back with a sigh.

Soon enough, he'd be back in civilization and all that entailed. He should enjoy the peace and quiet while he could.

Chapter 2

"**D**umbass."

Shelby muttered under her breath as she watched the black-and-white surveillance footage of the marina from last night. Based on Declan's reported bedtime, she'd started reviewing the video from a little after midnight to see what had caused the *Lady Jane*'s adventure. At the 12:45 timestamp, she had her answer.

The dumbass was Kirby Peterson. While she couldn't make out his face clearly, the idiot had worn his football practice jersey, and the huge number 18 showed up perfectly on the video. The other five with him weren't so easily and immediately identifiable, but Kirby had a posse, and that knowledge narrowed down the pool of possible culprits to a manageable few.

A huge yawn caused her jaw to crack under the strain, and she paused the video while she went to refill her coffee. Getting up this morning had hurt. After getting back last night, she'd done nothing more than slip off her shoes before crashing face-first back into bed. She'd said some very ugly things about Declan when her alarm went off at its usual time, most of which he deserved.

There was always a steady run early in the mornings, mostly from fishermen stocking up on bait, fuel, and ice for the day. This time of year, though, rentals for the Jet Skis and smaller day-sailers dropped off to nearly nothing, so at least she hadn't had to smile and deal with tourists in her sleep-deprived state.

But she was running strictly on caffeine this morning, and there was no nap for her in sight.

Sliding back into the battered leather office chair that had been her grandfather's, she cuddled the cup close, letting the aroma cut through the fog in her brain as she hit the play button.

Kirby and his gang—one of whom, from this angle, looked like Daryl James—were none too steady on their feet as they tripped through the yard. It was a wonder she hadn't heard them.

Shelby cut her eyes over at Cupid, sprawled belly up and snoring on her cushion beside the desk. "Some guard dog you are."

Cupid opened one eye, saw no reason to get up, and promptly went back to sleep. Next time Cupid went to the vet, Shelby was going to have Tate check her hearing. She was an old dog, but not *that* old.

One of the kids with Kirby grabbed the three-foot-long ponytail of another as she started to fall over her own feet. That ponytail almost definitely belonged to Mary Beth Carson, Kirby's girlfriend. *Three down, three to go.*

The suspicions she had just by the appearance of drunk-looking teenagers stumbling across her property were proven true as the footage played out as expected. Kirby and three others untied the boat, pushing it out of its slip, using one of the lines to pull it into the wider area past the dock before releasing it. If the tide hadn't been going out, the *Lady Jane* probably would have simply drifted over to the other side of the marina, running aground in the shallow water. Instead, dumb luck had the timing and positioning perfect to pull it straight out of the marina into the bay.

While she was angry at the kids, she didn't believe they truly meant any harm. They'd sprinted off—clumsily—as soon as the *Lady Jane* was floating free, probably never guessing they'd hit the jackpot of perfect conditions to put Declan or the boat at real risk. Kirby and company might be dumb and mischievous, but they weren't evil.

It also wouldn't have occurred to them that the person on the boat wouldn't know how to get back—because that just beggared belief. At worst, it was a prank, meant to inconvenience and startle.

Popping a disc into the drive, she burned a copy of the relevant footage. She'd take it over to the police station later and give it to Rusty. He could call a Come-to-Jesus meeting with the culprits and their parents and decide the best way to handle this to ensure it didn't happen again.

Bored kids, a small town, and alcohol . . . that was always a bad mix. Hell, that combo had led her to her share of stupid stunts, too. Granted, she'd never set a boat adrift, but Daddy would've had her hide mounted on the wall for even thinking about it.

She stood and stretched, very glad she didn't have a ton of stuff on her to-do list. She just wasn't one of those people who could bounce back after an interrupted night's sleep. But she did have stuff to do. High season might be officially over, but stragglers would stick around for a couple more weeks, making the most of the last warm days and smaller crowds. While the snowbirds were starting to arrive from their northern climes, they were more a boon for the town businesses and had little impact on the marina. South Alabama didn't get so cold as to completely shut down all water activities, but things were always very slow from November to February.

But November was still three weeks away, and things never came to a *complete* standstill, so tired or not, grumpy or not, she had to get to work. And at some point, she still had to go out and replace that wire on the *Lady Jane.*

She was going for her fifth cup of coffee when the door opened and Charlotte backed in, a decent-sized flower arrangement in her hands. While Charlotte's sister, Lannie, owned a flower shop and it was common for Charlotte to be carrying flowers around town for one reason or another, helping with deliveries, it wasn't common for her to be carrying flowers around *here.*

"Shelby?" Charlotte called, peeking out from behind the flowers.

"Over here," she answered. "What's all that about?"

"That's exactly what I was about to ask *you.* What aren't you telling me, and why haven't you?"

In the twenty-five years they'd been friends, Shelby could think of approximately two things she hadn't told Charlotte. And Charlotte had found out about those easily enough. "I have no idea what you're talking about," she said honestly.

Charlotte set the bouquet on the desk. "These are for you."

Shelby blinked. She couldn't remember the last time anyone had sent her flowers. "Are you sure?"

"Yes, I'm sure. Lannie called me this morning when she saw the order was for you. She figured you'd rather I deliver them than Marshall. You know how he gossips." Cupid came over, tail wagging, to greet Charlotte, who petted her absently. "Now, I need details. *All* the details."

"I have zero idea what you're talking about. Are you positive they're for me?"

Charlotte plucked the card out of the arrangement. "'Shelby Tanner, Bay Breeze Marina,'" she read smugly.

She still couldn't believe they weren't some kind of mistake. "Well, who are they from?"

"Oh, don't play dumb."

"I'm not playing. What does the card say?"

Charlotte unfolded the paper. *As if she hadn't read it already.* "'Thanks for last night. Declan.'" She grinned. "So who's Declan, what happened last night, and why oh *why* did my sister know about it before I did?"

Shelby wanted to kiss Lannie for calling Charlotte to make the delivery. Then she wanted to kick Declan for making such a provocative when-taken-out-of-context statement. Thank God Marshall hadn't read it—and he would have. And then he would have told people about it, putting a spin on it guaranteed to ensure that the whole town would be thinking . . . She looked over at Charlotte. Well, they'd be thinking exactly what Charlotte was thinking right now. "I'm afraid it's not nearly as exciting as it sounds. Declan Hyde is a customer whose boat got loose last night. I had to go get him sometime after three this morning and bring him back to shore."

Charlotte's face fell. "Well, that's not interesting at all."

Shelby refilled her cup and poured Charlotte one, too. "Told you."

"And here I was thinking . . ." She shrugged as she took the coffee with a nod of thanks. "Well, at least they're pretty. And that was very nice of him."

They *were* quite lovely, and they filled the office with a beautiful fragrance. While she was still grumpy about the whole thing, it *was* a very nice gesture. And they certainly brightened the place up. Of course, the place was pretty dreary to begin with, so every little bit helped. She leaned in to sniff one of the irises. Her favorite. "Yeah."

Charlotte perked up. "Any chance they could be . . ." She trailed off as Shelby shook her head.

"He's not flirting, if that's what you're asking."

"How do you know?"

"I just do. We spent a tense hour together *after* I'd been pulled out of a sound sleep. It wasn't fun."

"Oh." Charlotte knew how grumpy Shelby could be.

It wasn't like they'd really *talked* or anything, and Shelby wasn't the kind of woman men sent flowers to for no reason. Charlotte was, though. Boys had started sending her flowers in middle school. Lannie's flower shop had probably made a fortune off her sister's good looks alone. But Charlotte was so much more than just a pretty face, so it was hard to begrudge her the attention.

"But don't just assume that," Charlotte began, then caught herself. "Or do we not want this guy to flirt with you?"

"Probably not. A guy who is living—temporarily, I might add—on a boat that doesn't even belong to him?"

"Oh, good Lord." Charlotte shook her head. "How old?"

She shrugged. "Early thirties, maybe. He's rockin' the yeti look, so it's hard to tell."

Shelby waited while Charlotte filled in the rest of the blanks. She, too, knew the possibilities. "Recently divorced or just 'finding himself'?"

"I didn't ask. All I wanted to do was get him back to

shore before he got himself hurt." At Charlotte's look, she told her the full story.

Charlotte nearly choked on her coffee. "That might be the dumbest thing I've ever heard. Who lives on a boat when they don't know how to drive it?"

"Exactly."

"That's not safe. Is it even legal?"

"You know, I've been thinking about that. He doesn't need a license just to be *on* a boat, so if it never leaves the dock . . ." She leaned against the desk and sighed. "It's stupid, but I'm not sure it's illegal."

"Can he at least swim?"

Shelby laughed. "Let's hope so."

"Well, tie him up tight and maybe add a padlock so he doesn't get loose again. Can you sabotage the engine so if he does decide to give it a try, he can't get it started and get himself lost at sea?"

She shook her head and laughed. "That's only asking for disaster if he does go floating again. But I don't think he's silly enough to try that anyway."

"Oh?"

"He seemed so reasonable about the whole thing, you know. I think he's honestly just staying there."

"Then why a boat? Why not rent a house or a room or something? That would make a lot more sense if he's not going out on it."

"It's cheaper for one thing."

Charlotte peeked out the window at the *Lady Jane*. "Not when you add in the cost of renting that boat, too."

True. Declan had paid the slip rental, but she didn't know the financial agreement with the Farley family. "People are just weird, I guess."

Charlotte laughed. "And they all come to Magnolia Beach."

"Only the ones who can't afford to go someplace else. We're just the poor man's Caribbean."

"That should be the next Magnolia Beach tourism campaign slogan."

It was Shelby's turn to laugh. "I'll mention it to Ryan."

"I'm sure that will go over well. And unless you have something else to entertain me with, I'm off to work." Charlotte worked at the sea lab on Dauphin Island, in their outreach and education department, so her hours were variable and the occasional Saturday was just part of the job.

Shelby was just getting the coffee cups washed and put away when her father showed up. While he was semiofficially semiretired, he seemed to be having difficulty fully embracing the concept. Or at least that's what Shelby chose to believe—otherwise she'd have to accept that he didn't trust her to really run this place on her own. He homed in on the flowers immediately. "Where did these come from?"

"Good morning to you, too," she said.

"'Morning, princess." He leaned down to give her a kiss on the cheek. "Who sent you flowers?"

Now she wanted to go throw the silly things in the bay. And while a quick explanation of the night before answered his question, the curiosity on his face was rapidly replaced by a frown that furrowed deeper with each word she said. "You shouldn't have gone out after him by yourself like that," he scolded.

"What? Why not?"

"It's not safe, honey. What if he'd . . . *tried* something? Attacked you? You should have called me or one of the boys. Let us handle it."

While there were benefits to growing up in a big

family, there was a distinct disadvantage to being the only girl—no matter how enlightened they claimed to be. There was a severe estrogen deficiency in the Tanner family, and sometimes it truly sucked to be the only one in her generation without a Y chromosome. And while she could hold her own against any of the Tanner boys in any way they wanted to measure it, that age-old double standard could kick in at the most inopportune and frustrating moments. "I'm a big girl, Daddy. And it's part of my job."

"I shouldn't have rented him the slip. Not with you living here by yourself . . ."

Oh good Lord. She needed to shut this down quickly before it wound back around to "It's not safe for a young woman to be living out here alone," and eventually, "You should move back home."

"I took my mace with me, and he'd be fish food right now if he'd tried anything off base." The first part was a lie—which her father would never know—but the second part was the truth—and Daddy knew *that* perfectly well. He'd taught her how to defend herself *and* let her practice on Jamie and her cousins. "Instead, he sent flowers as a thank-you. I think that was very nice of him. And I know you've met him. Did he really seem like the mad rapist type to you?"

That was a rather low blow, and Shelby knew it, as Daddy would either have to admit he wasn't a good judge of character—which was something Michael Tanner prided himself on—or else admit he'd let a sketchy male live-aboard into his marina with his daughter sleeping just yards away.

The frown told her that he knew exactly what she was doing. "No, I guess not, but for both safety and liability issues, you're not to do something like that again. After all, if you'd run into trouble out there, who would have known to come look for you? Or Mr. Hyde for that matter," he added as an afterthought.

That was exactly why radios and cell phones had been invented, but Shelby kept that statement behind her teeth and graciously accepted her victory.

There was more muttering from her father, and later Shelby saw him not surreptitiously checking the locks on the doors as if Declan were going to try to sneak in one night while she was asleep.

But he didn't mention it again, so that was good. She'd take what she could get.

And it wasn't like Declan could really be *that* much trouble.

While there was a shower on the *Lady Jane*, Declan preferred to use the marina facilities, mainly because the water was hotter and the pressure more reliable. Plus the space was bigger, keeping him from banging his elbows against the walls every time he moved.

The marina's bathhouse wasn't anything fancy, just a squat cinderblock building that looked like it could turn into a humid oven on hot days, but it was clean, and since the marina itself wasn't very busy, it was always available and practically private. It wasn't as stylish as the facilities on the *Lady Jane*, but then, there was nothing fancy about *anything* at the Bay Breeze Marina. The best adjective he could come up with was "serviceable." Things were tidy and in good repair, but they lacked any kind of style.

He hadn't spent much time in the town, but what he had seen of it was a little eclectic, a mix of old and slightly less old, with brick and clapboard buildings lining clean streets, giving it a charm that was attractive to tourists who wanted that small, Southern town "feel."

But the marina was a hodgepodge of cinderblock and corrugated metal structures, built to be functional and service the boating and fishing populace, who probably didn't need or want it to be anything more.

It was a pity, though. That was a lot of wasted potential for such a prime location. But maybe that was what marinas were supposed to look like. His experience was limited to what he'd seen on TV and the one on Lake Michigan that Suzanne's father used to host company parties. That one was huge, with a Michelin-starred restaurant and multimillion-dollar boats docked in its slips. Maybe the average purely functional marina did look more like the Bay Breeze.

After watching the sunrise, he'd read for a while and taken a nap, and though it was getting late in the afternoon, he felt like it was early morning. His body clock was totally out of whack—a side effect of such an unanchored schedule.

He ran the towel over his face and hair. He needed both a haircut and a shave, but couldn't be bothered to do either. It was a small act of rebellion, too, against Suzanne, who hated facial hair of any sort. Now, he looked like a hippie, and he hadn't put on a tie in weeks. He wasn't even sure he'd brought one to Magnolia Beach.

It was quite freeing.

Clean and human-feeling, he turned off the lights in the bathhouse and headed back to the *Lady Jane*.

He found Shelby on the docks.

"I was just coming to finish that fix," she explained with a sunny smile. "Is now a good time?"

He hadn't gotten a good look at Shelby last night, due

to the situation and the darkness. She wasn't quite as young as he'd first assumed, but she wasn't much older, either, maybe in her late twenties, with open features and wide green eyes above high cheekbones dotted with freckles. A long blond braid hung loosely over one shoulder, but wisps had escaped to float around her face in the breeze. In shorts, a T-shirt with the sleeves rolled up to her shoulders, and hiking sandals, she had the uneven tan lines of someone who spent most of her time outdoors and didn't always wear sunscreen. She wasn't overly tall—maybe just to his shoulders—but her legs and arms were muscular and solid. Shelby was the textbook example of a wholesome, all-American tomboy girl-next-door. In fact, if not for the toolbox she carried, Shelby would not look out of·place at a gathering of summer camp counselors. It was cute. Maybe more than cute.

"Now is fine."

Shelby hopped aboard with an ease he had not yet mastered, making him feel clumsy in comparison. "I wanted to apologize for being so grumpy with you before. I'm a bear when I wake up."

"It's no more than I deserved."

"And thank you for the flowers. They're lovely."

"You're welcome."

"Can I offer you a piece of advice, though?" At his nod, Shelby's mouth twitched. "I'm guessing you're not from a small town, where everything is everyone's business, but for future reference, messages like 'Thanks for last night' on a bouquet from a man to a woman raises all kinds of speculation."

Shelby looked more amused than angry, so whatever speculation he'd unwittingly caused didn't seem to be too much trouble for her. "Noted. My apologies."

She shrugged. "No harm done. But you should know that this town runs on gossip and sweet tea. This won't take me long"—she indicated the stuff in her hand—"and it's not noisy, so it shouldn't disturb you. If you want me to, I can send a bill directly to the owner." She jumped from topic to topic without even a pause, but it wasn't jarring. The change from last night's terseness *was* jarring, though. But at least she wasn't holding a grudge, and for that he was grateful.

"I'll take care of it."

With a nod, she went to work. He left the cabin door open and piddled around aimlessly, unsure of what to do and why he was so undecided about it. Once again, he was sitting idle while Shelby worked. He certainly wasn't going to go watch Shelby fix whatever it was, but it felt weird to surf the Internet while she was being so industrious.

He wasn't a messy person, and the seeming chaos of papers and books was actually quite organized into piles of things he was reading for work and things he was reading for fun, but he tidied up a few things here and there, tossing his shower kit and dirty clothes into the bedroom and closing the door.

Seemingly mere minutes later, Shelby was already knocking on the door. "I'm done."

"That was fast."

"That was *easy*." She grinned. "Which also means it was cheap."

He waved her the rest of the way in. "I don't have much cash on me . . ."

She shook her head. "Don't worry about it right now. We'll get you an invoice in a day or two."

Gotta love a small town.

"I mean," she continued with a smile, easily walking

the line between businesslike and friendly, "it's not like you're going to take off on the *Lady Jane* or anything. And even if you did, the rent on the slip you'd forfeit far exceeds the cost of this repair."

"Very true." But Shelby didn't leave on that note. Instead, she looked around, fingers drumming against her thigh like she wanted to say something. "Shelby?" he finally asked. "Is something wrong?"

She took a deep breath. "Can you swim?"

The question came from out of nowhere, catching him by surprise. "Of course I can swim. Why—"

"That's a relief. But do you know where your emergency beacons are? How they work? Do you know how to use the radio? How to contact the Coast Guard?"

So that was the problem. "Shelby . . ."

"I know it seems a little crazy of me, but I just don't think it's safe for you to be on a boat and not know . . ."

That made him laugh. "You're a regular Suzie Safety, aren't you?"

Shelby stilled at his words, then one eyebrow arched up. "And proud of it," she said dryly. "Better to be a Suzie Safety than a dead idiot. And I certainly don't want to leave my family or the marina open to a lawsuit if something happens to you or this boat."

"I'll sign a waiver that releases you and the marina from all liability."

She frowned at his statement, then shook her head. "That's all well and good, but for your own and others' safety, I'm afraid I have to insist that you show familiarity with the emergency equipment on this boat and basic competency in operating it. That is," she said primly, "presuming you wish to continue your residency here at Bay Breeze."

He had to give her props. She wasn't cowed at all

and, in fact, had seemed to grow taller during her lecture. She might *look* like a camp counselor, but she was obviously not one to be fooled with. That competence he'd noted earlier extended beyond just nautical skill. The more she talked, the more interesting she got.

And she had a point he couldn't really argue with. Well, he *could,* but it was a good point and he wasn't *that* big of an ass. Plus, it was her marina, so she did have the right to lay down the rules. More importantly, he could tell he'd ticked her off, and he didn't want her angry at him. He had almost three more months here, and there was something about Shelby that warned him that he would regret trying to thwart her.

"Fair enough."

Her surprise was nearly comical, and he had to bite back a smile. Shelby's stance relaxed, and her attitude thawed immediately. "Oh. Okay, then." The little smile came back. "That was easier than I expected."

"You wanted me to fight you about it?"

"Of course not. I'm just not used to men who give in that easily."

He couldn't tell if the insult was intentional or not. "Well, while your argument is very sound, the fact of the matter is that I probably should learn more about boats. When I leave here, I'm moving to Miami."

"Illinois to Miami? That's a big change." His surprise at her knowing that must have shown on his face, because she quickly explained, "Your car has Illinois tags. So why not just go to Miami? Why stop off here?"

Because it's amazing what sounds like a good idea after half a bottle of tequila. "I have no job or apartment to go to in Miami until after the new year. And this was easier than trying to find a short-term lease in Miami and move all my stuff twice."

Her eyebrows pulled together. "And you couldn't just stay in Illinois until January?"

Ah, yes, small-town nosiness. "Well, it's a long story."

She waited for him to elaborate, but he didn't. Finally, Shelby nodded. "And it's probably cheaper to live here anyway, if you're out of work and don't have any family to stay with."

It was a clever way to fish for information, but he wasn't taking the bait. "Don't worry about my employment status. My rent is paid up, as you know, and I'm not going to starve out here."

Shelby held her hands up. "Not my business. This is as good a place as any to take a break, find yourself, write your great American novel . . ."

She said it with such distaste, Declan got the feeling she'd dealt with her fair share of wannabe hippies and Hemingways. "God, no. I'm not a writer."

Her relief was both obvious and amusing. "Oh, good, because then good manners would insist that I ask you about your book, and I really didn't want to feign interest."

That made him laugh. "At least you're honest." That statement got him a grin in return.

"And all the books?" She looked pointedly at the piles.

"I like to read."

"So if you're not a writer, what do you do?"

"I'm an architect."

Her eyebrows went up. "Cool. I've never met one of those before. Have I seen any of your buildings on TV?"

"Not yet." *But one day, maybe.*

She sighed dramatically. "You're being very cagey, and I give up." She leveled a look at him. "What are you doing here?"

"I told you, I have no place I need to be until after

the new year, so I'm just killing some time until my apartment opens up. I'm taking a long overdue and extended vacation."

"Well, that's nice for you. I hope you enjoy your stay in Magnolia Beach. So," she said briskly, rubbing her hands together, "shall we start with a recitation of the excellent safety features on board the *Lady Jane*?" She waved her arm around the cabin in an excellent imitation of a *The Price Is Right* girl. "That way, should you ever find yourself in a predicament like last night again, you'll feel comfortable sitting tight and waiting until a reasonable hour before calling me."

"*Touché.*" And that reminded him . . . "Did you find out how I got loose in the first place?"

"Drunk kids pulling a prank. I've already turned the video over to the local police. I'm sure they'll be in touch." She shrugged it off.

He nearly choked on her nonchalance. "You suddenly have a broad definition of a prank—especially since you've done nothing but lecture *me* about the dangers."

"And I'm sure there will be hell to pay for Kirby and his crew. But it was just a prank, and had it happened to pretty much anyone else, it wouldn't be much of a problem at all. *You* made the situation worse with your lack of basic knowledge."

She was just not going to let that go. "Maybe the marina should have better security," he challenged, but it was weak and he knew it.

The corner of her mouth twitched. "Well, I'm going to get Cupid's hearing checked."

He'd met the dog when it came out to greet him in the parking lot a couple of times. Cupid was an older dog, going gray around the muzzle, willing to come to anyone who might pet her, and it seemed, slightly deaf. She was hardly a deterrent to crime of any sort. *Gotta love small-town security measures.* "What will happen to the kids involved?"

Shelby shrugged again. "I'm hesitant to throw the book at them for simple teenage dumbassery—God knows I've done my fair share of stupid stuff—but that's up to the authorities. I'm sure Rusty or someone will come talk to you and let you know what charges can be pressed if you choose to."

"But you won't be pressing charges?"

She shook her head. "About the only thing *I* can get them for is trespassing. I know these kids, though, and they're not bad kids, just . . . bored, probably. And intrigued."

"Intrigued?"

"A reclusive hermit living on a boat? Who never seems to go into town? No one knows anything about him. What could he *possibly* be *doing* on that boat?" She shrugged again as she dropped the overdramatic tone. "I'm actually a little surprised it took *this* long for a bunch of them to get curious enough to come see what was up with you."

Shelby's questionable logic was giving him a headache. "So it's just chalked up to curiosity and harmless mischief?"

"Around here, kids have to make their own fun. That doesn't always end well."

"You certainly weren't quite so blasé about it last night."

"Last night, I had been woken out of a sound sleep and a very good dream in order to save your butt because of their stunt. I was grumpy and irritated at all y'all."

"Yet today we're all forgiven?"

"Rusty will make sure Kirby and his crew have a new religious awakening. You've already agreed to rectify your lack of knowledge. No one was seriously harmed, there's no property damage, and we all learned a valuable lesson and are taking steps to make sure it doesn't happen again," she chirped, sounding much like the camp counselor she resembled.

"We? And what did *you* learn?"

She shot him a smug smile. "To make sure live-aboards know what the hell they're doing *before* leasing the slip to them." She brushed her hands against her shorts. "So Monday after lunch? Say two-ish? Boating 101?"

He had to hand it to her. She had spunk. And he couldn't even be irritated at her heavy-handedness with him because she was being both rather reasonable in her arguments and perky about it, too. Shelby was definitely a "people person," able to get along and make friends with everyone—a valuable skill, he had to admit, and one he'd never quite been able to master.

He'd heard the jokes about how Southern girls could tell you to go to hell in a way that would make you look forward to the trip. It seemed it might be true. Her accent bordered on hypnotic—not too syrupy, but with enough of a drawl to rope him in.

"Two o'clock is fine."

Shelby flashed a brilliant smile at him. "Great. I'll see you then."

There was something about that smile and the tone of her voice . . . Why did he get the uneasy suspicion he was going to regret this?

Chapter 3

"If anyone wanted to wipe out the Tanner family, they could pick any Sunday at two o'clock and easily erase the entire bloodline," Eli grumbled as he unfolded chairs and set them around the table.

"If they want the *entire* family," Shelby corrected her cousin as she laid out silverware, "they'll need to wait until one of the big holidays when everyone's here. Hell, the whole immediate family isn't even here today. That leaves more than enough of the family to start repopulating the world with Tanners."

"Don't talk about repopulation too loud." Eli looked over his shoulder toward the kitchen, where all the women—other than Shelby, of course—were gathered. "Gran's on another 'We need a grandbaby' kick."

"Then tell Ryan to marry Helena and get on that." She said it quietly so Ryan and Helena wouldn't overhear. Their wedding date was a bit of a touchy subject. She wasn't sure who the holdout was, but her money was on Helena. She had settled in, but she still seemed a bit gun shy. Not that Shelby blamed her—she still had hearts and minds to win and that was a slow process in a town that had only had a year to adjust to the idea of a new Helena.

Plus, Ryan was so obviously insanely crazy about her, he couldn't be the one with cold feet.

Ryan and Helena certainly weren't a couple Shelby would have ever envisioned, but then she didn't know who could have. But Ryan seemed happy, so Shelby had come around. Whether Helena would continue to hold a grudge, well, that was hard to tell.

Eli snorted. "I'm not that stupid, Shel."

"That's debatable," she mumbled, then dodged the elbow he threw.

Most people would probably say there were enough Tanners in Magnolia Beach already—the younger generation didn't really need to start reproducing or else they might take over entirely. But it was true that most, if not all, of them could be found at Gran's on any given Sunday afternoon. Gran believed that the family Sunday lunch was the cornerstone of civilization, and it was nearly impossible—or at least very unwise—to argue with her about it.

Which was why every Tanner without a good reason not to be was here. Honestly, Shelby didn't mind all that much. The Tanner women—herself excluded—were known for their amazing cooking, and Shelby was not one to turn down a home-cooked meal. She even wore a dress every Sunday, much to the amusement of her brother and cousins, simply because Gran expected her to.

Of course, the boys had to dress up, too, so it wasn't like she was being singled out or anything.

The table in the parlor wasn't really big enough, but Shelby set it for six anyway. The true "adult" table was in the dining room, and with the four younger boys away at school, there was no reason to set up another table, so they'd just squeeze around this one. Sometimes when the extended family came, they'd have tables all over the place, but it was just the fifteen of them today.

For her family, this was a downright intimate affair.

Of course, with six around this small table—her brother, Jamie; cousins Ryan, Adam, and Eli; plus Helena and herself—*this* felt pretty intimate, too. And since things between Helena and Jamie—and Helena and Shelby, too—could still be a little awkward at times, the intimacy was a little uncomfortable.

But a lot could be ignored—or at least tolerated—for her grandmother's corn casserole and country ham.

Adam paused in buttering his roll to look at her. "You said you wanted me to rewrite something for you?"

She nodded and swallowed. "The slip rental agreement. I want it to have something that says we expect the renter to have a valid operator's license. Or some kind of proof they have basic know-how."

Adam looked at her as if she'd lost her mind, but Jamie was quicker to ask, "Who would—"

"Declan Hyde," she answered. "The dude living at the marina right now."

Ryan laughed. "So *that's* what Uncle Mike was talking about. Was there some kind of trouble Friday night?"

"What?" Adam asked.

Shelby sighed. "A bunch of drunk kids snuck into the marina Friday night and untied his boat. He was drifting out into the bay, and I had to go get him because he didn't even know how to start the thing."

Jamie looked pointedly at Helena, who dropped her fork and held up her hands. "Hey, I had *nothing* to do with that. I have an alibi and everything."

Ryan chuckled. "Yeah, I'll vouch for her where-abouts all night long." Helena made a face and smacked him on the arm.

"It was Kirby Peterson and his crew, actually," Shelby said.

Ryan frowned. He volunteered as an assistant coach for the football team and didn't like hearing his players were causing trouble. "How do you know it was him? Do you have proof?"

She nodded. "It's all on video. And Kirby wore his practice jersey. That made it pretty easy to identify him."

Ryan's frown deepened, and Helena made a sound suspiciously like a snort.

"Sounds like Kirby might be picking up your torch, Hell-on-Wheels." That was Eli's comment, but Helena liked Eli, so she responded only with a small smile and a lift of her eyebrow.

"He's welcome to try."

"Bite your tongue," Jamie said. "One Hell-on-Wheels is enough for any town."

Shelby turned back to Adam. "So I need you to add some fancy lawyer-speak to the rental paperwork—"

He smirked. "To keep the dumbasses out of your marina?"

"Something like that," she muttered, only she didn't really think of Declan as a dumbass. Sure, the situation was ridiculous, but he seemed—at least based on what little time she'd spent talking to him—to lack the true arrogance and stupidity needed to really claim the title. He was willing to admit the problem and take steps to correct it, so that had to mean something, right?

"Wait," Eli said in a tone that meant he'd just real-ized something. "You went out in the middle of the night to rescue some guy you don't even know *all by yourself*?"

All four of the boys were now staring at her in varying degrees of outrage and horror. She should have expected this.

"Shelby—"

"Are you insane?"

"What if—"

It comes from a place of love, she reminded herself, but it also came from the fact that none of them could get over stuff that happened over a decade ago, so she needed to shut it down fast. "And which one of you chuckleheads was I supposed to drag out of bed at three in the morning to do it instead?"

"I'd rather be dragged out of bed than have you do something so stupid," Jamie snapped back. "Did you even stop to think about what might have happened? Or did you just run off half-cocked as usual? I think we need to discuss who's the real dumbass in this situation."

She couldn't kill her brother in Gran's parlor, but . . . "Careful, I have a key to your house and access to a boat," she warned in a low voice. "They'd never find your body."

Helena was stabbing at green beans, a small smile on her face. Although she normally kept quiet in situations like this, choosing to stay out of family squabbling, she didn't even look up as she said, "My money's on Shelby, Jamie."

Jamie frowned in Helena's direction, but he was still too chicken to take her on directly. He'd tried it once, back when he was sixteen or so, and he was *still* pouting over the smackdown Helena had delivered in return. Of course, Ryan would kill him if he tried to take her on now, so Jamie was stuck in forced silence and acceptance.

Personally, she found that very amusing.

Adam cleared his throat. "That addition won't take but a minute or two. I'll e-mail it to you tonight."

"Thank you. You know," she said casually, playing with her green beans, "I was thinking we might want to consider allowing more live-aboards, particularly during the off-season."

"There's not enough space," Eli said immediately, like he knew anything.

"There is," she corrected. "We just would need to use our space more wisely."

"Dad doesn't like a lot of live-aboards. It doesn't always attract the most high-quality people. You don't want that, do you?"

His patronizing tone was enough to set her teeth on edge. The amazing thing was that Jamie was always the first to jump on anyone who dared treat her as though she was stupid, yet ironically, he was often the very first to treat her as if she *were*. It was infuriating. Not that Ryan, Eli, or Adam were much better. It was a miracle they let her run around without a leash, much less run the marina. She kept her tone neutral. "We'd just need to be very specific about the rules and careful who we lease to. Of course, we'd also want to consider sprucing things up, adding more amenities."

"The kind of people who use the marina don't want amenities."

She kept the sigh behind her teeth and concentrated on keeping her tone very, very casual as she turned back to Ryan. "Attracting a more varied clientele is not a bad idea, you know. Some of the captains running boats out of Bay Breeze are getting close to retirement. We need to be looking ahead."

"As long as there are fish, there will be fishing boats. Don't borrow trouble you don't need, Shelby."

And Ryan considered himself a forward-thinking mayor. Small-scale fishing was in trouble and not nearly as profitable as it used to be. She wanted to reach across the table and smack him. She'd been hoping that the feedback from them might be a little more positive, giving her some backing if she brought it up to her father. "None of you know squat about the marina."

"We know you," Jamie said. "You may have great ideas, but you don't always think them through, and you rarely *follow* through. It wastes money and time and then we'll end up with a mess when you decide it's not worth fooling with anymore and jump to the next thing."

Okay, that was a low blow and completely untrue. Well, *now* at least. "Are you saying I don't know what I'm doing? I've been running that place for years. No one knows it better than I do."

"No one is saying you don't, Shel." Eli was, as usual, trying to be the peacemaker, but his tone was more placating than earnest, and it made her want to throw something at him.

"It sure sounds like Jamie is."

"Jamie is going to shut his mouth," Eli insisted, and Jamie, who'd been about to argue something, actually did. "We're just saying there's no reason to mess with something that's already working."

But I could make it work better. Sadly, though, that wasn't an argument she was going to be able to make right now, not with all of them able to gang up on her and dismiss her. And since she couldn't shout or knock heads together in the middle of a family Sunday lunch, it would only frustrate her to continue banging her head against that brick wall. "Fine."

There was an uncomfortable silence until Ryan cleared his throat. "So what are you going to do about your current live-aboard?" he asked.

She'd lost her appetite, so she placed her fork on her plate and leaned back. "Teach him the basics, glue the *Lady Jane* to the dock, and pray he wasn't lying when he told me he could swim. I mean, I can't kick him out now."

"But why is he here?" Ryan asked. "I think it's safe to assume he's not here for the fishing."

"From what I understand, he's out of work and had no place to live, so a friend offered him the boat."

"That's a very nice friend," Adam muttered. "And not at all sketchy. Are you sure he's not cooking meth on board or anything?"

"That's a terrible thing to assume." Granted, *she'd* had a similar thought, but it had been fleeting.

"I was wondering the same thing," Jamie added.

"Well, y'all should be ashamed of yourselves. He's an architect. He says he has a job starting in Miami after New Year's, so I think he's probably just in a bad spot at the moment. And anyway, I've been in the cabin—when I made the repair yesterday," she clarified against the look on Jamie's face, "and I saw no indication of anything other than some Netflix binge watching."

"Sounds heavenly, if you ask me," Eli said with a sigh. "A long vacation of doing nothing followed by a nap and more nothing."

Jamie shook his head. "Real grown-ups don't take four-month vacations. The dude definitely sounds sketchy. 'Between jobs' is just a fancy term for 'unemployed.' How's he paying for that Netflix?"

Jamie was a CPA, so everything always came down to money. "Maybe he's independently wealthy," Shelby offered in explanation. "One of those trust fund babies or something."

"Here?" Jamie nearly snorted. "Trust fund babies don't vacation in Magnolia Beach."

"Well, it's not really our business, is it?" Shelby said. "His rental check cleared, and he's not causing any problems at the marina, so I say 'Live and let live.'" She wasn't sure why she was defending Declan, but Jamie was acting no better than Kirby and that lot—minus the late-night raid, of course.

"Just yards from where you live?" Adam asked.

Shelby shot him a warning look. "Let it go."

"I'm going to have to back Shelby on this one, too," Helena said reasonably, and from the looks on the boys' faces, they were surprised to hear her chime in. "She's an adult with a good head on her shoulders and you have no real cause to suspect this guy is up to something shady. If it were one of *you* guys living at the marina instead of Shelby, you wouldn't be having this conversation, so not only is it insulting, it's extremely sexist, too."

Silence descended on the table. Shelby's own surprise at Helena's defense of her left her gaping like a goldfish for a minute, but she finally cleared her throat and said, "Thank you, Helena."

Helena gave her a small smile in return.

There were small huffs and mutters as the boys turned their interest to their plates, but it was safe to assume the topic had been shut down—at least for today. And while Shelby was happy for that, it was annoying as hell, too. Why was Helena so easily able to cow them? Shut them down like *her* word was the final say on it, when they'd have sassed back if she'd said the exact same thing? *Ugh*.

But she'd take the win, unsatisfactory as it was, for now, so that she could finish her lunch in peace.

Declan had to admit that he'd never seen a more miserable-looking bunch of teenagers before in his life. Or a line of angrier-looking parents behind them, either, which probably had a lot to do with the miserable looks on those young faces. And, good Lord, they were *young*; when had he gotten so old that high school seniors looked like babies?

He'd been awakened this morning by the heart-attack-inducing method of having a man stand on the dock beside the boat and shout his name. Crawling out to find a uniformed police officer doing that shouting had nearly finished him off. Uncaffeinated, it took him a moment to realize he wasn't the one in trouble, and as Shelby had promised, the police were merely following up on Friday night's episode and needed him to come down to the station, which Declan promptly did.

He'd never been inside a police station before, and it looked nothing like what he'd seen on TV, but that was offset by the fact he was now in the ridiculous position of trying to look adultish and stern as a girl with a tear-streaked face turned huge puppy-dog eyes on him and swore on an imaginary stack of Bibles she'd never, *ever* do anything like that again.

The boy next to her took her hand in solidarity. "We're sorry. We didn't mean for it to be a problem. We didn't know you didn't know how to drive the boat or anything."

The earnestness in his voice did a better job of shaming Declan for his lack of knowledge than a direct assault would have.

The police officer, who'd introduced himself as

Rusty Jeffers, cleared his throat. "Miss Shelby has agreed not to press charges against y'all for trespassing on the property provided you understand you're not to be there in the future unless it's daylight, you're sober, you have an adult with you, and you have actual business with the marina bringing you there. Understood?"

Six heads nodded.

"Mr. Hyde, what about you?"

"Um, er . . ." What was he supposed to say? The kids looked scared half to death already, and from the look of their parents, they had good reason to. He cleared his throat and looked over at Rusty. "What are my options?"

"You could choose to press charges—reckless endangerment, malicious mischief, disturbing the peace—"

The kids were flinching with each word, and the girl looked on the verge of tears again.

"*Or* we could handle this informally, with them doing some community service while they prove to us they're serious about staying out of trouble."

Oh, thank God. He pretended to be thinking about it, then tried to look stern and serious as he finally nodded. "I could be satisfied with that."

The kids looked like Christmas had come early. There were mumbled, but heartfelt, "Thanks, Mr. Hyde," and the kids were ushered out by their parents and with an ominous-sounding promise from Rusty that he'd be in touch about the community service.

Declan felt himself deflate a little once it was just him and Rusty in the small conference room, which seemed much bigger now that everyone else had gone. He leaned against the table and sighed. "Could you really have charged them with all that?"

Rusty shrugged. He had average good ol' boy looks, burly and red cheeked—pretty much exactly what a small-town police officer should look like. "Hell, I can *arrest* them for anything I want, maybe even get them charged, but any decent attorney would get those charges dropped pretty quickly."

"Then why even offer me—"

"It scared the living hell out of them, didn't it?" he said with a laugh. "That was my intention."

It would have been helpful to be in on that plan. "What would you have done if I'd actually *wanted* to press charges?"

Rusty shrugged again. "Talked you out of it. They're basically good kids. Between whatever punishments their parents hand out and the shame of having to do community service, I doubt they'll pull a stunt like that again."

Declan felt like he'd been playing a really warped game of chicken. "And if you hadn't been able to talk me out of it?"

Rusty hooked his thumbs into his belt and raised an eyebrow at him. "You do know you can't actually *force* me to arrest people, right?"

"Guess not. But you didn't know I wouldn't ask."

"Shelby said you were a decent guy. I wasn't worried."

How could Shelby possibly know he was a "decent guy" off just two conversations? The alternative, though, was that she could have judged him to be an asshole after just two conversations, so maybe he should just leave that question alone and consider himself lucky. "Is there anything else I need to do or is this matter closed now?"

"I think we'll consider it closed. Hell of a welcome to Magnolia Beach, though. Definitely out of the ordinary. We try to be friendlier to our visitors."

"I'm sure."

Four bottles of water sat in the center of the table—far fewer than they would have needed earlier, but too many now—and Rusty tossed one his way before opening another for himself. Then he sat, leaned back, and stretched his legs out. "Since we know you're not here for the redfish and pompano season, what does bring you to Magnolia Beach?"

So more nosiness camouflaged as small talk, then. It seemed like he should just get used to it. "Just some R and R."

"This is a good place for exactly that. It's a quiet place—usually"—he nodded toward the door the kids had just walked out of—"and off the beaten path. A good place to go to ground if you need to."

The word choice threw Declan for a second, but then he caught on. *Oh.* This wasn't just small talk or simple curiosity. "No one's looking for me, if that's what you're asking. I'm just killing time, not on the run."

"Now what would make you think I thought otherwise?"

Declan bit back a smile. "No reason. Just wanted you to know that. I've obviously attracted a bit of curiosity," he said, echoing Rusty's earlier movement and inclining his head toward the door and the teenagers who'd just left, "but I assure you, there's nothing interesting about me to uncover. I'm just an architect from Chicago enjoying your temperate weather for a couple of months."

"There are other snowbirds in town and more are on their way." Seemingly realizing that Declan wasn't dumb enough not to know what he was doing, Rusty dropped the overly casual tone and said plainly, "Shelby says you're paid up through the first of the year."

"I'll start my new job in Miami shortly after that."

"Well, if you need some work in the meantime to make ends meet . . ."

Declan shook his head. "My finances are in good shape. I'm not rich, but I can afford the break. No need to worry about me."

Rusty seemed satisfied with his answers and Declan wondered if it was really going to be that easy. Then he realized that Officer Rusty had had plenty of time to run a background check on him and was probably just testing his story. "Well, that's good," Rusty said, pushing to his feet. "And a belated 'Welcome' to Magnolia Beach. I'm sorry we had to meet this way, and may the rest of your stay be uneventful."

"That's the plan."

As they walked through the small police station, Rusty turned conversational again, which after the last "conversation" had Declan on alert. "You know, you should come into town more."

"I've been to the library, visited a couple of stores."

"But I mean really get out. It's not healthy for a man to spend that much time alone. Things are kinda slow this time of year, but there's usually something going on."

He wasn't really one for church bingo. "I'll think about it."

"Well, just ask Shelby for suggestions. She'll know where to send you."

"She can fix boats and play tour guide?" He laughed. "That's a broad skill set."

"And nobody knows the waters around here better than our Shelby. If you decide you'd like to try some fishing while you're here, she can hook you up."

Shelby seemed awfully young to be the local expert. "That's a lot of water to know. I'm impressed."

"Well, everyone has their strengths."

That was a very odd statement. "So you know Shelby pretty well?"

"Of course. I've known her entire family my whole life. She's a sweet girl."

Now there was something a little patronizing in his tone that just seemed wrong. "Well, I certainly owe her one."

"I heard you sent her flowers. I'm sure she figures you're even—even if it was part of her job to come get you."

There was a note of censure in Rusty's voice. Declan wasn't sure if it was aimed at him or Shelby, but . . . Well, Shelby *had* warned him about the gossip the flowers could cause.

"But," Rusty continued, "can I offer you a piece of advice?" The new edge to Rusty's voice told Declan he didn't really have the option of saying no. "Since you haven't been in town much, you may not have heard much about the Tanner family."

This is just getting ominous now. "I can't say that I have, no."

"They're good people. But you should know that Shelby's the only girl, and the boys are a little protective of her."

And there's the thinly veiled threat. "And how many Tanner boys are there?" he had to ask.

"Eight." Rusty smirked. "And none of them are what you'd call small."

Jeez. That thin veil had just been jerked away. There was no doubt he was being told to stay away from Shelby. Since he hadn't had any thoughts in that direction, he felt unfairly vilified. Carefully and casually he said, "I doubt they'll have any reason to be concerned about me."

"I didn't think so." Rusty patted him on the back as he opened the glass doors and ushered him outside into the parking lot.

The sunshine and fresh air were a nice change after the fluorescent lights and recirculated air of the police station, and it made the last half hour seem surreal. He'd unwittingly participated in a small-town version of *Scared Straight,* been quizzed on the reasons for his residency, and watched a six-foot fence be erected around one of the few people he knew in Magnolia Beach.

Then he'd walked outside into a picture-perfect, small-town Sunday afternoon of clean, quiet streets and sunny skies.

This was a weird little town.

Chapter 4

Shelby was more than a little fed up with this town and everyone in it. She could handle—and understand—the fact she'd probably never outlive the "sweet, but not too bright" label she'd earned as a kid, but jeez, she was dyslexic, not stupid. She might not be the second coming of Albert Einstein, but there were certified idiots running around Magnolia Beach, and no one interfered with *their* business or assumed they couldn't do their jobs.

People just seemed to conveniently forget that the marina was a business, too, and that it was *her* job to run it. And while Pee Wee Jamison had run a charter boat out of the Bay Breeze Marina for the last twenty years, he had no actual stake *in* the marina and didn't get to tell *her* when or if she could adjust the agreement. His lease was up for renewal, and she couldn't let him ignore the new terms when no one else could. She'd even gone to his house to sit down one-on-one and explain the changes, but he'd spent most of the time explaining how she was wrong before sending her off with an "I'll call your daddy and talk to him."

That was just unnecessarily sexist and patronizing and had nearly caused her head to explode. But hell, she could barely get her own family to take her seriously, so how could she expect anyone else to?

Thirty minutes of arguing with Pee Wee—and the nickname had more to do with his intellect than his size, because God knew, *his* reading skills weren't exactly up to grade level, either—had her needing a drink. But drinking before noon would definitely cause talk and there was no way that talk would *not* get back to her parents.

She decided to self-medicate with sugar instead, so she swung in and parked in front of Latte Dah. Wrenching open the door, she was hit with the scent of fresh coffee, which always perked her up, and she headed straight to the pastry display, which looked a little bit like what she thought heaven would. *Calories be damned.*

Molly, the sweet and unbelievably perky owner of the coffee shop, popped up from behind the counter with a smile.

"Hey, Shelby. How are . . ." The question faded out as Molly caught sight of Shelby's face. "Someone needs chocolate." She pulled a cake pop out of the display and handed it over.

"Bless you." The cake pops were Shelby's current addiction, and Molly was really good about remembering things like that about her customers. The chocolate candy shell gave way with a satisfying snap and yummy sugary goodness melted onto her tongue. Shelby let the simple pleasure spread through her before saying, "I'm going to need about a dozen of these to go."

"That's a sugar high I really don't want to witness and something I really don't think I want to be responsible for, either. Everything okay?"

"Just people. *Annoying* people." She took another

bite of the cake pop and eyeballed a pink one with sugar sprinkles that might be strawberry.

"Who on earth would intentionally annoy you?"

"Pee Wee Jamison."

"Ah, well, I think he annoys everyone," Molly said tactfully. "I wouldn't take it personally."

"I guess that's true."

"Anything I can do?" From anyone else, Shelby might have doubted the offer was genuine, but Molly was just so sweet, it had to be sincere.

"Ever been told not to worry your pretty little head over something because the menfolk would work it all out?"

"Oh, good Lord." Molly's sigh was one of solidarity. "Here, have another. It sounds like you've earned it." Molly put the pink cake pop on a small plate and slid it toward her. "Coffee?"

Shelby slid onto one of the counter's stools. "Please."

Latte Dah wasn't very busy; the morning rush was over with, and only a few people were ensconced in Molly's comfy chairs or working at her tables. It was a place designed for relaxing—cool blue walls, carefully mismatched furniture, and a homey feel. Latte Dah provided caffeine, sugar, and ambiance, and if she thought Molly would let her, Shelby would move right in and live there.

Molly put a steaming cup in front of her, pushed the milk pitcher her way, and then sat down beside her at the counter. "I heard you had some excitement Friday night."

Molly wasn't a gossip and there was nothing in her voice to indicate she was looking for dirt of any sort. She didn't have to—due to the nature of the coffee shop business, Molly seemed to know pretty much everything that went on in Magnolia Beach anyway. If Molly hadn't heard about it by now, then the small-town grapevine would have to have been irreparably broken.

"How'd you hear about that?"

"Helena told me about it first, but Mary Beth Carson's mother was in this morning, too."

Shelby sipped the coffee, which was somehow better than what she made at home, even though she bought the beans from Molly directly. "I feel a little bad for Mary Beth. She's a sweet girl—I doubt it was her idea."

"That's what Patty was telling me. Mary Beth is all torn up over it, by both what they did and what could have happened. And she's embarrassed as well."

"Isn't that kind of the point of community service? The public humiliation?"

Molly's lips thinned into a line. "Probably. How truly Puritan of us." Then she shrugged. "Well, I think it's safe to say Mary Beth has learned her lesson—and will probably be breaking up with Kirby because of it."

"Her idea or her parents'?"

"I'm not even going to guess. But Patty wanted me to know because Mary Beth applied for a job here, and she's afraid I'd hold that against her once I heard."

"Will you?"

"Nah. Teenage stupidity happens, and I'm not that much of a hypocrite."

It was hard to picture sweet little Molly stirring up trouble of any sort, but she'd had some dirty laundry aired earlier this year that showed she wasn't above bad teenage choices, either. So she was probably a good role model for Mary Beth—showing you could be a teenage screwup and still become a productive member of society as an adult.

Shelby, of course, had no secrets at all, as every one of her sins had already been witnessed and discussed by the entire population. It was both irritating and liberating. She wasn't sure she wanted to examine why too closely.

"How's . . ." Molly's brow wrinkled as she thought. "Oh, what's his name? Donovan?"

"Declan," Shelby supplied.

"Declan, that's it. How's Declan after his adventure?"

"Fine. Wait, how do *you* know Declan?"

"I don't really know him—he's come in a couple of times for coffee to go. But he seems like a nice enough guy."

"Yeah. I think he is. Nice, I mean." She didn't have a lot to go on really, but Rusty had given her a full report of what happened at the police station yesterday.

"Just FYI, Helena says Ryan's not too happy about him living at the marina with you there so close."

"Yeah, well, Declan's been there over a month, so Ryan's concern is a little tardy at best."

Molly laughed, then got up as the bell over the door announced her next customer. Shelby picked up the pink cake pop and licked at the sprinkles. Whether it was the sugar or the caffeine or the atmosphere—or a mixture of all three—her blood pressure was equalizing and she felt much better.

This was what the marina needed. Well, not exactly this—it would need to be more café than coffee shop, but expanding this idea to include breakfasts and light lunches would work. They could offer little picnics for people to take out with them on day trips, and maybe attract some of the tourists over. And it would be a nice place to be a sort of Welcome Center for Magnolia Beach, attracting people in from the water. It wouldn't have to be fancy, just cute, like Latte Dah.

She took a bite of the cake pop. Of course, having easy access to treats like this all day long would play hell with her waistline, so maybe it was a good thing that that idea was doomed from the get-go.

Sam Harris, Molly's soon-to-be-sister-in-law if things between Molly and Tate continued at their current rate, arrived then, dropping her purse behind the counter and tying on an apron. "Hi, Shelby. Need a refill?"

"How about one to go? I need to get back to the marina."

"Will do. By the way . . ." Sam grinned at her. "I heard about your high-seas rescue."

Ah, the joy of living in a small town. "It's not nearly as exciting as that."

"It sounded pretty dramatic to me."

"Then whoever told you exaggerated a lot."

Sam's face fell. "Darn. I heard he sent you flowers and everything."

Damn. "That part's true . . ."

"*Oooh,* and?" Sam snapped a lid onto the go-cup before passing it over and leaned down on her forearms, ready to listen.

"There's no 'and.' It was just a friendly gesture."

Sam frowned. "That's a pity. He's cute. A little scruffy, but . . ."

"*You've* met him, too?" Maybe Declan had been coming into town more than she assumed.

"Just once when he came in for coffee." She sounded a little disappointed that they hadn't met more often.

"I'm sure Declan will be happy to hear he's so memorable."

"A guy coming in all by himself in the off-season tends to stick out. That'd be true even if he wasn't cute, and Declan is."

"True."

"I wonder what his story is?"

Sam was fishing, but Shelby wasn't taking the bait. "I couldn't tell you. You didn't ask?"

Sam shrugged. "It was early. He didn't seem real talkative."

"That's never stopped you before," Shelby teased.

Sam grinned in return. "Let me know what you find out. Like, does he like girls with Southern accents?"

"Will do." She pulled a twenty out of her back pocket. "Two cake pops and the coffee."

Sam nodded and went to get her change.

Outside, the sun was bright and the temperature was perfect. Buoyed by the snack and the coffee, her mood was much better than it had been earlier.

She might as well let Daddy handle Pee Wee. It was galling, but she couldn't change the mind-set of one old redneck. And it wasn't worth the stress for her anyway.

One day, things would be different, but today was not that day.

Damn. Now she needed another cake pop.

It had taken Declan a while to get used to the constant movement of the *Lady Jane,* but he had to admit it gave him a good night's sleep. That was the upside to living on a boat. The downside, though, was living in a marina, which on some days, could rival the city with the amount of noise. It was a different kind of noise, though, not the sirens and garbage trucks he'd long since quit hearing. One freaking seagull looking for his breakfast could be equally as disturbing as the morning traffic through the marina.

And, good Lord, these people got up *early*. Somewhere, in the back of his mind, he'd known that fishermen and other outdoorsy people started their adventures early in the morning, but it hadn't been a real thing until the first time a fishing boat had puttered past around dawn. He could only be thankful that the marina wasn't busier than it was. Summers had to be a zoo.

The occasional early-morning awakening only added to the time warp he lived in, keeping him constantly confused as to both the day and the time, so when his phone woke him up and he saw Suzanne's name on the display, his first reaction was panic. Then he realized it was nearly noon. The panic was replaced with confusion and wariness about answering.

He hadn't spoken to her in two months. Hell, she hadn't even been there when he'd moved his stuff out, and he'd simply left his key on the kitchen counter in lieu of saying good-bye. What would cause her to break her silence now?

Whether it was curiosity or masochism that caused him to hit the accept button, he didn't know—and he didn't want to examine it too closely either.

"Hi, Suz."

"Declan. It's good to hear your voice."

That was funny. She'd said she never wanted to speak to him again. "How are you?"

"I'm *good*. Feeling strong and whole again. How about you?" She was chipper, yet censuring at the same time. How *did* she manage that trick?

"I'm fine," he answered carefully. "I'm just surprised you'd call."

"Well, I've got some mail here for you," she explained. "Mostly magazines, things like that. I was wondering if you wanted me to forward it on to you."

He'd filed a change of address with the post office, forwarding his mail in care of the marina. To date, he'd received approximately two things. "Unless it's something that looks important, you can trash it."

There was a moment of silence. "I guess none of it's important enough, then."

Which Suzanne had to have known already and therefore had nothing to do with this call. If he waited just another second or two . . .

"Reid says you're living on a boat in Alabama. I couldn't believe it."

"Believe it."

"That's got to be . . . interesting."

"It's fantastic. So peaceful. Everyone should try it."

Suzanne laughed. They both knew she wouldn't last more than a couple of days outside the city. Hell, she panicked after a few days in the suburbs. Then she fell silent again. He didn't say anything, just let the silence draw out instead. Whatever the actual reason for this call was, she was about to get to it. He'd lived with her for nearly five years; he knew how this worked. And frankly, now he was curious to see what she'd say.

"Are you happy?" she finally asked.

He couldn't tell if that was a genuine question or a sarcastic one. Her tone wasn't clear. "Excuse me?"

"Did moving away make you happy?"

He wasn't sure how to answer that. "I guess. Things are a little strange right now—I'm kind of in limbo until I get to Miami—but I'm not unhappy." That was true, even if he wasn't sure it was the right answer.

"Dr. Stewart says . . ."

He rolled his eyes because Suzanne wasn't there to see it. To this day he didn't know where Dr. Stewart had received his medical training, but it couldn't have been an accredited school. The man was a quack, and Suzanne had been seeing him weekly for about twelve years. He fed her poor-little-rich-girl problems, massaged her ennui, assigned blame to everyone but her, and then purchased himself a summer home with the proceeds instead of simply telling her the truth: everyone had problems, but her life didn't exactly suck.

That had been Declan's job—at least for a little while. It hadn't gone over well with Suzanne *or* Dr. Stewart, and eventually, he'd given up.

". . . and that it's probably not even your fault that you're selfish like that."

Part of him wished he hadn't spaced out in the middle of that comment, but at the same time, it was probably a good thing he had. He'd never been on the couch with Dr. Stewart, but the man had diagnosed him via Suzanne's reports years ago. Whatever it was that had driven her to call, it was *entirely* his fault and due to a serious flaw in him—and probably something to do with his mother, too.

But he didn't live with Suzanne anymore, so arguing with her about the condition of his psyche seemed beyond ridiculous. "Suz, why'd you call?"

He heard her take a deep breath. "I need closure. I *deserve* closure."

Huh? "*You* broke up with me. *You* kicked me out. I'm literally on the opposite end of the country from you, and we haven't spoken in months. How much more 'closure' do you need?"

"Emotional closure, Declan. I need to know where we went wrong so I can heal and move on."

He gritted his teeth. "You just said you were feeling 'whole' again."

"*Almost* whole. There's a difference. I gave you five *years* of my life. I can't get that time back."

He hadn't considered it a waste of time . . . until now, and only because she seemed to. "Well, neither can I."

"Declan . . ."

He heard her voice break and that made him feel bad. Suzanne was self-centered, vain, and spoiled, but he had cared about her, lived with her, and even considered marrying her. "I'm sorry, Suz."

"That's all you have to say?"

She was on the verge of tears, but what else was he supposed to say? Well, actually he knew his role and his lines, and he had nothing to lose by giving her the victory she needed. "It's my fault. You deserve better."

"That's true. You're selfish and narcissistic, and . . ."

And obviously, a masochist. They'd already had this fight. He rubbed a hand over his eyes. "All I wanted to do was move. It's a better job and a great opportunity."

"For *you*. You never once discussed it with me. Asked me whether I wanted to leave my home, my family, my friends . . ."

"I made a choice. Just like you made a choice."

"You chose a job over me."

"And you chose your family and friends over me." It wasn't quite the same weight, but all choices came with costs, and neither of them had chosen the other. It was quite telling.

That silenced her. He could hear her breathing, so he knew she was still there. Finally, he heard her inhale. "That's not the same thing. At all. People are more important than some job."

A statement only an heiress could make.

"You need help, Declan. Serious help. At least I have family and friends to lean on. You have no one now. You're out there looking for something, but you don't even know what it is. That's why you can't be happy."

"I am happy, damn it," he snapped.

"Yeah, right. That's why you're living on a boat in some redneck town, alone, with no job and no friends."

That was not *why he was here.* "Maybe after living with you for so long, I need the break."

He heard her gasp at the insult, and he regretted lashing out at her like that. It was just easier—for her and for him—to shoulder the blame and let Suzanne get her closure. "Suz, I'm sorry. For everything. You're right. You deserve better than me, and I hope you find the right guy soon."

"I will. I hope you're sorry it's not you."

Well, that was about the best I could hope for. "I am," he lied.

Suzanne took a deep breath and sighed heavily. "Have a nice life, Declan. I don't know what you're looking for, but I hope you find it."

"Take care, Suz." But he was talking to a dead phone. Dropping it beside him on the bed, he stacked his hands behind his head and stared at the ceiling.

Suzanne's need to overpsychoanalyze everything always frustrated him, but it was just how she was. He knew that—and at first it had been amusing. A not-quick-enough-replied-to text showed a lack of respect for her. An offhand joke that fell flat was a sign he didn't appreciate her enough. And then she'd trace those slights back to his underprivileged childhood through a flow chart that made zero sense to anyone other than her.

She'd spent so much time examining his childhood and psyche that *he* certainly didn't feel the need to. What it came down to was that Suzanne needed to be adored and he wasn't doing that correctly. Or enough.

Suzanne was right, though: he had chosen a job over

her without much thought. And although it sounded terrible, he sort of knew, deep down, that Suzanne wouldn't make the move with him. It made him wonder now if that deep-seated knowledge had led to his accepting the job in the first place.

He shook his head to clear it. Good Lord, he was getting as bad as Suzanne, looking for reasons that didn't exist because there were *actual* reasons that decisions were made—none of which had anything to do with anything other than the right job offer.

Miami. Sun, beaches, all that great art deco . . . Who wouldn't choose Miami over Chicago? All that snow and ice and weeks where the temperature would make Santa want to move to Florida versus sun and surf? Miami had all the art and culture and nightlife of Chicago set to a salsa beat.

It wasn't like he'd asked Suzanne to move somewhere like . . . well, like Magnolia Beach. He snorted. Suzanne wouldn't be able to even *imagine* living in a place like Magnolia Beach. The only place to get sushi was run by a guy named Bubba, which didn't sound very authentic, and the few red lights the town boasted all went blinky at ten o'clock. Granted, the marina wasn't exactly in the center of the action, but he wasn't sure there would be much to do even if it was. He wasn't sure there even *was* any action in Magnolia Beach. Or a center, for that matter.

You're living on a boat in some redneck town, alone, with no job and no friends.

While all technically true, Suzanne's jab lacked oomph. Well, too much oomph. He *was* starting to get a little bored. But being alone didn't mean he was lonely. Suzanne was the one who needed to surround herself with people all the time, not him. *She* was the social butterfly; he was perfectly happy in his cocoon.

It was a carefully constructed cocoon, and he didn't need a shrink to explain that it traced back to his lonely days as a child, only to be perfected as he grew into a bookish, nerdy teen. That cocoon had been his shield against the teasing and bullying of the neighborhood kids and, later, the kids in his fancy prep school.

In college, he'd discovered the cultural idea of a hipster, and it had been an easy slide from awkward nerd to aloof hipster. Hipsters were at least somewhat cool.

While Suzanne needed to be the center of attention, he'd been perfectly happy on the perimeter. He didn't really like people—in general—all that much. Being stuck in the boonies would be a nightmare for Suzanne, but he had come down here looking *forward* to it.

But suddenly, the next eight or so weeks—which had seemed so short and easy to dismiss six weeks ago—loomed large.

And boring.

It wasn't that he didn't need or hadn't earned the time off. He just wasn't used to the inactivity. He'd spent his whole life with his eyes on his goal, and he'd worked damn hard to achieve it.

Study hard, get good grades, get a scholarship to get him the hell out of Detroit.

Study hard, get good grades, land a good job.

Work hard, move up the ladder, make a name for himself, get a *better* job.

Find the right girl, make the right friends, meet all the right people, get an even better job.

And if he did it all right, kept his eyes on the prize and his nose to the grindstone, eventually it would all pay off.

But now that he was almost there, the whole plan had ground to a halt, leaving him cooling his heels here and killing time.

Waiting.

And that was the problem. He was so damn tired of waiting, of getting ready for his life to actually start.

He should have just gone on to Miami, even if it would have meant multiple moves. He could be on a beach right now, making contacts, living the life he'd worked so hard to earn.

But in reality, that would be *more* waiting, just in a more expensive spot. And while his savings account was healthy, the cost of living in Miami without an income would burn through a hefty chunk of that pretty quickly. And he was not going to be poor again.

So he was stuck here, in Magnolia Beach.

Waiting.

His stomach growled, giving him a reason to get out of bed, and he pushed himself upright. His hand landed on the book he'd been reading last night. When he'd gotten home from the police station yesterday, he'd found it propped against the cabin door—a thin, dull-looking book with a badly Photoshopped cover picture of a family on a pontoon boat and the uninspiring title of *Responsible Boating*.

While there was no doubt Shelby had left the book for him—her name was printed on the inside cover in block letters—there had been no note accompanying it. With nothing else to do last night, he'd read it, assuming Shelby expected him to, but it had been as frightfully dull as the cover promised.

That didn't exactly bode well for today's lesson, but he wasn't dreading it either. It was a pretty day, and it wasn't like he had other pressing plans. And it didn't hurt that his instructor was the funny, interesting, and lovely Shelby Tanner.

He didn't *have* to wait around, alone in a redneck town with nothing to do and no one to do it with. He needed to make the most of the situation, learn to adapt, and bloom where he was planted—even if he was just killing time.

It beat the hell out of the alternative.

Chapter 5

Shelby was prompt, arriving one minute early for his lesson in what he was beginning to think was her uniform of shorts and T-shirt. "You ready?"

"As ready as I'll ever be."

"Try not to sound so excited," she said as she climbed aboard and dropped a backpack onto one of the seats. "It'll be painless, I promise. It might even be fun."

"Am I going to be tested on this?" he asked, handing her back the book as she got settled.

"Did you read it?"

"Yes."

Shelby grinned and slid the book inside her bag. "Then no."

"Then why did I read it?"

She shrugged. "I just wanted to offer you a head start since you don't know all that much. I didn't want you to feel stupid or get overwhelmed."

While that was kind of her . . . "So you'd have tested me on it if I'd said no?"

"How? I'm not a licensing official of the state of Alabama. I can't 'test' you on anything. But it does make this easier—if nothing else, I know you won't be a pain in the butt about learning."

"Will I be ready to take the boating license test when we're done?"

"God, no," she scoffed. "I'm just hoping you won't drown. Or wake me up again," she added with a smile.

"I'm glad to know you have such low expectations."

"I'm just being realistic. Basics first."

In reality, safety was first, as she showed him where life jackets and beacons and radios were stored and how they worked. It was a full hour before Shelby even untied the boat from the dock. Actually driving the boat wasn't completely unlike driving a car, only it handled much differently, and it wasn't long before he was feeling pretty proud of his ability. He wasn't ready to captain anything, but in the highly unlikely chance that he found himself accidentally floating away or in some other kind of emergency, he now had a clue of what to do.

Interestingly, though, that was pretty much what he was doing *now*—floating outside the entrance into Mobile Bay. He could still see land if he looked behind him, but the Gulf of Mexico stretched out in front of him all the way to the horizon. He shut off the engine and turned to Shelby with a grin. "That was easy."

"You did well." She sat back and turned her face to the sun, stretching her legs out along the cushioned seat. She rolled her shirtsleeves up to the shoulders and stacked her hands behind her head as she basked. She had nice arms and *great* legs, toned and strong, and he didn't mind the view at all. The sporty tomboy look was really growing on him. "But don't get too cocky about your newfound skills. You're nowhere near ready to strike out on your own," she cautioned.

"I wouldn't dream of it. But I won't have to wake you up again. I promise."

"That's excellent. The *Lady Jane* is really user-friendly—even for newbies. It's got all the latest tech, especially designed to keep or get you out of trouble."

"It?"

Her eyebrows pulled together over the frames of her sunglasses. "Huh?"

"You called the *Lady Jane* an 'it.' I thought boats were always 'she.'"

Shelby made a face. "Don't be silly. It's an inanimate object. It doesn't have a gender."

What little knowledge he thought he had about boats was being shot down quickly. "I thought it was tradition or something."

"It's an antiquated idea as well as completely sexist. And ridiculous."

He laughed. "Why don't you tell me how you really feel."

She fake-smiled at him. "You really don't mean that."

"All right, then." It seemed Shelby had some strong opinions to go with those strong legs, and she had no problem speaking those opinions. He liked that. His earlier conversation with Suzanne made him far more appreciative of Shelby's honest, straightforward style. He waited for her to say something else, but she just sat there basking in the autumn sun—which was rather nice, but a bit anticlimactic. After a few minutes of quiet nothing, he finally asked, "So now what do we do?"

"If you had any gear on board, we could fish, but . . ."

There might be gear on board—somewhere. The *Lady Jane* was, after all, a fishing boat, and there were all kinds of hidey-holes he hadn't bothered to inspect. "You like to fish?"

"Yes, I do. I take it you don't?"

"I don't really like to see my food when it's still alive."

She smirked. "Fair enough. Then I guess we'll just do this for a little while."

"This?"

She sighed. "Have you never even been on a boat before?"

"Of course I have." Granted, they were party cruises on the lake, but . . .

"Well, this is kinda what you *do* on a boat. You relax. You enjoy the sound of the water and the feel of the breeze and the warmth of the sun . . . It's supposed to be peaceful. Very Zen. So just close your eyes and breathe."

Suzanne had also been very into finding her Zen, but as far as he could tell, that involved yoga classes and guided meditations with the improbably named Guru Scott. "You're not going to chant, are you?"

"No." A small smile on her face, she exhaled deeply. He couldn't tell if her eyes were closed or not behind her sunglasses, but he assumed they were. "Now just breathe for a minute."

He felt weird doing it, but he tried. It was a nice day, and he tried to concentrate on that as they sat quietly for a few minutes. Then he realized they were still moving. "Shouldn't we drop anchor?"

She sighed and he heard the exasperation. "Nah. It's too deep." He must have made a sound, because Shelby looked at him over her sunglasses. "Are you worried we're going to hit something?"

He could see a few other boats, but none close enough

to be considered a danger at the moment. "I guess not. But we *are* drifting."

"We won't go far. I promise."

"I guess I'll have to trust you. Officer Rusty says that no one knows the waters around here better than you."

The corner of her mouth twitched. "That's very kind of him to say so."

He couldn't help noticing she didn't argue with the truth of the statement. He liked people who were sure of their skills and didn't claim false modesty when it was unwarranted. "I'm not sure I'd call him 'kind.' I mean, he scared the hell out of those kids and then tried to scare me, too."

"Well, the kids deserved it—and needed it, probably—but how on earth did Rusty scare you?"

"I said he *tried*. There was a little grilling on why I was here."

"You can't really blame him for that. It is a little odd."

"I'm not the only person to ever winter in Magnolia Beach," he reminded her.

"But you're the first snowbird *I've* ever met under the age of seventy."

He adjusted his sunglasses and mirrored Shelby's posture, trying to relax. "And here I thought small towns were supposed to be friendly places."

"They are. And *we* are. But *because* it's a small town, suspicious behavior stands out more."

"How have I been behaving suspiciously?"

Without looking at him, she held up a finger. "One, you're a little young to be a snowbird, and they usually come in pairs anyway. Two,"—another finger went up—"you don't go into town much, so few people have met you, and no one knows anything about you. Three, the *Lady Jane* isn't your boat, so you're not here for the fishing. And four, when Rusty asked me, all I could tell him was that you kept to yourself and didn't have visitors, but that you'd sometimes leave and be gone all day. If you were a police officer, what would *you* make of all that?"

When she put it that way . . . "I guess that does sound a little suspicious."

"So what *are* you doing here?" She sat up. "Honestly."

"Did Rusty ask you to find out?"

"No, but I am curious."

"I told you. This is my first vacation in years. I'm vacationing."

"I thought you said you were unemployed."

"Between jobs," he corrected.

She waved a hand. "Same difference."

"Not really." He might not be able to see Shelby's eyes behind her sunglasses, but he could practically hear them roll. He sighed. "It's a long story."

She smirked and tucked her legs underneath her, tailor-style. "I've got some time."

"And it's not terribly interesting."

"I live in a very small town. I think you'd be surprised at what I can find interesting." She crossed her arms over her chest, an expectant look on her face, and waited.

He could just wait her out, but he had a feeling he'd lose this standoff. "A guy I know from college recommended me to a guy he knows in Miami who will have an opening at his office in January. I interviewed and they offered me the job—and it's a great one with more money, better position—and I accepted. But when my current employer found out I was planning to leave . . ."

"They fired you." She seemed to be considering something. "Okay, while technically still unemployment, I'll give you 'between jobs.'"

"How kind of you."

"I try. But that wasn't a very long story at all."

"Nor very interesting. I warned you."

"But still . . . why not stay in Chicago then? Why come here?"

"Aside from all the snow in Chicago?"

"Well, you won't see *that* here, but I'd think even the prospect of snow wouldn't be worse than being all alone in a town where you don't know anyone."

He hesitated, even though he had no idea why. "It seemed like a good idea at the time."

There was another of those moments when Shelby seemed to be considering what he'd said, and those moments were making him increasingly uncomfortable, as she seemed able to fill in all the things he *didn't* say, too. Her mouth twitched into an almost-smile. "Ah, there's a woman back in Chicago."

There was no sense denying it. He just shrugged.

"Why'd she break up with you?"

Why'd she automatically assume Suzanne had broken up with him? She was right, but . . . *Jeez.* He was starting to rethink his earlier admiration of her straightforward style. "You have no problem asking people very personal questions, do you?"

Shelby laughed. "None at all. There are no secrets in small towns, and I'm just naturally curious."

He had nothing to lose. "When I told her I'd taken the job, she told me she didn't want to move to Miami."

Shelby's eyes widened. "You accepted a job in Miami and didn't check with your girlfriend *first* to see if she was okay with it?" She shook her head sadly. "Men."

He was *not* going to respond to that.

"Is she an architect, too?"

"No, Suz is a corporate art curator."

"And that is . . ."

"She buys art for companies as investments. Usually from new and upcoming artists she thinks will hit big and make their early work valuable."

"Sounds impressive. And risky. What happens if the art doesn't appreciate?"

"She works mostly for her father. She's got job security, regardless."

Shelby looked at him over her sunglasses again. "I'm not one to look down my nose at people who work for their parents."

"I'm not judging people for working for their parents. But Suzanne likes to be beautiful among other beautiful things. Her father indulges her on that."

"That's a bit harsh," Shelby scolded.

"Suz is kind and sweet and beautiful. She might not have a lot of depth, but that's not entirely her fault. She is what she is."

"Were y'all together a long time?"

"Nearly six years."

Shelby frowned. "Yet you say she's shallow. That doesn't speak too highly of you."

"Because I say she's shallow or because I was with her even though she was?"

Shelby laughed. "Both, actually."

"I don't mean it as an insult. She had many good qualities, and I did care about her."

Shelby didn't look convinced, but she still nodded. "So is that why you hide on the boat all the time? Are you nursing a broken heart?"

Boy, Shelby had no filter at all. It was a bit disconcerting. "I'm *not* hiding. I'm *vacationing*. Catching up on all the TV and books I've missed. Sleeping. Studying Florida building codes."

"That's fair enough, but you should really try spending some time in town. Meet new people, stuff like that. It would help you get over her faster."

The funny thing was, he was already over Suzanne. That last phone call had proven that. He had no doubt that if he hadn't accepted the job in Miami, he'd still be with her, but after the initial shock, he'd been fine. He really didn't miss her beyond the strangeness of being single when he'd been part of a couple for so long. His heart *wasn't* broken, which was good, but Shelby was right in that it didn't say much for what kind of person he was to have been with a woman for that long and now wonder why he'd been with her at all.

"I could introduce you to some people," Shelby offered.

"That's okay. I'm quite enjoying the alone time."

"Aren't you bored? Or lonely?"

"I have plenty to keep me occupied, and since I don't really like people all that much, I'm not lonely, either."

Shelby's eyebrows pulled together. "How can you not like people?"

He wasn't sure how to answer that. "'I have not the talent which some people possess of conversing easily with those I have never seen before.'"

Shelby looked at him blankly.

"*Pride and Prejudice?* Mr. Darcy?"

"Oh. I've never read it. I kind of remember the movie, though." Shelby didn't call him a nerd outright, but he assumed it was implied in the tone. "Still, that much alone time isn't healthy."

"And you're an expert on mental health?"

She snorted. "I don't need to be an expert. Humans are social creatures. Solitary confinement has been proven to cause psychosis," she said primly.

"I'm good," he assured her. "No need to worry about me."

"Forget you. I'm worried about *me*. If you snap and go all axe-murdery, *I'm* your nearest neighbor."

The statement was both earnest and ridiculous and it made him laugh. "If you think that's a possibility, I'm surprised you're not worried about being out here with me."

An eyebrow arched up over her sunglasses. "Are you saying I need to be?"

Was she flirting? "Maybe."

"Well, I can take care of myself."

So much for that. "It doesn't matter as I've already been warned to stay away from you by a man wearing a gun."

That got her attention. "*Excuse* me?"

Her indignation made it almost impossible for him to keep a straight face. "Rusty made a point of telling me about your eight brothers ready to kick my ass."

"I cannot believe him." She shook her head disgustedly and muttered something under her breath, punctuating it with the most exasperated sigh he'd ever heard. Then, resigned, she offered, "And it's just one brother."

He laughed. "So Officer Rusty lied to me about eight Tanner boys guarding your virtue?"

"No. There *are* eight Tanner boys. Seven of them are cousins, though. And four are away at school right now anyway."

"I like those odds much better."

"Oh, you do, do you?"

"Yeah." Although until two minutes ago, he hadn't actually thought about it. Maybe it was the fact Officer

Rusty had put Shelby off-limits that suddenly brought her to his attention. She was certainly pretty—very earthy and real. Suzanne had first fascinated him by her cool aloofness and classic beauty. But Shelby now had him rethinking his "type." And while she was friendly and her voice had a teasing tone to it, it was hard to tell if she was being flirty or not.

She laughed. "Those odds are still not in your favor."

Well, that answered *that* question. He was a little more disappointed than he expected to be. "Rusty said they were big."

"Well, their egos certainly are. At least the older ones," she amended. "I'm working on making the younger ones a little less . . . well, less Tanner-ish."

"Tanner-ish?"

"Loud-mouthed know-it-alls bordering on insufferable."

"Sounds charming."

Her sigh was one of the long-oppressed. "And yet everyone still likes them."

"Except you."

"No, including me," she admitted. "They irritate the snot out of me, and I want to smack them half the time because they're all up in my business *all* the time, but they're family. You know how that is."

She seemed to be waiting for his agreement, but he couldn't relate. "I've got one sister. She's six years older and lives in Colorado, so we're not exactly close."

"And your parents?"

"My mom died four years ago. I haven't seen my dad since I was a kid."

She blanched. "I'm so sorry."

"No need to be."

"Still, I apologize for being so rude and flippant."

After a long moment, she asked, "So no other family in Chicago?"

Boy, she just can't help herself. But it wasn't irritating. She seemed genuinely, honestly curious and without an agenda. "No, I moved there for grad school and stayed to work. I've got some extended family in Upstate New York, but I grew up in Detroit, so I don't know them very well . . ."

"Wow. I can't even imagine." It almost sounded like she felt sorry for him.

He needed to change the tone of this. "You know, it makes the holidays so much easier. No stress about trying to get home or the family dramas."

She took the change in tone. "That would be easier. Sometimes I think I'm related by blood or marriage to about half of Mobile County. It gets complicated."

"That must make it hard to date—even without Officer Rusty running interference."

She smirked. "There's a reason Southern family trees don't always branch."

Unfortunately he'd just taken a drink of water, and her words nearly had him spewing it everywhere.

But Shelby had moved on as if she hadn't just said something outlandish and was now gesturing toward the shore. "Why don't you show me what you've learned and take us in?"

It was a hard turn from the previous conversation, and it took him a second to switch gears. "I thought we were going to sit here for a little while. Breathe and find the Zen and all that."

"You're the one who's on vacation, not me. *I've* got work to do. I left Harvey minding the office, but I can't stay gone too long."

He was a little disappointed to have the outing end.

The isolation must have finally gotten to him. But whatever the reason, he *had* been enjoying himself.

All things considered, he did pretty well going back in. There were several more boats in the marina then there had been when they left, and there was a small crowd milling around near the building, making him realize she really did have work to do.

The *Lady Jane* bumped against the dock a little harder than he'd intended, but all in all, it wasn't a bad performance, and Shelby's praise, while not excessive, was genuine.

She showed him how to secure the ropes—and double-checked them, he noticed—then dug into her backpack, pulling out a certificate, a smiley face sticker, and a Bay Breeze Marina water bottle like the one she'd been using and handed them to him.

"What's this?"

Her mouth twitched, but her voice was serious. "It's what we give to all the people who complete the Magnolia Beach basic boat safety class."

The water bottle was full of M&Ms. "Really?"

"Well, the average age of the participants is usually about seven. But your certificate has been signed by the mayor and everything," she said brightly, pointing to the signature of Mayor Ryan Tanner. *She was related to the mayor.* Somehow, that didn't surprise him.

"So, congratulations." She stuck out her hand, forcing him to juggle the items in order for him to shake it. It was the first time she'd touched him, and he was surprised by the little frizz of electricity that shot up through his arm. There was a brief moment where Shelby's eyes widened as if she'd felt it, too, but it was gone as quickly as it happened.

With a small wave and a "See you around, Declan

Hyde," she headed up toward the building, already talking loudly to the crowd gathered there.

There was something about the way she said it that rather implied she wasn't planning on it. He flipped the top of the bottle open and shook M&Ms into his mouth.

That little electric shock had woken something up inside him—something he hadn't felt in a very long time. It was strange, but good, too.

And odd. He didn't quite know why.

Maybe the next few weeks might not be so boring after all.

Chapter 6

The Bait Box was definitely a local's bar. Although tourists weren't *un*welcome there, Magnolia Beach catered to families in the summer and snowbirds in the winter, so they didn't get a lot of out-of-town folks just wandering in for a beer and the limited entertainment on offer.

It was also a bit of a dive, which Shelby kind of liked, but that tended to limit its appeal to outsiders. Scuffed and blackened hardwood floors, cheesy neon beer signs, and the aroma of stale beer and fried foods created a certain kind of ambiance—and that ambiance would never be described as "classy."

But it was comfortable home turf, *her* turf, where Peter the bartender not only knew what she liked to drink, but also special-ordered it from the brewery in Mobile just for her.

Monday nights were always slow, keeping both the noise level reasonable and the pool tables available so she and Charlotte could play without people hanging over their shoulders.

Charlotte was currently trying to knock the seven ball into a corner pocket by banking it off the side rail but finding little success. As the cue rolled past where Shelby was leaning against the table, she caught it and sent it back to Charlotte to try again.

"Thanks." Charlotte frowned as she lined up the shot again. "It shouldn't be this hard."

"Aim here." Shelby put her finger on the rail where the cue ball needed to hit. Even with the shot lined up correctly, the cue somehow bounced off and rolled in the *opposite* direction of the seven. Shelby had to laugh. "Well, *that's* certainly not easy to do."

"Ugh. I suck at this." Charlotte held up a finger in warning. "And don't say 'It's just geometry.' I damn near failed geometry and you know it."

Shelby bit back the smile. Shortly after Shelby had finally gotten her official dyslexia diagnosis, Charlotte had discovered that dyscalculia was an actual thing. She'd immediately diagnosed herself with that, blaming it for her math struggles. Shelby appreciated the show of solidarity for what it was. Math was the one subject she'd done pretty well in and was the only thing that managed to salvage her GPA. So she'd gotten Charlotte through their math classes, and Charlotte had gotten her through pretty much everything else. Together, they made a great team.

Charlotte lined up the shot one more time, aiming again at the place on the rail Shelby indicated, and this time, the cue ball ricocheted into the seven, sending it rolling slowly into the pocket. It wasn't the cleanest shot, but it got the job done. *And we still make a great team.* "There you go."

"About damn time." Charlotte leaned her stick against the table and reached for her beer. "I think I'll drink for a while. It couldn't make my game any worse. So what about my proposal?"

"I know half a dozen captains who'd be more than capable to do it, but not for the money y'all are offering. It's barely enough to cover fuel costs, much less their time. I can make those kinds of arrangements for your team—that's no problem—but you'll have to come up with more money before I could even ask anyone in good conscience."

Charlotte sighed. "That's what I thought, but this new director wants good science done cheap and that's just not possible. He is possibly the tightest guy I've ever met. He'd squeeze a nickel until the buffalo burped."

"You *have* met my brother, right? The boy wants a PowerPoint presentation on profit and loss before every trip to the freaking grocery store." Charlotte started to laugh, but Shelby interrupted her. "Seriously, when we had that storm damage last year, Jamie wanted to see full written estimates with labor and supplies itemized before we could start the repairs."

"That's just typical bean counter stuff."

"Not when you're hiring your *cousin* to do the work."

Charlotte snorted. "We should get Jamie and Director Cheapo together."

"Trust me, you do not want Jamie anywhere near your program. He'd drive you just as insane as he drives me."

"You do know that really good small business accounting programs exist, right? You could fire him."

"It's not my marina, so it's not my place."

"*Yet.*"

It was a point of some contention for Charlotte that Shelby could run the marina, essentially giving her parents early retirement, yet not really be in charge. Shelby appreciated the loyalty and vote of confidence, but that's just the way things were. "And, God willing, it won't be for another twenty years or so."

Charlotte blanched at the realization of what she'd just implied. "Of course."

"Until then, it's important to Mom and Daddy that Jamie play *some* role in the family businesses. But because he's such an indoor cat, he's not interested in much beyond the books. And I hate doing the quarterly taxes anyway."

"There are other accountants."

"Oh, and that wouldn't make Sunday dinners at *all* uncomfortable. Anyway, I need Jamie and Daddy both right now."

"Because . . ."

She sighed. "Some of the older men won't even talk to me. Especially the ones from out of town. They all want to speak to the 'man in charge.'"

"Why?"

"One, because I'm female, and two, because I'm young. Therefore, I couldn't *possibly* have a clue as to what I'm talking about. They pat me on the head and call me sweetie, and then look around for a man to talk to." She couldn't help snorting. "It seems I need the beard."

Charlotte's nose wrinkled up in distaste. "That's just . . . *wrong.*"

"I know. But the good ol' boy mentality is still strong in these parts. You know that."

"But they all know you."

"And that's part of the problem. I've got a lot to live down. Folks who can remember the Homecoming Parade disaster of my sophomore year don't exactly see 'Competent Businesswoman' when they look at me."

Charlotte winced. She'd been partly responsible for that fiasco, but folks tended to remember Shelby's role more—if for no other reason than it'd been so much more visible. "But still . . ."

"I know. But some of the captains are just resistant to change. They did their business with my grandfather and then my father. They expected Jamie to take over, not me, and they're just more comfortable talking to a man."

Charlotte rolled her eyes and sighed before reaching for the rack and pulling balls out of the pockets. "Let's play before I get any more depressed. You break."

Shelby was lining up her shot when Charlotte let out a low whistle. "Well, hel-*lo*, handsome," she murmured, her voice suddenly half an octave lower and slightly purring.

She looked up to see Charlotte looking a little glazed. "What?"

"A really, *really* hot guy just walked in."

Here? As if. "Oh, don't tease."

"Honey, he is no joke." She fanned herself. "*Hummina.*"

Shelby took her shot, the balls scattering nicely even though nothing fell in. Straightening up, she said, "Okay, where?"

Charlotte tipped her beer bottle a fraction of an inch in the direction of the bar. "He's talking to Peter. Be casual."

It felt silly, but Shelby casually made her way to Charlotte's side of the pool table, where she'd have a good view of the bar and anyone at it. The only person she saw was Jimmy Green, who, while sweet and funny and kind, was *not* best described as "hummina." "Don't be mean. Jimmy's a good guy." And he'd had a major crush on Charlotte since about second grade.

"Not Jimmy. The guy Jimmy is blocking. *Move*," she muttered, as if she had telekinetic powers.

"Are you about to ditch me?" Whoever this hunk of burning love was, she had no doubt that Charlotte could land him like a lazy fish—which was fine, except that it would put an end to their evening. "Because if so, I'm not going to order another beer."

"I think I'll just appreciate him from here for now—provided Jimmy will just *move.*"

Jimmy did move at that moment, opening up the view to the man behind him. He was leaning against the bar and had his back to them, so Shelby couldn't tell much beyond the fact he was tall and broad-shouldered and had a cute butt cradled in some very lucky Levi's. His hair was dark and curled against his collar, and as he turned to speak to Peter, something about his profile seemed familiar . . .

She nearly bobbled her beer.

Charlotte noticed, which turned her attention away from the bar. "Are you okay?"

"That's Declan."

There was a moment of blankness while Charlotte tried to place the name. "The Declan who sent you flowers? The one practically living on your front porch?" At Shelby's nod, Charlotte added, "Oh, honey, I kinda hate you a little right now."

Shelby couldn't be too concerned about that at the moment. Damn, the boy cleaned up *nicely.* Untamed, his hair had just stuck crazily out around his head, but brushed back and under control, it showcased a high forehead and chiseled cheekbones. It was still a little too long, but that length took the yuppie edge off, giving him a slightly rakish vibe.

And he'd shaved. She hadn't realized how much that one little thing could completely transform a man. Gone was the straggly Yeti look, revealing a strong jawline and smooth skin.

Have mercy.

"Seriously, Shelby, you shouldn't hold out on me like that. A man that pretty is hanging out in this 'burg and you couldn't share the joy with your very best friend?"

"I didn't *know*. He didn't look like *that* before." But then Peter was pointing in their direction. Declan's head followed Peter's finger, and when he saw them, he smiled and headed in their direction.

Her knees might have wobbled a bit. It was unsettling to say the least. This was *not* the same scruffy guy that had been living in her marina. It couldn't be.

Pull it together.

"Hi, Shelby."

"You shaved," she blurted out, and then wanted to bite her stupid tongue.

"Yeah. I was way overdue." He ran a hand over his newly smooth jaw, and Shelby wanted to do the same. The man had a dimple in his chin, for goodness' sake, and she had a nearly overwhelming urge to stick her pinky in it. Or maybe her tongue.

She heard Charlotte clear her throat. Then after a second, she sighed and stuck out her hand. "Hi, I'm Charlotte."

"Declan. Nice to meet you."

The inane introductions going on snapped Shelby out of her daze and reminded her of her manners. "Sorry," she muttered, taking over. "Charlotte is a friend of mine. Declan is renting a slip in the marina right now." *Well, that wasn't any less inane.*

"Shelby told me about you," Charlotte said, deploying her dimples at maximum wattage.

"Well, we met under rather embarrassing circumstances—at least for me. I may never live it down."

"Probably not," Charlotte said, laughing. "But it's a good story."

Did Charlotte just toss her hair? A weird feeling hit Shelby in the stomach. It took her a second to identify it as jealousy. Of *Charlotte*, of all people. Her very best friend. Shame landed on top of the jealousy, and none of it made sense.

"A good story for Shelby to tell, maybe. Although I kind of hope she doesn't." His smile was self-deprecating, but not sheepish, and it was ridiculously sexy as well.

Charlotte looked at her with a "say something" smile, but Shelby was gawking and having a hard time making sense of this situation. Why was he *here*? Looking like *that*? Her brain was jumping around like she'd forgotten to take her meds this morning, and she had nothing to add to the conversation at the moment.

When she didn't say anything, Charlotte's eyes narrowed the tiniest bit before turning back to Declan with those dimples on full display. "Do you play, Declan?" she asked, inclining her head toward the table.

"A little."

"Why don't you take my shot, then? Shelby broke, but the table is open. I'll go to the bar and get another round for us." After giving Shelby a look full of instructions Shelby wasn't sure she could carry out, Charlotte headed to the bar.

"So what are you doing here?" she asked, trying to sound only vaguely interested, as Declan chose a cue and chalked it.

"You seemed worried about the potential damage to my mental health and your personal safety from my hermit-y ways, so I decided I should take your advice to get out and meet some people."

"But you said you don't like people."

"I like you," he said offhandedly enough to get her

attention but still be considered noncommittal. "And I can still meet them," he continued. "You know, have a drink and maybe play a little pool." He paused to look over the table, finally choosing stripes and sending the nine ball rolling easily into the pocket. It wasn't a particularly hard shot to make, but it had been cleanly done. He looked up. "Sorry. I forgot to call the shot."

"We're not that picky on the rules. It's just a friendly game."

"Good to know. Twelve, side pocket," he called anyway. That ball went in, too, making her wonder if he played more than just "a little," but she definitely liked watching him bend over the table, so it wouldn't be a hardship or anything. "You look different, too, you know," he added almost offhandedly.

She pushed her hair back over her shoulder before realizing what she'd done and felt the flush rise up her neck. *Thank God it's dark in here.* At least Declan couldn't see it. But then he gave her an assessing look from head to toe that only increased the heat in her face. "In fact, you look very nice, Shelby."

"Well, even this dive has a dress code." That was a complete lie, because it wouldn't be a dive otherwise. "I can't come in here looking like I do at the marina."

"Don't get me wrong, I like that look, too. Fourteen, off the fifteen, corner pocket."

Was he flirting? She didn't really have a "look." At work, she dressed for comfort in things she didn't care about getting anything from bilge water to fish guts on. Quick-drying was also a plus. Even Charlotte tsked and rolled her eyes at her euphemistically titled "work wardrobe," and she *knew* how Shelby spent her days. The usual crowd at the Bait Box wouldn't blink an eyelash if she showed up looking like she'd crawled out from under the dock, but Charlotte would. Jeans and a cute top weren't exactly fashion-magazine-worthy, but it wasn't enough to draw attention to herself, either. It was both the upside and the downside to living in Magnolia Beach: everyone knew her, and therefore barely anyone ever noticed her. So flirting or not, the attention from Declan was certainly flattering.

The green-striped ball rolled right to the cusp of the pocket before stopping. Declan merely shrugged. "Your shot."

She checked the table. The four ball was an easy shot, thank goodness, as she had no assurance she'd be able to hit anything more complicated. Across the table, Declan perched a hip on the stool and crossed his arms over his chest, the beer bottle dangling easily from his fingers. With a big cheesy smile and a waggle of his eyebrows, he asked, "So you come here often?"

"Actually, I do. There aren't a lot of other options."

"True. But it did make it a lot easier for me to find you."

The casual statement caused her to miss the cue ball entirely. "Damn it."

"Take a do-over." As she started to protest, Declan held up a hand. "It's just a friendly game, right?"

Forcing herself to focus—she did not want to look like a fool—she was able to sink the ball on her second try. Pretending to really study the table, she asked—very casually, of course—"You were looking for me?"

"I was. You said you'd introduce me around, and in order for that to happen, I had to find you first."

Oh. It made sense, but she couldn't deny his very rational reason wasn't a bit of a hit on her ego at the same time. "Well, it's a little slow in here tonight, so it wouldn't take long at all for you to meet everyone. It's busier on the weekends, though, with live music and sometimes some dancing."

"We'll have to give that a try."

Declan seemed determined to keep her wobbly. To throw off her game or something else? Not that it mattered, as it was completely working. She'd been aiming for the three, but missed it entirely, hitting the ten instead. The ten then rolled over to the corner pocket, knocking in the fourteen before rolling in behind it. *Lovely*, she thought as she heard Declan try to cover his laugh with a cough.

Charlotte chose that moment to return with Jimmy, Eli, and Todd in tow and hand her a bottle. Shelby immediately turned it up like she'd been sober for a month. "So how's the game going?"

Shelby had no freakin' clue how to answer that.

He'd succeeded in flustering Shelby. In a way, Declan felt bad about it—even while at the same time he was enjoying it—but it only seemed fair. He'd been flustered the moment he'd seen her tonight.

While she still had that wholesome, all-American, girl-next-door look, the tomboy was gone. She was very casually dressed, in snug-fitting jeans and a silky tank-top thing that floated to the tops of her thighs, but her hair was loose, hanging in a shiny blond curtain over her shoulders and those toned biceps. If she was wearing any makeup, it was subtle, undetectable under the lights of the neon signs. The effect was feminine, yet not fluffy or overdone. Shelby looked right at home, classing up the joint without looking out of place.

He hadn't been lying to her, either. That look *did* work for him. More than expected and possibly a little *too* well.

On second thought, though, Shelby's look should have been exactly what he'd expected. The Bait Box was more of a place to *be* rather than a place to be *seen*, but it wasn't the Bay Breeze Marina, either. He'd stepped up his game tonight, too, but it wasn't exactly a big step, even compared to how he'd been living the last few weeks.

But the look on Shelby's face had been totally worth it. Her fluster was just a bonus.

She'd been so competent and assured at the marina, and while not necessarily acting superior, she was definitely amused by his lack of knowledge and enjoying it a bit too much. Knocking her off her stride, even a little, was satisfying payback—however immature it might be.

Shelby's friend Charlotte returned from the bar with their drinks and handed a bottle to Shelby, who accepted it gratefully. Charlotte and Shelby seemed like close friends, but they were an odd pair. No one who had ever met Shelby would describe her as quiet or retiring, but Charlotte was the kind of woman who demanded attention. From her glossy curls and lush curves to her elegant manicure and chandelier earrings, she looked like she belonged anywhere other than a dive like this. Standing next to Shelby, Charlotte seemed almost comically overdone in comparison.

There were three men on Charlotte's heels. Since the Bait Box didn't seem like a meat market—and Shelby and Charlotte had been playing alone before his arrival—he had to assume she had invited them over.

"Declan, this is Jimmy, Todd, and Eli."

After shaking his hand, Eli moved past him to stand next to Shelby—not in a possessive way, but unmistakably warning him, nonetheless. Jimmy, on the other hand, was practically worshipping Charlotte with his eyes—something Todd seemed to find amusing and Charlotte tolerated with an ease that told Declan she'd been dealing with that for a long time.

There were all kinds of stories and undercurrents, like he'd walked into the middle of a soap opera—which, he realized, he kind of had, in a way. These people had known each other for a very long time and had story lines he had no clue about.

He wasn't exactly sure how he felt about Eli's nonaggressive but clearly made warning, but Shelby wasn't paying Eli any attention one way or the other, so he wasn't going to press that just yet.

There was friendly chitchat and a little ribbing—it seemed the story of his rescue was making its way around town, in part due to the community service being done by those kids—but nothing he couldn't handle. "Well, Shelby took me out on the *Lady Jane,* and I'm now a graduate of the Magnolia Beach Basic Water Safety Program. I've got a certificate signed by the mayor and everything."

The others laughed, but Eli's eyebrows pulled together as he looked at Shelby. "Really? I thought we talked about that."

Shelby barely glanced in his direction. "*You* talked. I ignored you."

"Shelby . . ."

"Well, you're not the boss of me, so shut up."

"So whose shot is it?" Charlotte interrupted, her voice forcefully bright.

"Declan's," Shelby offered, shooting Eli a look Declan couldn't decipher.

"Which technically makes it Charlotte's," he corrected. "You're stripes," he said, and handed over the cue.

Charlotte surveyed the table. "Which means I'm winning for once. Maybe I should keep letting you play for me. Shelby normally kicks my ass."

"The eleven is wide open," Jimmy said, motioning Charlotte over to his side of the table.

Declan would have recommended Charlotte try for the fifteen, but he wasn't wanting to help her line up her shot, either, which Jimmy obviously was.

"Having an off night, then?" he asked Shelby. She looked at him blankly. "The game? Kicking ass?" he clarified.

Her shoulder moved an inch in what might be considered a shrug. "It happens."

"And here I thought you were setting me up to hustle me."

Shelby started to smile, but Eli had overheard and took exception to his remark. "Shelby doesn't need to hustle people."

Her smile flattened out as she rolled her eyes. "Go away, Eli," she said, without even looking in his direction. "There's got to be someone else in here you can annoy."

While Charlotte seemed to handle her admirers with a mixture of humor and indulgence, Shelby wasn't pulling her punches. Declan couldn't decide if he liked that or not. There was obviously a history between Shelby and Eli, making him feel a little like an interloper—whether it was true or not.

There was a small groan that told him Charlotte had missed her shot, and Shelby looked over to give her friend an encouraging smile before handing her cue to Eli. "Why don't you play for me. I'm off my game tonight anyway." Under her breath, she added, "And he's a better match for Charlotte anyway."

Eli heard the comment and frowned, but he took the cue and walked to the end of the table—although not before sending a warning look in Declan's direction.

Shelby saw it and sighed. "Ignore him. It's so much easier that way."

Eli did not strike Declan as someone easy to ignore. He was a big guy, maybe an inch or so over his own six feet, with burly arms that spoke of a serious commitment to the gym. Added to his hovering over Shelby . . . "So what is the story there?"

"Huh?" She looked genuinely confused.

"You and Eli? Is he an ex or something?"

Shelby nearly spit her beer. Coughing, she wiped a hand over her mouth. "*No*," she stressed once she got her breath back. "Eli is my cousin."

Now that she'd said it, it made sense. And now that he knew, he could see the family resemblance—which was pretty strong and not something he should have missed. "One of the eight I was warned about. Jeez, are they all that big?"

"In general, yeah. It's all that fresh sea air and sunshine we get here. Grows 'em big, you know."

"Then what happened to you?" he teased. Shelby wasn't dainty or fragile, but in comparison to Eli . . .

"Every litter has to have a runt."

"If you're the runt . . ." He took a moment to appreciate her from head to toe again. "That's a very impressive litter."

Shelby might have blushed a bit. It was hard to tell in this light. "Impressively annoying, maybe."

"I think it's nice that they care so much."

"Something only someone without family all up in their business would say." Then her eyes widened. "I'm so sorry. That was really rude."

"How?"

"With your mom passed . . . I mean . . . everyone's family is different and you may have very good reasons why—and I'm sure you do—that you're not close to them and you might . . ." She paused to clear her throat. "I'm just going to stop talking now."

"You didn't offend me, Shelby."

"Oh. Okay. No, I mean, I'm glad I didn't." She dropped off into mutters before drinking deeply from her bottle.

A cheer went up at the table, and Declan looked up to see Charlotte doing a happy dance and getting high fives. One solid red ball remained on the table. She'd won.

"Good for you, Lottie!" Shelby leaned across the table—he tried not to look, but he didn't try *too* hard and failed anyway—to give her a high five as well. Then she turned to her cousin, who was leaning on his cue, and mouthed, *Thanks*.

The corner of Eli's mouth turned up, but he just shrugged. No one else seemed to notice the exchange.

"He let her win?"

"Probably. But if he didn't, he can salvage a bit of pride by thinking that I think he did. Either way, I'm glad. Charlotte could use the ego boost. She's had a tough couple of days at work."

Shelby had a good heart, both for her friend and the cousin she was annoyed at. It was more than he could guarantee from himself. "But you won't throw a game for her?"

"I can't. She'd never believe it. And Jimmy is too busy trying to impress Charlotte with his skill to figure out how to tone it down, and Todd's just too inherently honest to throw any kind of game for any reason."

So Shelby was a good player, meaning he had flustered her. That boded well. But the razor-sharp analysis of her friends . . . "You know them all that well, huh?"

"Yeah. I told you, it's a small town."

"And what do they know about you?"

"Pretty much everything. We all grew up together."

"I'll remember that."

Her eyebrows knitted together. "Why?"

Declan didn't have to answer that question as Jimmy interrupted them. He was removing balls from the pockets and rolling them to one end of the table. "You want to play, Shelby? We can do doubles. Me and Charlotte against . . ." He trailed off as he looked at the other three men. "You can pick your partner."

"There are other empty tables. Why don't you just go get your own balls to play with?"

Thankfully, Todd and Eli snickered, too, so Declan wasn't left alone feeling twelve years old. Shelby shot them an exasperated look, which changed to embarrassment as she figured out why they were snickering, and then morphed back to exasperation. "I'm not sure any of y'all are old enough to be in here."

Eli grinned. "Age ain't nothin' but a number, Shel."

"Obviously."

Charlotte interrupted. "I think it should be boys versus girls. Me and Shelby against whichever of you want to take us on." She threw an arm around Shelby's shoulder and tossed her hair over her shoulder, lifting her chin in challenge. "So? Who thinks they can take us?"

Declan might have heard Eli mutter something like "Oh my God," as he placed his cue on the table and held up his hands. "I'm out."

Charlotte grinned. "Smart man. Cowardly, but smart."

Jimmy looked less enthused about his doubles idea since he'd lost his chance to team with Charlotte. Todd had pulled out his phone and seemed intent on whatever he was typing.

Cocking an eyebrow, Charlotte pinned her stare directly on Declan, making him a little uncomfortable. "So, what about you? Think you could handle us both on your own? Or should I just let you and Shelby go at it?"

"Lottie . . ." Shelby scolded. "Be nice."

"I thought I was." She winked at him. "What do you say, Declan?"

"I'm game. If Shelby is, of course." The sharp arching of Shelby's brow as she opened her mouth to speak warned him of a protest. "But she says she's off *her* game tonight," he added before she could make that protest. "I wouldn't want to take her on if she's feeling less than her best."

"Shelby *is* the best," Charlotte said lightly, even though he could feel the weight of her words.

"Enough. Both of you." She slid out from under Charlotte's arm. "Look, it's getting late, and I have an early morning tomorrow. I think I should head home."

"It's only eight thirty," Charlotte protested.

Belatedly, Shelby remembered that it was Charlotte's turn to drive tonight, which would cut her evening short. "You stay, though. I'll get Eli to run me back."

"I was actually going to take Jimmy up on his doubles idea, and Todd and Eli would make a better match for our skills," she protested. Then, with the most angelic smile he'd ever seen, Charlotte said, "Maybe Declan could take you."

He covered his laugh with a long drink from his

bottle. Charlotte wasn't even trying to be subtle now, and the looks Shelby was giving her would slay a lesser creature. "Declan might not want to leave just yet."

"What makes you think Eli does?" Charlotte shot back.

He saw a muscle clench in Shelby's jaw. "Eli won't mind. Trust me."

"I don't mind, either. Really. I need to get up early in the morning, too," he added, even if it wasn't technically true, "so an early night isn't a bad idea. Just give me a second to settle up at the bar."

He left Shelby whispering furiously at Charlotte, but by the time he paid his tab, Shelby was waiting by the door, a sweater draped over her shoulders and a serene smile on her face. She waved at someone as they made their way out into the parking lot.

She looked a little surprised as Declan opened the door for her, but she didn't say anything as she settled in. Once he was in the driver's seat, though, she turned to face him. "It's very nice of you to drive me home, and I'm sorry that Charlotte is such a pest and caused you to cut your evening short. I know they will all be there for a couple more hours at least, so if you want to drop me off and go back, they'd be happy to have you join them."

"It's my pleasure. Charlotte is amusing, and I have no need to go back. Even though your friends seem like very nice people," he added so as not to give offense. "Honestly, I only came out tonight to see you."

The look Shelby gave him had him reconsidering everything that had happened this evening in a completely different light, because he'd obviously read something *very* wrong and was now stepping all over it. "I mean, you wanted me to get out and meet people. This way you know I did."

Shelby nodded. "I think you'll find that people in Magnolia Beach are quite friendly, and we're used to tourists. They'll talk to you and make sure you have a good time. You don't need me around to break the ice."

"Good to know," he said, because he didn't know what else to say.

The marina was on the outskirts of town—not that Magnolia Beach was big enough for even that to be much of a trip—and the traffic at eight thirty on a Monday night was nonexistent. He couldn't justify going slowly, even if he wouldn't mind drawing out the drive.

"You need to slow down," she warned. "There's a speed trap right around this corner."

He eased off the gas, coasting to a nearly crawling thirty miles per hour, but sure enough, they passed a police car that had been hidden by the curve. "Thanks."

"Just in general, you should assume they mean the limits they post on the signs—especially in small towns."

It was a neutral, safe topic, and he grabbed hold of it gratefully. "I take it speeding fines are an important source of revenue to the Magnolia Beach city budget."

"I wouldn't say that. It's just what else are they going to do?" She waved her hand to encompass the quiet empty streets. "We don't exactly have an epidemic of crime that needs fighting."

"You have a point. But that's a good thing."

"Of course it is. This is the kind of place where most people don't even lock their doors."

"And that's exactly the kind of thing you should mention to the slightly suspicious guy living in your marina," he teased.

She laughed. "Well, at least we'd know where to start looking if that crime wave suddenly takes hold."

He pulled in and parked next to Shelby's rather battered-looking Jeep, and her dog appeared from behind one of the buildings to greet them—well, her. Cupid merely sniffed in his general direction as Shelby squatted and rubbed her ears. "Hey, Cupid. Who's a good girl?" she cooed.

Declan vaguely wondered why Shelby had given a female dog a male name, but then decided it made as much sense as any other pet name.

Shelby stood and briskly brushed her hands against her thighs. "Well, thank you for the ride home. I appreciate it."

"You're welcome. Thanks for convincing me to go out. It was fun."

"There's a contra dance at the Methodist church tomorrow night. I know it sounds like something for just old people, but it's usually a pretty mixed crowd. If you're looking for more things to do, that is."

Was that an opening? "Are you going?"

"Ah, no, I'm busy. But it's easy and fun to do."

"I'll consider it."

"Good night, Declan."

He nodded. "Good night."

Shelby pulled a key out of her pocket and unlocked the office door.

"I thought you said people don't need to lock their doors around here."

"Well, there's this suspicious guy living nearby, you know." Then she flashed that grin at him as she went inside, taking Cupid with her. He heard the door lock behind her.

Well, that was pretty clear.

Chapter 7

"I swear, Shelby Tanner, you make me want to strangle you sometimes." Charlotte sat back on her couch and swirled the wine in her glass.

"Ditto." Shelby indicated the piles of flyers for First Methodist's upcoming bazaar, which she'd somehow been roped into helping Charlotte fold and stuff into envelopes. Charlotte's mother wanted them done by tomorrow, and Shelby, sucker that she was, hadn't been able to resist Charlotte's cry for help.

Chester, Charlotte's fat ginger cat, sat in the middle of the mess on the coffee table, helpfully batting at the unsteady stack of envelopes ready to be sealed like it was not only his job, but his *duty*, to knock them to the floor. "This is your project. You could at least help, you know."

Charlotte sighed and lifted Chester off the table, settling him into her lap as she sat and picked up a sheet of mailing labels. "The boy was totally flirting with you, and you just sent him back to his boat like nothing?"

She didn't need to ask which boy. Charlotte was all about Declan, wedging him into the conversation whenever she could and not even trying to be sly about it. "He was not flirting with me."

"Oh, *please.* I've seen you nearly frog-march people to the altar after less-obvious signs of encouragement. If you want to be a matchmaker, you should really start with yourself."

"I gave up matchmaking after the Helena and Ryan fiasco. People will just have to find their own romances from now on."

"That's probably smart. I love you, but you weren't very good at playing Cupid."

Shelby couldn't be offended since it was true. But Charlotte had to be high to think Declan could be interested in her. Not when Charlotte was also standing there, all dimples and shiny hair. "Have you thought that maybe he was trying to flirt with *you* and you just brushed him off instead?"

"I wish." Charlotte's heartfelt sigh was almost funny. "Honey, he could not have given less of a damn about me. It was painfully obvious exactly why he was there and who he wanted to see. Why do you think Eli was so bowed up about it? I'm surprised the poor boy didn't strain something."

It was flattering to think that Charlotte might be right. But then, Charlotte was also on her third glass of wine. "Even if he was—and I'm not saying I think he was—Declan's a tourist."

"So?"

"*So*, why start something with an expiration date on it?"

"*Everything* has an expiration date on it. That's just life. Hell, even life has an expiration date. You take your opportunities when you can."

"Don't try to be philosophical."

"Okay. Then let me remind you that *that's* the joy of

tourist boys. They leave. No muss, no fuss. A good time is had by all, and there's nothing awkward afterward."

"But most tourists leave in a couple of weeks. He's here for a couple of months."

"All the better to enjoy that lovely piece of man candy nice and slow."

"You know he's unemployed, right?" That should deter Lottie. She didn't like freeloaders of any sort.

"Again I say 'so'? I'm not saying you should marry him or anything."

Charlotte could be a little too tenacious sometimes. "He's a tenant at the marina."

"So? There's nothing unethical about sleeping with a tenant as long as you're not trading it for rent."

"It's not professional behavior. I have a hard enough time getting people to take me seriously as a business-woman without giving them an actual reason to grasp on to."

Charlotte rolled her eyes. "Then don't stand in the middle of Front Street and announce who you're sleep-ing with. Be discreet. Keep it on the down low."

Shelby snorted. "Because *that* always works. No one ever knows anything about anyone else's private busi-ness around here." Chester jumped back up on the cof-fee table, and Shelby shooed him away. "We have nothing in common."

"Talking is highly overrated. There are much better things to do with your tongue."

"Lottie!" She could feel the flush rising up her chest, but Charlotte only smirked. She cleared her throat and tried to sound serious. "You're operating under a huge assumption anyway."

"That he wants you? That's not an assumption. I read

that news off the flashing neon sign over his head. I mean, really, Shel. Why else would he decide *now,* after all this time playing hermit, to wander into the Bait Box? It's some kind of coincidence that he decides to do that just a couple of days after meeting you for the first time?"

"Maybe he was just lonely and bored." She decided to skip over the fact that she'd practically badgered him into getting out to meet people.

"Then you're doing a good deed. Showing kindness and charity to a stranger who's alone. Hell, it's practically your Christian duty."

Shelby nearly choked. "My *what*?"

Charlotte just smirked and shrugged.

"Okay, you need a remedial Sunday school class. *And* I'm cutting you off." Shelby reached over to take her wineglass.

Charlotte moved it out of her reach. "And when was your last date? I don't mean hanging out, either. I mean an actual date."

Shelby had to think. Colby Bryce had asked her out . . . jeez, had it really been a year ago? How depressing. "A while."

"You've had a chance to look over every eligible male Magnolia Beach has to offer, so don't tell me you're holding out for one of them."

"No, but . . . You never know, we might get a sudden influx of eligible men."

"How?"

She thought for a moment. "Shipwreck?"

Charlotte laughed. "Fingers crossed. But until then, Hot Dude wants you. Take advantage of that." She started to take another drink, but stopped and gave Shelby a questioning look. "Unless there's something you're not telling me about Declan? Has he done something skeevy I need to know about?"

"No," Shelby assured her. "But I know he just broke up with someone. He told me. He downplayed it, but he could be rebounding." *Plus, she's some rich, gorgeous, supermodel art curator. Talk about not even in the same league . . .*

"And?" Charlotte rolled her eyes. "I'm still not seeing the problem, Shelby. He's gorgeous and funny and *totally into you.* Go for it."

Maybe playing dumb would work. "Go for what?"

"*Declan.* You should be rockin' his boat right now, not hanging out with me and Chester."

Guess not. "Can we talk about something else, please?" Her face was growing warm. It wasn't like she hadn't thought about it. In fact, she had thought about it a little *too* much last night, at the expense of a decent night's sleep and some vivid dreams.

"You're blushing."

She felt her face get even hotter, and she reached for her glass. "Hush."

"You *are.*" Charlotte's grin was both smug and mocking. "That means you're attracted to him."

There was no sense denying it. "I'm not blind. He's quite pretty."

"Then what is the problem?"

All Shelby could do was shrug.

"You're young and beautiful and unattached. So is he. You're attracted to each other. He seems nice. There's no bad here."

"How do I know that anything he's telling me is true? I don't actually know for certain that he really is anything he says he is. He could be on the run from the law, or trying to avoid child support, or . . ."

Charlotte waved that off. "You know as well as I do that Rusty has at least run his tags and checked him out, if not run a complete background check on him by now. If there was something sketchy, you'd know. He's obviously educated and has some form of financial support. It all adds up to 'yum.' He's perfect fling material."

That much was true. "I'll think about it."

"Don't think too long. You said yourself that there's an expiration date. He's going to leave, and you'll be kicking yourself that you didn't take the chance while you had it."

"The chance for what?"

"To have sex with him," Charlotte said bluntly. "To have hot, sweaty, toe-curling sex with the hot guy living in your marina. Not only do you need it, you deserve it."

Oh, just the thought . . . "And what if he's not interested?" She'd die of embarrassment if she made a move and found out she'd been right all along and Declan *wasn't* interested in her.

"I'm solid in my faith that he is, but on the off chance he's not, so what? You lose nothing. And look what there might be to gain," she said with a smile.

"I'll take it under consideration. Now get to work."

"Go. Now. I'll finish this."

Like she was just going to go run to the marina, get naked, and climb onto his boat. She wasn't *that* desperate.

But boy, it was tempting. "Stick and seal, Lottie, stick and seal."

"You know, sometimes I think you were a lot more fun unmedicated."

"Seriously, are you high? Because I can't believe you just said that."

At least Charlotte had the decency to look abashed.

"Sorry. That came out all wrong. You know I didn't mean it."

Shelby grabbed another stack of envelopes. "That's what I thought."

"It's just . . ." She stopped and took a deep breath. "You've just swung so far in the other direction, trying to prove to everyone that you're a responsible adult, that you're sucking all the joy out of your life. I mean, have you heard yourself tonight? You're trying to talk yourself out of having any fun at all with this guy with a whole list of reasons that are nothing but weak, lame excuses. You let everyone beat you up until you finally believed it, and now you're second-guessing and over-analyzing every decision you make. Don't let people shame you out of enjoying your life, Shel."

Ouch. "That's not it, Lottie." *Or at least not all of it.* "It just takes forever for people to change their opinions. Look at Helena Wheeler. She left town for ten years and is now a responsible, tax-paying adult dating the freakin' mayor, and my brother *still* accused her of setting Declan's boat loose."

"Your brother is a dork."

"True, but that's neither here nor there."

"Well, I've got a newsflash for you. Not sleeping with Declan Hyde isn't going to make anyone suddenly realize that you're not the same screwup you were at fifteen. So if you want him, go for it. The absolute worst thing that could happen is that the sex might not be great, but something tells me that's not going to be a problem."

"Like I said, I'll take it under consideration. Now, can we please just finish this?"

Charlotte pursed her lips, but remained silent. Since both of them had made their point, the topic was dropped for the moment, but Shelby knew it wouldn't be forgotten that easily. Charlotte would bring it up again and again until Shelby had some sort of satisfactory answer to give her.

She just wasn't sure what that answer would be.

When the last envelope was stamped and sealed and she was on her way home, only *then* did Shelby let her mind drift back to Charlotte's idea.

There were far worse ideas floating around out there—she had to admit that much. And Charlotte was right; dying of embarrassment aside, she didn't have all *that* much to lose.

And she wasn't a prude, unable to consider the idea of a fling. Growing up, she'd had many a good time with tourist boys and even a couple of discreet, slightly inappropriate relationships as an adult before without regrets. It was one of the few benefits of living in a town that got a lot of out-of-town visitors on a regular basis.

The rush, the excitement, the chemistry of a new relationship was addictive. There wasn't time to get bored with someone because they left long before the newness could fade. And God knew it was pretty much impossible to find "new" in Magnolia Beach otherwise. She knew everyone so well that the chemical rush was never there, able to get anything off the ground.

She was living in a town of broken-in comfy shoes, and Declan was a flashy, sparkly, expensive pair, the kind of which she didn't see in Magnolia Beach very often.

So what was holding her back?

Less than a hundred and fifty miles separated New Orleans from Magnolia Beach, but Declan felt he'd traveled a lot farther than that.

It wasn't really fair to compare the two—New Orleans

was a much larger city, a multicultural and esoteric experience, while Magnolia Beach was just a small town. The things that attracted people to places like Magnolia Beach would keep them out of New Orleans, and while New Orleans had history, Magnolia Beach felt trapped in time.

But New Orleans felt small compared to Chicago, so it was a matter of perspective, really, and personal taste.

He loved the architecture, though, especially in the French Quarter and the Garden District, the mishmash of styles and eras that somehow still seemed to work.

And New Orleans came with the bonus of a really late lunch with his college roommate, Eric, which in addition to the nostalgia and camaraderie such things always entailed, had the added bonus of proving both Suzanne and Shelby wrong: he knew people, he had friends. *So there.*

Although they kept in touch on social media and the occasional e-mail, Declan hadn't seen Eric since his studies had taken him to Atlanta for graduate school and then to Duke for a tenure-track position in their English Department. Luck had him in New Orleans today for a conference on the Harlem Renaissance, and Eric looked every inch the cool young professor. Declan felt rather scruffy in comparison. Eric called him on it almost instantly over their muffalettas and beers. "You need a haircut."

Since Eric's head was completely shaved . . . "And you need some hair."

"Nah, this is much easier." He grinned. "And the ladies love it. Trust me."

"If there was a chance I'd look like Shemar Moore instead of Charlie Brown, I might consider it. But I might as well enjoy the freedom while I can."

Eric shook his head. "I still can't believe you're living on a boat in South Alabama."

"No one can. Not even me, most of the time."

"And you thought architecture was a safer major. I told you that you should have majored in English with me instead of just minoring."

"I think that would have substantially *increased* my chances of living on a boat in genteel homelessness. At least this is only temporary." He meant it to be funny, but Declan could see the look of doubt and concern creeping across Eric's face. "Seriously, it's a vacation of sorts. I'm not homeless and broke, trying to put on a brave face while I lie about it on Facebook."

"Honestly?"

"I swear. I can even buy your lunch today."

Eric seemed relieved, if not fully convinced. "Well, if you'd majored in English, you could be writing a book right now. You'd be able to call it a 'sabbatical,' and no one would question it."

Except for Shelby, who seemed to have a healthy skepticism of writers.

"Who?"

Declan didn't realize he'd spoken aloud. "Shelby. She runs the marina I'm living at."

"And she doesn't like writers."

"It's a beach town. I imagine they get a lot of those. I see her point."

"So what are you doing instead on your sabbatical?"

"Reading. Watching TV. Day-tripping. Sleeping."

Eric, whose work ethic and energy levels shamed the Energizer Bunny, couldn't hide his distaste. "Until January? That's more than just a vacation."

"I know. But it sounded good in theory."

"Getting bored yet?"

"Honestly, yeah, I was, but things are starting to pick up. Shelby taught me how to operate the boat and introduced me to some of her friends . . ."

"So you and Shelby are . . ."

"Nothing."

"Because . . ."

That was a good question, and thankfully Eric's phone rang before Declan had to answer it. Shelby was hard to read, and a rebuffed pass might make things awkward for him at the marina later. He had to live in what was basically her backyard for another two and a half months—he didn't want her to be wary of him or get branded a creepy pervert.

He didn't need *that* getting around Magnolia Beach. And it totally would.

At the same time, he couldn't deny he found her attractive. Plus, she was interesting, totally different than most other women he'd dated, and the complete opposite of Suzanne. No dating site would have ever matched them, but there was something about her that sparked in him—and *not* just because he was bored or lonely.

He was able to distract Eric from further conversations about his current situation—or Shelby—with questions about Eric's classes and research, and Declan left with a list of books he now wanted to read. He wasn't sure about the depth and breadth of the African-American literature section at the Magnolia Beach public library, but he could be optimistic and at least see what they had.

But his long, late lunch with Eric, while great, had him leaving the city during rush hour, adding an extra half hour to the drive back to Magnolia Beach. After a day of mostly walking around New Orleans followed by hours spent on the road, he was glad to see the entrance to the marina.

Shelby's Jeep was there in its usual place, but the lights were off in the upstairs part of the building where her apartment was. She'd left the outside lights on, though, creating puddles of light and giving him plenty to see by as he made his way through the parking lot.

Although the marina might be noisy in the mornings, it was nearly silent in the late evenings, something that had been hard for him to adjust to but he had grown to enjoy.

But as he walked by the main building, he heard humming. And singing. It was a little off-key and the words were unintelligible, but it was music.

And it was coming from above him.

There, on the porch that looked out over the marina, was Shelby. She had her feet propped up on the railing, and her toes were wiggling in time to whatever was playing in her headphones.

He still couldn't identify the song, as Shelby alternated between mouthing the words, humming, and the occasional "la-la-mmm." She had a notebook of some sort in her lap, and she was sketching, pausing every now and then to tap out a beat with the pencil.

It was cute.

The oversized headphones framed her face, and her hair was twisted up on top of her head in a messy knot. It wasn't exactly cold, but it was chilly by Southern standards, and she had on a long-sleeved T-shirt and sweatpants to combat the breeze coming in off the water.

He wasn't sure how long he stood there watching her, but when she reached for the beer bottle beside her, she finally saw him, jerking in surprise and nearly overbalancing in her chair.

She righted herself, pulling the headphones off and clearing her throat. "Declan! You startled me."

"Sorry."

"How long have you been standing there?"

"Not long."

A second later, he heard a jingle of tags and the sounds of toenails on the decking. Cupid's shaggy head peered down at him, then she turned to Shelby and woofed.

"Yeah, I could have used that warning a little sooner," Shelby muttered as she reached over to pet the dog. "Are you just getting back?"

He nodded. "I drove over to New Orleans today."

"That sounds like fun. This is actually a good time of year to go. It's not quite so hot and sticky."

There was a moment of uncomfortable silence, then he shrugged. "Well, I guess—"

"Would you like—" Shelby said at the same time. "Sorry. You first."

"Go ahead."

She cleared her throat. "Um, would you like a beer?"

His pulse kicked up. "Sure."

"Come on up."

The sign on the gate at the bottom of the stairs said, "Private," but it wasn't locked and the latch was easy to release. Cupid greeted him at the top, and Shelby closed her sketch book, carrying it inside with her. She returned a second later without the book, but carrying a bottle by the neck, which she handed to him as he took the chair beside hers.

"What were you drawing?"

"Nothing. Just doodles. I'd been inside the shed all day working on inventory and needed to clear my head."

He propped his feet on the railing, too, and leaned back in his chair. "Nice view." From this vantage point, he had a clear view of all the boats bobbing in their slips and all the way out to Mobile Bay until it blended into darkness.

"Yeah. I had Ryan add the deck four years ago when I moved in. It gives me a good view of everything going on."

"Surveying your kingdom?"

She smiled. He could tell she really loved it here. "Just my little part of the world."

"It's nice. Very peaceful."

"Right now it is. Come spring and summer, though, people are actually on their boats, so it can get noisy, even at night."

"Yet you still live here."

She took a sip of her beer. "Someone needs to be on the property in case of emergencies. Before I moved in, we'd have staff taking turns crashing on a cot in the office."

"And now you're on call twenty-four/seven."

"Honestly, it's not usually much of a problem. And it's a good trade-off. I live rent-free, we save money not having to pay staff just to sleep, and they get to go home to their families every night."

"You don't get lonely out here?"

"No. I have Cupid." At the sound of her name, the dog padded over to Shelby and dropped her head into Shelby's lap for a scratch behind the ears. "And I stay pretty busy during the days, so it can be nice to be alone."

"See, alone time isn't bad," he teased.

"No it's not. But self-inflicted solitary confinement can be."

"I spent the day in New Orleans," he protested. "Plenty of time with all walks of humanity."

"That's not quite the same thing. What took you over to New Orleans?"

"I went to visit the architecture. To look at the buildings and the houses."

"Is that normally what you do when you're gone all day? Go look at buildings?"

"Yep. Some people like to look at nature, some people like to look at art. I like to look at buildings."

"The old ones or the new ones?"

"Both. For different reasons. I walked through the French Quarter, downtown, and some of the Garden District. And then I had lunch with a friend."

"So you *do* have friends." Shelby's eyes widened as she mocked him. "I *knew* you couldn't be serious about not liking people."

"Eric was my college roommate. I didn't really have a choice. I had to live with him."

"And he lives in New Orleans now?"

"No, he was in town for a conference. He lives in North Carolina now."

"That's nice, though. You had a chance to catch up."

"But there's a lot I didn't get to see because I met up with him, so I'll need at least another trip or two. I also want to go back and drive through some of the Katrina-damaged areas."

Shelby wrinkled her nose. "Disaster tourism. That's tacky."

"But educational for me. I'm moving to South Florida, after all. Hurricanes are a possibility. Plus, sustainable and low-impact design is one of my interests. Some of the rebuilding has really incorporated interesting ideas."

She shook her head. "You don't have to go all the way to New Orleans to learn about hurricane damage. Hell, you could talk to people here. We've been hit plenty of times."

"Let me guess, you could introduce me to some people?"

She smiled as she nodded. "The historical society, the mayor's office—they'll all have lots of before and after photos, stats, and more details than you probably want."

"And you?"

"I've been through a few. We evacuated before Katrina, though, and went to stay with friends in Montgomery. There was a lot of damage, but we were pretty lucky."

"You sound nearly blasé about it."

She shrugged. "Every place has its natural disasters—tornadoes, floods, blizzards. No matter where you live, there's some way Mother Nature can kill you. Hurricanes are just the price of living on the coast," she said very matter-of-factly. "Want me to teach you how to make a hurricane emergency kit, too?" she teased.

"Maybe."

There was another moment of quiet as they both drank. "So," Shelby finally said, "where else have you been to look at the buildings?"

"Mobile, some of the plantations. There's a lot of variety in a relatively small driving area."

"And what do you think of Magnolia Beach? In your professional opinion, that is."

He hesitated. "Just a typical small town."

She'd heard his hesitation. "You think it's ugly."

Great. Now I've insulted her. "No," he said carefully. "Just . . . architecturally un-notable."

To his surprise, she laughed. "Fair enough. We have other things going for us." There was pride in her voice.

"You like it here, don't you?"

"Yeah. Why? Do you think that's weird or something?"

"To me, yes. I can't imagine living in a place this small."

"You haven't given it much of a chance, hiding out on the *Lady Jane* and all."

"I'm not hiding, for goodness' sake." He was getting exasperated at her insistence, but then he caught her small smile. She was doing it on purpose. "You tell me, then, what's so great about Magnolia Beach?"

"It's a close-knit community of good, friendly people."

"That sounds like an ad campaign."

She acknowledged that with a tilt of her head. "It was, actually, but that doesn't make it less true."

"And that's why you like it here?"

"It's home," she said as if that explained everything. "It's where I belong. I've got my family, my friends, my dog, and a really excellent Internet connection for everything else."

"That's enough for you?" Belatedly, he realized that could sound insulting.

She took a long drink before answering. "Of course not. I have goals and plans. But I've got a firm foundation here—a happy life to support those goals and plans, so anything more is just gravy." She shrugged a shoulder, "But then, I'm also not the person living on a boat in a town where I don't know anyone because I'm in between jobs and have nowhere else to go. I think you're the one who needs to be having long thinks about what's 'enough' out of life."

Yeah, he'd insulted her. *Smooth move.* "It's only temporary. And I wasn't saying there's anything wrong with living here. It's just not for me."

"But Miami will be?"

It had to be. "That's the plan."

"City boy."

He couldn't tell if that was meant to be an insult or

not. "Born and raised. Give me smog and noise and traffic and crowds."

"Ugh. I guess all this peace and fresh air and open space must just be hellish for you. Poor thing."

There was no way he was going to respond to that and insult her again. "I just prefer the activity level. There's always something to do in the city."

"You're just here at the wrong time. We're coming off high season, so the whole town is a little hungover from the summer. There's always something happening from April through September because of the tourists. We get some downtime before things pick back up after Thanksgiving and on through New Year's, and then we'll rest and recuperate until mid-March when it all starts again. Things may seem a little slow right now, but that's good. And once you know people, there's always something to do anyway." Then she smiled. "And if nothing else, you can do this for a while." She waved a hand out at the expanse. "Nothing at all."

"I'm not really the be-one-with-nature type."

"But you've been doing a lot of nothing lately and you seem to be enjoying it."

"It's a different kind of nothing. And honestly, I am starting to get a little bored. A four-month vacation sounds great in theory, but there's only so much TV one man can watch."

"Then you'll have to find something to do. Want more suggestions? I'm afraid there will be people involved, though. Not a lot doesn't involve people around here."

That was the opening he was looking for, and he wasn't going to pass it up. "I like food. Are there any good restaurants around here?"

"Oh, definitely. We have to feed all those tourists somehow."

"What's your favorite?"

She didn't even pause. "Miss Marge's for the basics— and make sure to try her Three Berry Pie—the Frosty Freeze for burgers, and Bodine's for seafood. It's pricey, but their crab cakes are *divine*. Harry's is great, but they're only open during the season." She glanced at the watch on her wrist. It was oddly delicate and feminine for someone like Shelby. "But it's getting kind of late. Most places are closing by now."

"No, I'm not hungry now. I was just thinking maybe you could go with me sometime." Her eyebrows went up. "Eating alone all the time gets old," he explained.

He thought he saw her mouth twitch, but it was hard to tell. Then she sat there for an inordinately long time—much longer than it should take to respond to a simple question. "It's just a dinner invitation, Shelby, not a complicated existential postulation."

She laughed. "That might be a little easier."

"How?"

"Going out to eat with you . . . People will talk. Especially after the whole flower fiasco."

"So?"

"I have to decide if it's worth it."

That was a statement he hadn't expected. He had no idea how to respond.

His confusion must have shown on his face because Shelby laughed. "I told you this town runs on gossip. It's better not to give people things to talk about."

Another point in favor of the anonymity of the city over a small town. "That's a bad way to live your life."

"It keeps us out of trouble, though."

"Are you saying I'm trouble?"

She gave him an assessing look. It was a little disconcerting, to be honest, but then she smiled. "Probably."

He wasn't sure if that was a good thing or not. Shelby could move from open and forthright to cryptic and unreadable in a distressingly quick moment. "It's just a friendly dinner with one of the few people I know in town."

"Pity."

He nearly fell out of his chair. Shelby, though, kept her eyes on the horizon as she turned up the bottle for the last drop, making him wonder if he'd misheard her. It was impossible to tell from the look on her face. He turned his eyes to the water, too, and casually said, "Tomorrow. Seven o'clock. I like crab cakes, so that Bodine's place."

"It's a date." Shelby stood, putting her face in the shadow and making it impossible to tell what she was thinking. "See you then."

He wasn't entirely sure what he'd just agreed to, but he placed his half-empty bottle on the table and stood as well. "See you tomorrow."

This was surreal, bordering on farcical, but Shelby was already walking away, Cupid on her heels. At the door, she paused and turned. "Good night, Declan."

"Good night, Shelby." Then she was inside, leaving him on her porch wondering what the hell had just happened.

Shelby's hands were shaking, and she was surprised she'd been able to play it as cool as she had. She was definitely out of her wheelhouse. She heard Declan's feet on the stairs, and then the opening and closing of the gate at the bottom, meaning she was safely alone now. The bravado that had buoyed her failed right then, and she sank into a chair, all the air coming out of her in a big huff.

Cupid came over to see why and whined as she put her head in Shelby's lap.

"I'm okay," she muttered absently as she petted her, but she wasn't sure she was. She'd spent the last couple of days in high school crush mode, egged on by Charlotte and the fevered imaginations of her own twisted brain.

Hadn't this been the reason she'd been out there in the first place? After intentionally avoiding him for two days, she'd parked herself on her porch tonight, knowing he couldn't get back without her seeing him. She hadn't been fully decided on her course of action at the time, but she'd made the first step.

And now she had a date with Declan. It sent little happy jolts through her bloodstream, but at the same time, it wasn't like the competition was real tough for her right now. He'd met, what, maybe ten people total, in the time he'd been here? And she'd practically badgered him into "getting out." She didn't want to think that she was just convenient, but at the same time, should she really question her luck? The boy was gorgeous, and he'd asked her out to dinner.

The ego boost was flattering no matter how she wanted to temper it, and she was proud of herself for taking the plunge. She'd let Charlotte's badgering convince her that Declan might think she'd rejected him outright and might not make another move. She should be grateful her little plan had worked.

It might be crazy, but after all the thought she'd given this the last couple of days, no one, not even herself, could accuse her of being heedless or impulsive. She had that much going for her. And while she was a little floored that she'd actually done it, the excitement of possibilities was rapidly starting to overtake the shock.

Of course, that assumed that Charlotte was right about Declan's intent. He'd flirted and asked her out to dinner, but that meant only slightly more than nothing. She might be making a big deal out of nothing at all. Maybe what she saw as "flirting" was just his way of being friendly, and she was reading way more into this than he intended. It wouldn't be the first time she'd jumped into something she'd misread and was left looking foolish. At least he'd be gone later if it turned out she was wrong. It had taken her months to be able to look Quinn Haslett in the face after that Valentine's Day fiasco five years ago.

Argh.

But misunderstood or not, she had dinner plans for tomorrow night. And she'd just have to deal with whatever that might or might not mean.

She'd hope for the best and deal with whatever happened.

Because Charlotte was right. She had nothing to lose.

Chapter 8

Bodine's was an unassuming-looking place in one of the Victorian-style houses on the Mobile Bay side of Magnolia Beach with nice views of the water. It was cozy and classy, but infused with that laid-back attitude that permeated everything here. Declan was glad he hadn't worn a tie.

Though it was the off-season, the restaurant was busy, so that was a good sign. Even so, they got a table easily—possibly because the hostess greeted Shelby with a hug and said, "I'll tell Chris you're here."

"Chris?" he asked as they fell in step behind the hostess on their way to the table.

"The manager. He's a friend."

Not only did she know the hostess and the manager, but she waved to the bartender, spoke to half a dozen tables, and stopped to hug at least three other people.

Declan knew he shouldn't be surprised, really, but good Lord, did Shelby really know *everyone*?

"I'm sorry I didn't introduce you," she said as she placed her napkin in her lap, "but we'd never have gotten to the table if I did."

"I'm surprised you're ever able to accomplish anything."

"It can be a challenge sometimes, especially when you're in a hurry and just need to do something really fast, but it would be rude not to at least speak."

"And I guess you can't be rude."

"A little politeness and small talk never killed anyone," Shelby said airily. Then she dropped her voice. "The thing is, these people *also* know my mother and my grandmother, and if they find out I'm being rude to people for no reason, *they'd* kill me."

"It must be like having Big Brother watching you all the time."

Shelby raised an eyebrow. "If you're not doing anything you're ashamed of, what does it matter who sees you do it?"

For some reason, that felt like a compliment. "You have a point. So what's good here?"

Shelby hadn't even opened her menu. "Everything. I'm going to have crab cakes, but there's nothing bad on the menu. The snapper and the grouper are both really popular, too."

Seafood was definitely Bodine's specialty, but it had the requisite steak and chicken entrées, too. It all looked good, and with this many locals in the place, he had to assume it was. While Shelby had described Bodine's as "pricey," the place was a steal by Chicago standards. He might not be counting pennies these days, but he wasn't so far gone from those times that he couldn't *not* look at prices, either. Everything was just cheaper in Alabama— another reason for folks to winter down here, it seemed.

"Hey, Shelby." Their server, a young redheaded woman, appeared with ice water and a basket of steaming hush puppies. "I haven't seen you in a while."

"I've just been busy. How are you?"

"The same."

"Caroline, this is Declan Hyde. He's staying at the marina this fall."

Caroline's eyes widened. "*Oh*. Nice to meet you."

The tone of that "oh" told him exactly how she'd heard of him, and the twitching of Shelby's lips meant he was right. The infamy bordered on ridiculous, really, but he just answered with, "Nice to meet you, too."

They ordered, and once Caroline left, Shelby leaned forward to say quietly, "I may not have introduced you on the way in, but everyone will know who you are when you leave."

"I don't doubt it. I only wonder if I'll ever live it down."

She shook her head. "Your grandchildren will be able to come visit and hear that story."

"Jeez. All I wanted was a nice, quiet vacation. So much for anonymity."

Shelby's forehead wrinkled. "I guess I should have asked first. We could have gone someplace out of town if you wanted to be incognito."

"You're conflating two different things. I'm not trying to be all man-of-mystery, and I don't have anything to hide. I'm just not used to being infamous, so it's a little weird. Cut me some slack."

"I refuse to believe you've always lived the life of a hermit." She leveled a look at him over her glass. "Everyone knows people."

"There's a difference between having friends and knowing everyone within the city limits," he teased.

"Even in big cities you have to know your neighbors, at least."

"I was a student with at least one, if not two, part-time jobs for almost ten years. I barely had time to sleep, so

I certainly didn't have time to get to know my neighbors."

Shelby blinked in surprise. "Wow. I didn't know it took so long to become an architect. My uncle is a doctor, for goodness' sake, and it only took him a little longer than that."

He shrugged. "Well, you don't want buildings falling on your head, do you?"

"Definitely not. That would be bad." She leaned forward. "But what about when you were a kid?"

"Why does this bother you so much?" he countered.

"Well, I'm a curious person by nature to begin with—"

"I'd have gone with nosy."

Shelby shrugged that off. "You wouldn't be the first," she said, picking up a hush puppy. "But I've never lived anywhere other than here, so it doesn't take much to interest me. Plus . . . it's just *weird*."

That made him laugh. "Have you stopped to think that maybe Magnolia Beach is the anomaly?"

"Oh, I know we're not exactly the norm for anything, but I can't wrap my head around living someplace and not knowing your neighbors."

"I knew who they were, but I didn't *know* them."

"How is that even possible?"

"Well, we didn't exactly hang out on our front porches. The weather in Detroit six months of the year makes that a problem."

"And the other six months of the year?"

He thought about not telling her—or at least softening the truth—but what did it really matter now? "We lived in a pretty rough part of Detroit when I was a kid. I didn't necessarily *want* to get to know my neighbors, and they certainly didn't want me in their business."

"Oh. I'm sorry."

Well, *that* shut her down. Not that he minded. It wasn't a topic he particularly enjoyed, and in fact, avoided whenever he could. "Do you always ask people so many questions? Or is it just me?"

"I'm afraid I interrogate everyone. Honestly, that's the best part of living in a tourist location. I get to meet all kinds of people."

"Well, I guess if you know all the residents already, that makes sense. Interrogation tendencies aside, you have good people skills."

She grinned. "Why, thank you, sir."

Caroline reappeared with steaming plates that smelled amazing. His stomach growled in response, causing Shelby to smile. "Go ahead. Try it."

He took a bite of his fish, which melted in his mouth and slid down his throat in lemon-buttered goodness. "This is delicious."

"Told you." She took a bite of her crab cakes, making a blissful face as she swallowed. "So where'd you go to school?"

He bit back a smile. At least she found him interesting and wanted to know more. That boded well. "University of Illinois at Chicago. You?"

"Magnolia Beach High."

"No college?" That was a little surprising. From what he'd been able to gather, the Tanner family seemed to be fairly well off, so money probably wasn't a limiting factor, and with a doctor and a mayor in the family, they probably valued education, *and* she'd mentioned younger cousins away at school. It just seemed odd that she hadn't gone somewhere. But then, he was the first in his family to go to college—and he'd nearly killed himself to do it—so he was probably more touchy about it than most. He couldn't imagine *not* wanting to go to school.

She shook her head. "I've always known I wanted to take over the marina. I didn't need to go to college to learn how to do that."

Maybe it was practicality, then. "Well, from what I've seen, you're good at it."

"I try."

There was something odd about the way she said it. It wasn't false modesty or self-deprecation, but he couldn't put his finger on exactly what was off about her tone. "Officer Rusty sang your praises."

"If you want to know where to find fish, yes, I'm your girl. That's all Rusty really cares about." Shelby was actually squirming a little. He'd hit a nerve, but damned if he knew how or why. A split second later, her voice and posture changed completely. "But that's just one of the things I like about my job. I get to be outside. I couldn't stand being cooped up in an office all the time. No offense," she quickly added.

He still didn't know what had just happened there. "None taken. I'm just not the outdoorsy type. That's why I design buildings, you know. To keep all that outdoors away from me and other sensible people. No offense," he teased.

She laughed and shook her head. "You'd get along well with my brother. Jamie will happily stay inside on the most beautiful of days. We think they might have switched babies at the hospital."

"A Tanner oddity?"

"Definitely. We all like fishing and camping and the outdoors, and my cousins all play pretty much every sport there is. Most of them have office jobs now, but Jamie is the only one who intentionally remains indoors, delicate little flower that he is."

"Is that how you see me? A delicate hothouse flower?"

She gave him an assessing look that was almost frightening in its intensity, almost as if she really were judging the depth of his psyche. Then she shrugged. "I don't quite know *what* to make of you, Declan Hyde."

Was that a good thing? "Um . . ."

"So that's why I'm here."

That was an even odder statement. "Excuse me?"

"I have to admit that I'm very curious about what makes you tick," she said gravely, like he was a specimen on a slide to be analyzed, but then that grin broke through and she winked at him. "Plus, you're kinda cute."

"Well, I don't know quite what to make of you, either, Shelby Tanner," he countered, trying to mimic her accent. "But you're more than just kinda cute."

Her cheeks turned pink. "Are you flirting with me?"

"You're just now figuring that out? I must be terrible at it."

"Maybe I just don't get Yankee-style flirting."

"First of all, I'm not a Yankee. I'm from Michigan."

She waved a hand airily. "Same difference. You're all Yankees to me."

He'd argue geography another time. "Second—and let me be very clear about this—I am very much flirting with you." He put down his fork, leaned forward, and pinned her with a stare. It was time to get serious, and he had absolutely nothing to lose. "You are beautiful and funny and have amazing legs. I'm being a gentleman and keeping my hands to myself, but it's a hell of a fight. I'll sit here and talk to you all night long if you like about any subject you want, but it's not going to keep me from wondering if you taste as good as you look and hoping you'll let me find out. Soon."

Shelby's eyes were round and getting bigger with each word.

"Tell me you're not interested, and we'll go on like we were before. I'm a big boy, and I can handle it. I'll go back to my hermit cave on the *Lady Jane* and leave you alone. Or I can keep trying to flirt with you until you decide about me. I'm willing to put in the effort. I can't offer you anything permanent or even long-term, but you know that already. I'd like to make the most of the time I will be here. With you, if that's possible."

Shelby swallowed. He might have thought he'd just been flirting with the idea, uninvested either way, but the reality was proving much different.

"I want you. I'm not trying to be crude, just honest." He sat back in his chair and picked up his glass. "And now you know my objective, so there's no chance of a misunderstanding. How it plays out from here is entirely up to you."

He could literally see Shelby's pulse fluttering in her throat, and her breath was quiet and shallow. He'd shocked her—hell, he'd shocked himself—with his bald words, but he was dead serious and couldn't regret speaking the truth. He wanted to think that she was at least somewhat affected by his honesty, because it had had quite an effect on *him*. If she shot him down, he'd back down quietly, but he couldn't help hoping.

Shelby blinked. Twice, and the lips that had parted slightly in surprise when he started speaking closed as she cleared her throat and swallowed hard. She didn't say anything, but neither did he. He'd told her the ball was in her court, so he had to let her make the next volley.

But she seemed to be taking an inordinate amount of time deciding. When she reached for her glass, Declan had a momentary worry she was about to toss it in his face. But she just calmly took a sip, dabbed her lips with a napkin, then grabbed their waitress as she walked by. "Can we get the check, please?"

Caroline looked at their half-eaten plates, obviously confused and concerned. "Is everything okay?"

Yeah, that was the million-dollar question. He realized he was holding his breath waiting for Shelby's answer.

Shelby's eyes met his. Then she smiled before cutting her eyes back up at Caroline. "Yeah. Everything is great. There's just something we've got to go do."

He couldn't get his wallet out of his pocket fast enough.

I can't believe I just did that.

Her heart was pounding in the base of her throat, and she seemed to be having a difficult time getting oxygen to her lungs. It was making her light-headed.

But there was a slow burn warming her low in her belly, fanned by Declan's words. His simple, honest, and raw words. The little voice in the back of her mind told her she should be offended, but she couldn't draw up any outrage at all. Flowery declarations were way overrated, because that clear, simple "*I want you*" was about as swoon-worthy as it came. If she didn't know half the people in this room, she'd do one of those table-clearing sweeps like in the movies and crawl across the rubble into his lap.

They were making enough of a scene as it was, though. Caroline was visibly concerned, and Shelby had no idea how she was going to explain herself tomorrow.

But honestly, she didn't really care right now.

Declan barely glanced at the check before throwing some bills on the table and pushing to his feet.

He seemed remarkably calm, though, making her wonder if she'd hallucinated the last bit of that conversation, but then he looked directly at her and the heat nearly scorched her skin.

So, no. That had really happened.

She forced her face into what she hoped was a calm, neutral look, but inside she was grinning like an idiot. Walking past people she knew and saying quick good-nights was the hardest thing she'd ever done, especially since she felt like she had the truth tattooed across her forehead. And when Declan's hand landed on the small of her back to guide her, the simple, rather gentlemanly gesture felt like a brand landing on her spine.

She couldn't quite believe that Declan had all but propositioned her outright in the middle of Bodine's, but she really couldn't believe she'd been rash and brash enough to *agree*.

The parking lot was decently well lit—enough, at least, to find a car easily—but there were pockets of deep shadow from the beautifully landscaped trees and bushes around the sides. Declan had parked in the back of the lot when they arrived, directly under one of the lights, and his SUV looked lit up like a landing pad. Declan, though, walked right past his car into the shadows beyond, nearly dragging her with him.

She stumbled as her feet left the asphalt, and Declan grabbed her waist to steady her. "You okay?" he asked as the shadows swallowed them.

She wasn't pulling in enough air to answer, so she merely nodded.

She expected to be pounced upon, was looking forward to it even, but Declan merely smiled. "Good." His hands came up to brush her hair back from her forehead, then slid slowly down her face as he exhaled, making a small growling sound low in his throat.

His thumbs traced along her jawline and down over her neck while his eyes searched her face with an unnerving intensity. *What the hell was he waiting for?* The anticipation was killing her. Her hand was shaky as she placed it on his chest, but she could feel the heavy pounding of his heart under her palm.

She felt his hand tighten, pulling her a little closer as his thumb edged her chin up a fraction of an inch. Then, with a sound somewhere between a sigh and a groan that was possibly the sexiest thing she'd ever heard, Declan moved his head toward hers.

He has the softest lips. That surprising thought was the first to register. It was nice, almost gentle, and a startling contrast to the strength in the hands holding her in place. And it was frustrating, a teasing taste of what she *really* wanted, like a cookie held just out of reach.

She let her hand slide over the strong plane of his chest, down and around to his waist. Declan's breath caught as her fingers trailed over his ribs, and she was rewarded by being pulled fully against him, causing her to rise up onto her tiptoes to wrap her arms around his shoulders and anchor herself there.

And then everything changed.

He'd been holding himself in check, and the full force of his kiss nearly knocked her off her feet as his tongue tangled with hers, making her both dizzy and completely focused on the sensation at the same time. A tug on her hair exposed her neck, giving him access and the taste he'd claimed earlier to want.

This kiss . . .

This kiss was . . .

Mercy.

Every inch of her skin was alive and tingling where it touched him and needy and screaming where it didn't. His arms tightened around her, nearly lifting her off her feet, and she brought her hands to his cheeks to force his mouth back to hers for more.

A lot more.

She wasn't a delicate virgin flower prone to swooning, but she could definitely see what caused such things. When Declan finally put her back on her feet, she nearly fell over. His hands on her hips kept her upright until her equilibrium returned, but even then, she wasn't in a hurry to move. She looked up to see him staring down at her, his hair sticking out in crazy angles from where she'd dragged her hands through it. He was breathing hard, and while his stance looked relaxed, she could feel the tension in him, and his fingers were moving restlessly along the waistband of her jeans.

And yet she still couldn't get enough air in her lungs to actually speak. She had to settle for a weak smile in his direction.

As her heartbeat finally slowed to a steady rhythm, she found her voice. But that didn't mean she knew what to say. Finally, after it seemed as if they'd been standing there like fused statues for ages, she managed to speak. "You didn't get to finish your dinner."

"This was better. It's what I really wanted anyway."

It wasn't an eloquent compliment, but the evident sincerity of the statement and the huskiness of his voice were definitely swoon-worthy.

He dropped a kiss on her forehead. "Should we go before we cause a scene?"

That snapped her out of her impending swoon. Granted, they were off to the side, in the shadows, but they weren't exactly hidden from anyone. *Crap.*

"I think we should."

That got her a grin.

Declan held the door as she got in, then climbed in the driver's side. The awkwardness descended as she got settled, as if the universe was giving her both the hint and the opportunity to back down.

"Dinner was good. I like that place."

She bit back a laugh. "You didn't get to eat much. You'll probably be hungry later."

"I'll be fine. But we should definitely go back sometime. I'd like to see the dessert menu."

This was both so normal it bordered on farcical, and so awkward it was about to become painful, but once on the road back to the marina, Declan casually reached over to take hold of her hand, twining his fingers through hers.

It was sweet, and it felt natural. Almost easy. At the same time, it held a promise, enough to keep her motors running and heighten the anticipation, making the whole thing surreal.

But it was exciting, too. The close intimacy of the car, the way he was holding her hand, the quiet murmur of the radio, talk of a second date—it was straight out of a how-to-date instruction manual. But that kiss . . . That kiss knocked everything sideways.

Just-one-of-the-guys Shelby Tanner didn't get kisses like *that*. She felt very femme fatale—and a little cheated, actually, by all the other kisses in her life that hadn't been like that.

Just the memory of it—hell, she didn't need memory;

she was still floating in the afterglow, still feeling the neediness crawling under her skin, asking for more.

And she totally wanted more. She could feel her nerves humming as they got closer to the marina, closer to the time she'd be able to *get* more.

Declan's thumb was now stroking her palm, making that neediness worse, honing the edges, and whetting her—

Why the hell was every single light at the marina on?

The pleasant musings of her libido stuttered to a stop as Declan turned into the parking lot. The place was lit up like a Christmas tree, and she sure as hell had not left it like that.

"What's happened?" Declan asked.

"I have no idea." But then she saw the car parked out front, and cold water splashed over what was left of her simmering thoughts. "Damn it, Adam's here."

"Adam?"

"A cousin." *An annoying, obnoxious cousin with terrible timing.* She wrenched open the car door before Declan had the car fully in Park.

Adam must have heard the car, because he opened the door to the office a second later. "Hey! Where've you b—" He stopped, and his eyes widened as Shelby heard Declan's door close behind her.

"Out," she answered. "What are you doing here?"

Two figures blocked the light behind Adam in the doorway before morphing into Jamie and Eli. *Just great.* Cupid wound herself through the group, tail wagging, obviously excited to have the whole freakin' family around.

"So you went out, huh?" Adam, at least, seemed to find this amusing.

"Yes. We went to get something to eat." Once Declan caught up to her, she made introductions. "Declan, this

is Adam and my brother, Jamie. You've met Eli already."
Since they were well aware of who Declan was, there
was no need for an explanation there. There were polite,
manly handshakes and sizing ups, and Shelby wanted
to pull her hair out. "Again, I ask why you're here."

"We're looking for Grandpa's old tackle box," Jamie
answered. "Dad says it's somewhere in the office. Or
maybe the shed."

"Do you have to get it right now?" *Because there's
sex I could be having at the moment.*

"Gran wants, we fetch," Adam said cheerfully, making her want to kill him. There was no way he didn't
know how much she didn't want him here right now,
and he was obviously enjoying getting to be a giant wet
blanket.

Declan cleared his throat. "Well, I'd be of no help
at all, so I'll leave you to it. I had a nice time, Shelby.
Thanks." He kept his hands in his pockets and barely
nodded his head in her direction as he spoke. Although
it was the right move considering the circumstances, it
still felt like a bit of a slight. Then he turned to the boys.
"Good luck finding it. Good night, everyone."

Aaaargh. She could cheerfully strangle all three of
them. Maybe Declan, too. But short of telling Adam,
Jamie, and Eli that they really needed to get lost so that
she could get naked—and that would *not* go over well—
she was stuck. *Maybe she could get them out of here
quickly . . .*

"Well, let's find it." She stomped past Eli, elbowed
Jamie out of the way, and scanned the office, picturing
the small tackle box in her head and eliminating some
places just on size or the fact she knew what was there.
Daddy was a bit of a pack rat, though, and there were
drawers and at least one storage closet that probably

hadn't been cleaned out in forty years. And the shed was even worse . . .

She sighed, which got her a look from Jamie. "Why so testy, Shelby? You don't have to help us look. Go on about your business."

Oh I wish. "And just leave you all to dig through stuff, moving it all around where I'll never find anything again?"

"We'll be careful. You'll never know we were here," Adam added.

"So I can sit upstairs and listen to you all riffle through everything? Yes, that's a relaxing way to spend my evening."

"She's just pissy because we've interrupted her date," Eli said over his shoulder as he opened a file cabinet.

That got her looks from both Adam and Jamie.

"*No*," she corrected, "I'm pissy because I don't come to *your* homes or offices and dig around in your stuff uninvited and unannounced. It's called boundaries, people. Respect." She dragged a step stool over to the storage closet and climbed up to peek at the higher shelves.

"You were on a date? Really?"

He didn't need to sound so damned surprised. Stranger things had happened. She didn't even turn to look at Jamie as she answered, "I went to dinner." That wasn't a lie. She didn't have to admit that it had also been foreplay. "People have to eat, and it's not fun to eat alone all the time."

"Did he know it was 'just dinner'?" That deep question came from Eli, of all people.

"Excuse me?"

"Hey, I saw him the other night at the Bait Box. The guy is totally into you."

Both Jamie and Adam stopped what they were doing to stare at her. "Interesting. And was Shelby into him?" Jamie asked.

"I think so. She let him drive her home."

Adam smiled. "Well, that does explain her current attitude."

"Hello, I'm standing right here."

"Do you like him, Shel?"

She nearly fell off the step stool. "What?"

Eli leaned against the file cabinet and looked at her. "Are you interested in this guy?"

She opened her mouth, but no sound came out. Clearing her throat, she tried again. "That's really none of your business." She'd tried for aloof and frosty, to put him in his place, but the words came out shaky and defensive at best, and she wanted to lock herself in the closet the second she heard them.

Adam laughed. "The judges will accept that as a yes."

Jamie frowned. "I'm not sure I'm on board with that."

"No one really asked you, did they?" Eli rebutted before she could.

"Pardon me for being a little concerned that my sister is hooking up with some random dude."

"I'm not—" She started to deny it but then realized that was exactly what they'd interrupted.

But Adam was quicker. "What's the harm if she is?"

"The *harm*?" All Jamie needed was some pearls to clutch and he'd be the picture of scandalized affront.

"Oh, grow up. She's a big girl."

"That's my *sister* you're talking about."

"Every woman is someone's sister," Adam said. "Don't be a hypocrite, Jamie. It's not a good look for you."

Okay, now they're just baiting him. But she couldn't

find her voice to stop this. She simply could *not* believe this was actually happening.

They were all talking over each other now, and she wasn't convinced one of them wasn't going to take a swing, and then there'd be blood and explanations she'd have to make, and *dear God*, had one of them just brought up someone's virginity? *Please don't let that have been about me.* She wasn't sure if she should be outraged or crawling under the desk in embarrassment. Finally, she put two fingers in her mouth and let loose an ear-splitting whistle. Cupid barked twice at the noise, and the boys stopped their squabbling to look at her as if she'd lost her mind. "Enough! Would y'all please stop talking about me like I'm not even here? Or like any of this could possibly be any of your business?"

"Oh, the professional meddler finally gets a taste of her own medicine, and she doesn't like it," Jamie snarked. "The irony just burns. Welcome to *our* world."

And just like that, they were a united front again.

She rolled her eyes, and there, like a saving grace sent from heaven above, was Grandpa's tackle box, tucked in with some old ledgers being used as a stand for the electric fan near the window. She grabbed it almost desperately and shoved it into Jamie's hands. "Here. Mission accomplished. Good night and go away."

"So you can get back to your date?"

"I hate all of you."

Eli grinned. "You don't mean that."

"But I *did* mean 'go away.' I'm done with y'all tonight. And if you don't go, I'm going to call Gran and tell her all about how her rosebushes ended up dead that time."

It was a powerful threat, and she knew it. It was her ace in the hole, and it worked like a charm, making all three of them clamp their mouths shut so fast that she nearly laughed and ruined the whole thing.

Eli cleared his throat. "Good night, Shel. Thanks for finding the tackle box."

"Good night, boys." She forced herself to smile. "Sleep well."

The low talk that drifted back to her as they left was unintelligible, but she'd made her point. She wasn't sure she'd won, necessarily, but she didn't exactly know what she'd been trying to win, either.

Calling Cupid back inside, she closed and locked the office door, then made a point of turning off all the exterior lights—including the one in the parking lot—before they were even in Adam's car.

It was petty, but so be it.

Date or not, battling with her very own Three Stooges had ruined her evening, killing the spontaneous and exciting momentum. Now, in the glaring fluorescent lights of the office and the wake of the Tanner boys, her rash enthusiasm seemed a little tawdry.

She puttered around, putting the things the boys had moved around back into place, but she kept glancing at the big window that faced the slips. Declan was out there, on the *Lady Jane*. Was he waiting up, expecting her to come rushing down there once her family left? Or had the arrival of the Tanners thrown a wet blanket over his engines as well?

Damn it. She knew how to be spontaneous and she knew how to be calculating—spontaneous just seemed better somehow when it came to things like this. Not only was it more exciting, but taking the time to be calculating only highlighted the absurdity and the possible pitfalls.

Declan had been pretty clear what was on offer. And that kiss boded very well for how good he'd be and how much she'd enjoy herself. But being forced to look at that offer soberly and without the chemical reaction muddling her brain made it seem cheap. If she took Declan up on his offer now, she certainly couldn't claim later that she'd been caught up in the moment.

Stupid boys. Always ruining her fun.

Well, she thought, *at least they didn't show up twenty minutes later.* A mid-coital arrival of her family . . . She shuddered. It could have been worse.

But, damn it, tonight could have been a lot better, too. She'd hate to think she walked out on half a plate of crab cakes for nothing.

Yet she couldn't help but keep looking out the window.

The *Lady Jane* had a light on.

Chapter 9

Declan now understood the meaning of the term "cockblocked." The three Tanners, however unintentionally and accidentally, couldn't have done a better job if they'd tried.

He wondered if he'd done the right thing, leaving like that. It was obviously what Shelby's brother and cousins had wanted him to do, but he'd been trying to take hints from Shelby. Her clear discomfort with finding her family on her doorstep like that had been his cue that his presence wouldn't be helpful. Or wanted.

It was frustrating, yes, but disappointing, too. It felt like a genuine loss. The abrupt interruption of the endorphin high left him feeling deflated, empty. He liked Shelby, and the chemistry was potent, unlike anything he'd felt before.

But then, he'd never met anyone quite like Shelby before, either.

He flopped onto the couch and toed off his shoes, letting them fall where they may. Then he draped an arm over his eyes. Shelby's scent still clung to his clothes, causing a spike in his blood pressure each time he inhaled.

Not that he needed the scent of her to relive it. He could easily remember the taste of her mouth, the texture of her skin, the silk of her hair in his fist. The way she'd melted into him . . . He wasn't the romantic type, but that had been one amazing kiss.

But what was he supposed to do now? Try to figure out when the extraneous Tanners had left so he could go back up there? Hang out here and hope Shelby showed up on her own? Accept that the moment was gone and resign himself to another night of Netflix?

And a really cold shower?

The thing was, he didn't know Shelby well enough yet to figure out the correct answer to that question. And the things he did know about her made it impossible for him to guess. She could be both competent and silly, practical and dreamy, turning on a dime. It made her fun to talk to and hang out with, but it also meant he had no idea what she'd do next. Which wouldn't be necessarily bad—and some might even say made it more exciting—but it made deciding what to do right *now* next to impossible.

How long would it take for her to get rid of her family anyway? If he went out on deck, he could see the building easily, maybe watch for the lights to go off inside, but he'd have to either sit out there like a stalker or else pop in and out like a gopher in a hole.

But even knowing when they left wouldn't necessarily tell him what he should do. It simply took him back to his earlier unanswered questions of waiting here—possibly for no reason—or going back up to the building—when Shelby may have changed her mind and might object to the equivalent of him showing up for a booty call.

He had no real reason to dislike the Tanners—and he had to assume their appearance here was simply a coincidence—but that didn't stop him from being very pissed at them.

How long had it been? He had no idea. His brain was circling around his frustration with unanswerable questions, and there was no telling how long it'd been spinning. And he hadn't exactly been checking the clock this evening, either, so he had no idea what time they'd gotten back here.

Was that a knock?

Fully aware it could be just a hopeful hallucination, Declan still leapt off the couch and covered the short distance to the cabin door before the echo had completely faded.

And Shelby was there, her hair floating wildly around her face in a sudden breeze. Her smile was a little shy, but her tone was exasperated. "Sorry about that."

He looked over her shoulder, up to the building, which was now dark. They'd left, then.

Seemingly aware of what he was doing, Shelby laughed. "They're gone, thank goodness. Quite the buzzkill."

I beg to differ. All the want had slammed back into him at the sight of her. If anything, it was worse than before, with a sharper edge from the waiting and uncertainty. Shelby, though, while she was *here*, was holding herself a little awkwardly, staying the hand that really wanted to reach for her.

Her smile began to falter. "Um . . . Can I come in?"

"Of course." He pulled the door open and stepped back a bit, allowing her to pass. She'd come to him, which boded well, but there was enough uncertainty on her face that made even reaching for her seem disrespectful enough to get his face slapped. "Sorry for the mess."

She shook her head. "It's fine. Are you okay? I know

the Three Stooges kind of got in the way earlier, but now that they're gone, I kind of hoped our evening could continue." Her smile seemed uncertain. "Unless, you don't—"

He'd never moved so fast in his life, closing the space between them in less than a heartbeat and grabbing hold of her like his life depended on it. His sanity certainly did. His mouth landing on hers stopped her words, and her arms immediately twined around his neck, kissing him with an intensity that made the earlier one in the parking lot—it felt like it was *ages* ago—pale in comparison. It made his legs go weak, and he caged her against the wall to stabilize himself before he fell over.

Shelby was no shy Southern belle; she met him head-on, matching his passion with her own, which only fanned his desire more. He couldn't get enough of her taste, her lips, the side of her neck, the slope of her shoulder. He wanted to strip her and bury himself inside her, but at the same time, he didn't want to move from this one spot, where she was pressed against him, her hands sure as she slipped the shirt buttons out of their holes and spread the fabric wide to skate teasingly over his chest.

He sucked in his breath as her thumbs smoothed over his nipples, and he felt her smile under his lips. With a groan, he managed to get his hands moving, grabbing the hem of her shirt none too gently and pulling it up and over her head in one quick move. Shelby took care of her bra herself, then echoed his sigh as skin met skin, rubbing her chest gently against his.

That snapped the last thin thread of his control, and he reached under her hips to boost her up, loving the feel of those strong thighs wrapped around his waist.

The main cabin of the *Lady Jane*, while perfectly suitable for his other needs, wasn't designed for this—

the couches were too narrow, the carpet on the floor too thin. But it wasn't far to the bedroom—thankfully—and soon he was on his back with Shelby covering him like a hot, exciting blanket.

Shelby's hair fell around them in a blond curtain, blocking out the light from the main cabin and tickling his skin. She was no delicate flower, either; the physical nature of Shelby's job had sculpted and toned her body into long, sleek muscles draped in soft skin that twitched and shivered under his fingers.

He liked having her on top—the access it gave his hands, and the freedom it gave her to move against him. It was raw and unfiltered, and the obvious pleasure it gave her was a powerful aphrodisiac to him.

The snap and zip of her jeans gave way easily, and he was somewhat surprised to see that the tomboyish and no-frills Shelby favored rather lacy panties. It put a smile on his face as he traced across the top edge, and her belly contracted under his fingers.

She cocked an eyebrow when she saw his smile, then she mirrored his movements, releasing the snap and zip of his jeans and letting her fingers tease along the waist-band of his boxers, then raised the stakes by planting soft, sucking kisses on the sensitive skin.

He lifted his hips, letting her slide his jeans down, then taking over and kicking them away. Hers were more difficult, though; the snug fit he'd admired earlier caught low on her hips, trapping her. After a moment of wiggling—which nearly killed him—Shelby dropped to the bed beside him, cussing as she tried to shimmy out of the denim.

"Damn it, I'm trapped." Then she dissolved into giggles. "That's a bit of a mood killer."

"Not at all," he replied. He pretended to study her. "It's kinda sexy, you all trussed up like that."

She shrugged a shoulder. "Hey, whatever floats your boat." After an experimental wiggle, she snorted. "It's going to make certain things a little difficult, though."

"Allow me." Grabbing her belt loops, he wiggled the jeans down a little farther, trying to concentrate on what he was doing even though Shelby's movements to "help" were far more distracting than helpful. Once midway down her thighs, it got easier, and he was able to pull them the rest of the way off without a problem, turning them inside out, and tossing them away.

He went to grin at her, but froze. Bathed in the dim light, Shelby's skin glowed against the dark blue sheets. Her hair puddled around her head like an old-fashioned artist's halo. Those perfectly shaped limbs were displayed like an early birthday gift just for him, and her lips were swollen and pink. It was an earthy and lush picture, and it fired his blood, making the want a nearly painful thing.

Shelby pushed up onto her elbows as her eyebrows pulled together. "Declan?"

He couldn't quite get words out yet.

"Is something wrong?" When he didn't answer immediately, Shelby reached for the corner of the sheet.

The uncertain look on her face finally freed his vocal cords. "Don't." That had come out a little harsh, so he cleared his throat. "I'm just admiring the view."

"Oh." She lay back down, bending her knee into a pinup pose and draping her arms over her head. She met his eyes for a moment, then squirmed under the continued scrutiny. Exasperation took over, shattering the facade. "Okay, now you're making me nervous."

She might look like a centerfold, but she was still

Shelby, and he laughed as he joined her on the bed again, trailing his fingers over those strong legs and pulling her underneath him.

Relief flooded through her. For a moment there, she'd thought Declan was reconsidering his options now that he'd seen her naked. Although she would have had to kill him, it still would have been a mortal blow to her ego.

She knew she wasn't conventionally sexy—she didn't have the hourglass curves or the svelte thinness of beauty queens—but Declan seemed appreciative of what she did have and was taking his sweet time exploring what was on offer.

And, *mercy*, he was exploring it thoroughly. Mind-scrambling, thigh-shaking, toe-curling thoroughly.

It was *bliss*.

She was very glad the marina was empty because she wasn't sure she could keep quiet. Declan's mouth muffled her voice as he explored her with his hands, but when his lips retraced his path, she was left biting her lip and moaning into the pillow.

While she'd started off on top and in charge, Declan had flipped the script, and he seemed in no real hurry to relinquish his control. She wanted access, wanted to do her own explorations, but when she tried, Declan pinned her wrists to the bed and kissed her hard, and she was more than happy to acquiesce to the demand.

She felt beautiful, worshipped, feminine, and she let herself float on the sensations. And Declan was a feast for all her senses—warm planes of skin stretched over defined, but not bulky, muscles, the crisp hair on his chest and legs that both tickled and titillated, the spicy scent of his soap . . .

Poetry should be composed about this man and his skills. Epic poetry.

And that thought made her giggle.

"Huh?" Declan pulled back to look at her, and the expression on his face made her laugh harder.

"I'm sorry," she managed to choke out.

An eyebrow arched up. "Should I be offended?"

She snorted, then clapped a hand over her mouth in embarrassment. *Pull it together.* "No. Really. Please continue."

Declan crawled up the bed and leaned on an elbow beside her. "Not until you tell me what's so funny."

Damn it, she was ruining the best sex of her life with a giggle fit, but at the same time, she saw Declan's lazy smile. Maybe the sex didn't have to be serious to be epic. "Nothing."

He trailed a finger over her hipbone. "Tell me . . ."

She rolled toward him and propped her head on her fist. "Things got a little dramatic there for a second."

"Dramatic?" He blinked in surprise. "That wasn't exactly what I was going for."

"*Good* dramatic." Under his continued stare, she grew increasingly uncomfortable until she couldn't stand it any longer. "I suddenly felt the need to compose odes to your prowess, okay?"

Declan stared at her blankly for a second, then collapsed into laughter himself.

She gave him her best frown. It didn't work. "Stop. I know it's silly, but be flattered. My brain doesn't normally scramble like that."

"Then I am flattered." He scooted closer to her, leaving just the tiniest sliver of air between their bodies, close enough for her to feel the heat of his skin. "Poetry, huh?"

She nodded as he pushed the hair back from her face and leaned close.

"Do you like poetry?"

The seriousness of the question caught her off guard. "I guess."

"I like poetry. I minored in English. Did I tell you that?"

She shook her head. It was an inane conversation, better suited for having over coffee in someone's kitchen, not naked in bed. But the earnestness in his voice made even this topic feel important. "I figured I could go back for my master's and teach if the architect thing didn't come through."

The determined, purposeful movements of his hands were certainly giving her an education. Hell, as long as he kept moving like that, he could talk about anything he liked. *For now.*

"*'License my roving hands and let them go,'*" he whispered, his breath hot in her ear. "*'Before, behind, between, above, below.'*"

His hands were doing exactly that, and the idea of poetry no longer seemed quite so funny.

"*'O my America! my new-found land, My kingdom, safeliest when with one man mann'd. My mine of precious stones, My empery, how blest am I in this discovering thee.'*"

Shelby couldn't quite breathe. Not all the words made sense, but she got the gist easily. His voice was deep, husky, and hypnotic, and her skin felt hot and overly sensitive everywhere he touched.

"*'To enter in these bonds is to be free. Then where my hand is set—'*"

Shelby gasped as his hand settled and the room spun.

"*'—my seal shall be.'*" He kissed her then, a hot, hungry kiss that felt both sweet and carnal at the same time, as he draped her thigh over his hip and pulled her close, sliding inside her with agonizing slowness.

She could feel the tremors starting already, gradually building from the inside out as Declan moved slowly at first, then growing in intensity as he flipped her to her back and increased his pace. She anchored herself the best she could, wanting to prolong the feelings for as long as possible, but it was too much.

She lost touch with reality—hell, she may have even blacked out—and by the time things came back into focus, Declan's head was buried in her neck, his whole body heaving as he tried to catch his breath.

She let her fingers splay across his back, feeling the sweat pooling in the dent of his spine. He'd worked hard, and she was immensely grateful for his efforts.

With one last deep breath, Declan pushed up onto his elbows and shook the hair out of his face. She helped, brushing the long strands back. He might think he needed a haircut, but she was kinda liking it long and scruffy. After one more kiss—sweeter this time, less carnal—Declan rolled off her onto his side, draping one arm over his eyes, and sighed.

This was always the awkward part. Should she leave? Did he want to talk? Cuddle? Was he one of those guys who was going to fall asleep any second now? She was sated for the moment, but there was a low-power humming still in her muscles, and honestly, she wouldn't mind staying to explore this a little more. But she didn't want to come across as clingy and desperate nor did she want to insult him by jumping up and beating feet out of there, either.

And the longer he lay there, not saying anything, the more awkward and unsure Shelby felt. A hookup should really leave quickly and without fuss, but a friendly fling could hang around. Unfortunately, while Declan had been clear about some things, she could now wish they'd been a little clearer about others . . .

Okay . . . She edged gently toward the side of the bed, nearly jumping out of her skin when Declan's hand landed on her arm. "Do you have to go?"

"I guess not."

Mercy. That boy's smile . . .

"Good."

"He quoted *poetry* to you?" Charlotte sat cross-legged on Shelby's bed as Shelby rushed to get ready. Somehow, she was always the one running behind, even though her beauty regime took about a third the effort as Charlotte's. And while Shelby wasn't sharing *every* intimate detail about last night's adventure, *that* one was definitely BFF share-worthy. Even if, based on the look on her face, Charlotte was having a very hard time believing it.

"Yeah." She could hear the sappy sigh in her voice. Maybe Charlotte hadn't noticed. The idea of poetry might be distracting enough.

"*Actual* poetry? Not something he made up himself or read on a greeting card once?"

"I had to Google it this morning, but yeah, *actual* poetry. Seventeenth-century British poetry at that."

"Wow. I'm not sure how to process that. Was it romantic or smarmy?"

"Believe it or not, it was *sexy*."

Charlotte fanned herself. "A hot nerd. That's my fantasy, you know. I just might swoon."

"I nearly did." Shelby dug for her mascara. In the mirror, she could see Charlotte's eyebrows go up, questioning her primping.

"Do you think it was a line? You know, his signature 'panty-melting' move, perfected with his bros for picking up girls?"

Well, *that* would take some of the swoon out of the memory. But in a way, she almost wished it had been a line. Guys smart enough to reel off poetry at the drop of a hat . . . that was new. And a little intimidating. At the same time, though . . . "It didn't seem like it. But either way, it worked. Like a charm."

Charlotte clapped her hands like a little girl. "Yay, you! I'm so happy. And just to put it out there, I told you so."

"Yeah, yeah, whatever." Charlotte could gloat all she wanted. Shelby was still floating on enough afterglow and endorphins to be magnanimous about it.

"So tell me why we're going to a football game, then? Why are you not down on that boat making some waves?"

"Because it's homecoming, and we'd already planned it. I'm not going to ditch you like that." She frowned at her hair. She'd tried curling it, but it was flat again already.

"Consider me ditched, honey. He's only here for a short time. You should make the most of it."

The fact Declan was only here for a short time kind of made it even more important *not* to make too much of it. There was a line between having a good time and setting yourself up to be miserable later. She'd watched Ryan fall into that trap just last year when he'd fallen for Helena, only for him to be miserable when she left. She'd seen her friends—even Charlotte—overinvest in the chemistry and hormones of tourists, only to crash when vacation was over and everyone went back to their usual lives. A fling with Declan was a nice distraction, but not worth standing up her real friends over. Plus . . . "And have everyone in Magnolia Beach wonder where I was? Or, God forbid, come looking for me when I don't show up?"

"They'd never think to look on the *Lady Jane*."

Actually, that would probably be the *first* place Jamie would look for her. And the thought of that . . . *ugh*. "Well, I'm glad you're so accommodating, because Declan's coming with us tonight."

"To a high school football game? Why?"

"Because it's better than sitting alone watching Netflix?"

"You could offer him something better to do."

"Don't tempt me." Her hair was just going to have to do. It certainly wasn't going to get any better, and she'd spent far more time on herself tonight than she had for any other football game, ever. It was a little embarrassing. At least Charlotte hadn't called her on it.

"Seriously, Shelby, that has to be the worst date idea ever."

"It's not a date. We're friends."

Charlotte rolled her eyes, but Shelby ignored it. "I offered to introduce him to some people, show him around a little, so he wouldn't have to spend all his time alone. That's what I'm doing."

Charlotte looked confused. "But you could be having sex. You're priorities are way out of whack, girl."

"It is possible to enjoy someone's company *out* of bed as well as in it. Declan's smart and nice and interesting, and he thinks *I'm* interesting. We talked for over an hour last night just about random stuff. It was fun. I really do think that he was starting to get lonely and needed to get out."

"So you're taking him to a football game."

"A home game is a quintessential small-town experience. He said he was looking forward to it."

Charlotte crossed the room and fluffed Shelby's hair. "*I'm* going to safely bet it's only because *you'll* be there. You look great. If you need a distraction for cover to escape early, just let me know." She handed Shelby a jacket. "I'll just think of that sexy poetry and swoon."

She grabbed Charlotte by the shoulders. "Do not embarrass me. Or Declan. In fact, I'm swearing you to silence now. I don't need everyone in town knowing . . . well, anything."

Charlotte rolled her eyes. "You went to dinner last night. You're taking him to the game tonight. People will talk, and there's nothing you can do to stop that."

"True, but all they can do is talk. Unless *you* give them something meaty, talk is cheap." She heard footsteps on the stairs. Declan was on his way up. "Behave and be nice," she warned.

"Of course."

Somehow Shelby wasn't fully convinced, but she waved Declan in as he knocked.

There was an awkward moment, as she wasn't sure how to greet him. When she'd left him last night, there'd been a long, lingering kiss, but it was perfectly natural considering what they'd just done. Now, though, she wasn't sure. A hug? A kiss on the cheek? A handshake? *Lord, I'm losing it.*

But Declan seemed almost as unsure, his eyes flicking to Charlotte, then back to her. But then he smiled and briefly squeezed her hand. "Hey," he said quietly.

It was simple, yet it worked for her. A little too well. "Hey."

"Hi, Charlotte. Good to see you again."

"And you, Declan." Charlotte's tone carried a wealth of meaning that no one could misunderstand. "Ready for the game?"

"I guess. I've never been to one before."

"A high school game or a homecoming game?"

Declan smirked. "A football game."

Charlotte's eyes widened. "Ever?"

"I'm not big on sports in general."

"Well, don't tell anyone else that. It'll be easier for you if you just claimed to be an atheist."

Declan looked to Shelby for an explanation. "We're a little fanatical about football around here."

"I'm aware of that. I do watch TV."

"Well," Charlotte said dramatically, "I'm going to go powder my nose and then we'll go."

It was an obvious ploy to leave them alone for a minute, but Shelby wasn't going to object. Neither was Declan, it seemed, because the moment the door closed, he leaned in for a quick kiss. "I wasn't sure if I should do that in front of Charlotte or not."

"She knows."

His eyebrows went up. "How much does she know?"

She had to bite back a giggle. When had she gotten so giggly? It was terrible. "The important stuff," she hedged.

"Was it a good report, or do I need to hide in shame?"

She couldn't help grinning. "You got high marks across the board."

"Good." He kissed her again, a little more thoroughly this time.

Fighting the urge to fan herself, Shelby had to admit Charlotte might be right. Now going to the game didn't seem like such a great idea. It actually sounded kind of stupid.

"And seriously," Declan asked, just before she decided to cancel the plan, "atheism will go over better than football neophyte?"

You have no idea. Either way, Declan was going to stick out like a sore thumb. Although he looked yummy enough to set Shelby's pulse pounding, a critical eye would see he was totally out of place. He wasn't overdressed or anything or even wearing the other team's colors, but there was something off—jeans a little too tailored, his hair a little too coiffed, even the way he held himself marked him as a "City Boy" better than a flashing neon sign above his head. "I wouldn't bring either topic up. Just cheer when everyone else does, okay?"

Charlotte danced right along the edge of needing a muzzle all the way to the school. Shelby barely felt the heat of one blush subside before the next double entendre sent the blood rushing back to her face. Thank goodness the darkness hid most of it. And while Declan seemed to take it all in stride, Shelby was really reconsidering the prudence of bringing him tonight.

As they walked toward the entrance, Shelby pulled on Charlotte's arm. "I hope you got all that out of your system on the way here. Don't make me kill you in front of witnesses."

"I'll be good. I promise. Hey, Lacey!" Charlotte sprinted ahead to greet her. Of course Lacey was in a crowd of folks, and they all turned at the sound of Charlotte's voice, which put Shelby and Declan right in their line of sight, too.

Wherever Lacey was, her husband, Howie, wouldn't be far away, and since Howie was one of Adam's closest friends, of course Adam was there, and because the universe was just messing with her, of course Eli and Jamie were right there, too. Along with half a dozen other people, all of whom seemed to find her arrival with Declan quite interesting.

Yeah, maybe I didn't think this through all the way.

Chapter 10

Every stereotype he'd heard about Southerners and football had been proven true in the last hour. Crammed into the stands with what seemed like the entire population of Magnolia Beach, Declan got the full effect: the marching bands, the cheerleaders, the sideline quarterbacking, all of it.

And he was having a great time.

It was surprising, yes, but crowd mentality was obviously a real thing, even for the less enthusiastic. Here was practically an entire town, turned out to support their youth. What could be more wholesome than that? Plus, their enthusiasm was contagious.

And Shelby really did seem to know everyone and took the time to introduce him to people. It was a little disconcerting how many of them not only already knew who he was, but also knew about him—where he was from, what he did for a living, even what kind of car he drove. Shelby found it amusing that it seemed weird to him. "Slow news week in a small town. You're the most exciting thing around," she'd explained with a shrug.

It was a beautiful clear night—he was beginning to

think that Magnolia Beach only had beautiful weather—with a slight nip in the air that clearly said it was fall, even if the days were still pretty warm. While the locals were in jackets—a few were even wearing hats—it wasn't nearly cold enough for him to need one. And packed into the stands like sardines, it felt warmer than it actually was.

But when Shelby scooted close to him claiming to be chilled, he decided he liked the thinness of Southern blood.

Shelby excused herself at halftime when the visiting team's band took the field, leaving him alone in the crowd of her friends. They'd certainly been friendly enough, if overly curious for his comfort, making Shelby's earlier assertion that this was a friendly place, welcoming to tourists, seem true.

Then suddenly, he was surrounded by Tanners.

Jamie took the seat recently vacated by his sister, and Eli took the other side, with Adam stepping in front of him, blocking his view of the field. There were two younger boys with them, their features the younger versions of the other three. *More cousins.* How many did Shelby say she had?

It was a show of strength, obviously meant to put him on edge. He found it funny—mainly because they'd waited until Shelby went away to make this show. If Shelby wasn't going to be cowed by them, he certainly wasn't.

But before any of them could say anything, a dark-haired woman pushed her way through. After one look at Jamie, he was vacating his seat for her, and she smiled at Declan as she sat.

"Hi," she said, sticking out a hand. "I'm Helena. Please ignore them." There was bluster from the Tanners, but Helena ignored it. "You must be Declan."

He searched through his memory banks, but Shelby hadn't mentioned a Helena. And she certainly didn't look like any of the Tanners, even if she held the same amused and exasperated tolerance of the others as Shelby did. "Nice to meet you."

"I'm Ryan's fiancée. Ryan," she explained, "is Shelby's cousin, and Adam and Eli's brother."

He appreciated her mapping the family tree. "The one who's mayor."

"Exactly. He also volunteers as the assistant coach for the football team, so he's in the locker room right now instead of backing up the rest of the Avengers. You know Jamie, and the JV squad behind him is Tucker and Joe, who should really be tucked away safely in their dorms at school instead of here annoying people." She flicked her eyes in the general direction of the others and sighed. She leaned in as if she were going to share a secret, but then spoke loudly enough for everyone to hear. "The Tanners can be an acquired taste. Don't let them see you sweat, though."

He wasn't sure what to say to that, so he stuck to a much safer topic. "Congratulations on your engagement. When's the wedding?"

Helena's lips thinned to an invisible line as the Tanner boys howled with laughter. "Yeah, Helena," one of the younger ones asked, "when is that wedding going to be?"

"On a date when I'm sure *you'll* be back at school, Tucker Tanner," she snapped icily.

"That's a rather fraught topic," Adam added unnecessarily—and a minute too late to keep Declan from stepping in it. "But we've got a pool going if you want in on it."

Helena's mouth dropped open. "You do not."

That just made them all howl louder.

Helena cleared her throat with some force, and turned back to him. "So you're an architect?"

"Yes."

"Magnolia Beach must feel like the Sahara of the Bozart to you."

Having already put his foot in his mouth once already about the wedding, he worried this might be a loaded statement. She was, after all, the mayor's fiancée and a resident of the town. She probably thought it was great. "It has its charms."

Helena laughed at him. "How diplomatic of you. It is quite the definition of Mayberry Americana, isn't it?"

"And that's its charm. It's an eclectic mix of styles, yet it creates a pleasing aesthetic that the residents like. Ultimately, that's what's important."

"An eclectic but pleasing aesthetic," Eli echoed. "You should put that on the website, Helena."

Since Helena was ignoring Eli, Declan did, too. "My taste isn't what matters. Good design is about function and form that's appropriate to the location and what it'll be used for, and the tastes of people who hire me. If you come to me and ask for an office that looks like a spaceship with a tree growing out of the top, that's what I'll design for you."

Helena laughed. "Hopefully, you'd try to talk me out of that. But I know what you mean. I do web design work for people and they're all 'use nine colors and six fonts and make every third item move,' and while I try to explain how downright ugly that would be—in the nicest possible way, of course—"

"Of course."

"I'll still do it—knowing I'll have to redo it when they decide it's terrible. How do you—"

Eli coughed.

Helena sighed. "Oh, all right. You seem like a decent enough guy."

That was a rather abrupt change of topic. "I like to think so." He didn't know what else to say.

"Good. Just don't mess with Shelby."

His jaw nearly fell open. One of the younger Tanners laughed.

Helena cleared her throat. "I mean, you can 'mess' with her—"

"Hey now—" That might have been Jamie protesting, but Helena held up a hand.

"Just don't mess with her head. Be nice and don't hurt her feelings."

Once again, he felt unfairly vilified. At the same time, this was her family, and they cared about her. Some leeway had to be given because of that, but still. . . . "I hadn't planned on it."

"Good." Helena smiled broadly. "Then these nice gentlemen will knock off the caveman crap and leave you two alone." Again, there was muttering, but Helena spoke firmly both to him *and* them. "No need to worry about them now."

He wanted to say something snarky, but prudence—he was vastly outnumbered, after all—held his tongue.

"Not that there'd be much of you left for them to fight over after Shelby was done with you," Helena added.

He nearly choked. Neither her chipper tone nor her polite smile had changed a bit, which somehow made the warning feel even more sinister.

Helena patted him on the shoulder. "So we're done here now. Enjoy the rest of the game."

"Oh, no, we're not even a little bit done," Jamie said.

Helena held up a hand. "Don't you dare start, Jamie. We agreed I'd handle this."

"You agreed, Helena, not me."

Helena sighed and rolled her eyes. "Behave."

"Let him talk, Helena." That was from one of the younger Tanners.

Helena turned on him with a killing look that had *Declan* pulling back out of the line of fire. "*You* may keep your lips zipped, Joe Tanner. It's bad enough the others think they get some kind of say-so in Shelby's business, but I will not let you think you get one, too. And wipe that smile off your face, Tucker," she snapped. "Shelby is an adult, and you are not. You'll treat her with respect."

Joe and Tucker wisely directed their attention elsewhere, but Helena wasn't done. She turned on Adam, Eli, and Jamie next. "Do y'all not see what you've done? You treat Shelby like a child and now the Wonder Twins there think that they can, too. It's appalling. I'm surprised she hasn't killed you all in your sleep. God knows I would."

"Butt out, Helena—"

Declan could tell he was witnessing a family issue, one that had depths he was completely unaware of. Whatever was going on, whatever it was Jamie wanted to say and had caused Helena to run interference *before* turning on the Tanners, went well beyond the general familial posturing of protectiveness. But he didn't know what was going on, and the bickering he was witnessing now made no sense. It also made him a bit uncomfortable.

"What the hell is going on?" Shelby's arrival caught the others by surprise and silenced them pretty quickly. She sent a pointed look around the group and frowned.

"Like I can't figure it out myself. Deliver me, Lord, from my idiotic family. Sorry, Declan." She sighed disgustedly and shook her head, waving Eli out of his seat so she could sit next to Declan. Intentionally ignoring the others, she spoke only to Helena. "Hi."

A whistle and a crash of cymbals welcomed the teams back onto the field, and just like that, the matter dropped. He did see Shelby throw an elbow at her brother once, though, followed by a low-pitched spat that culminated in another elbow thrown at Adam and some seriously threatening eyeballing of her other cousins.

He seriously did not understand the Tanners. But Helena was marrying into the family, so they obviously weren't too bad, even if she did say they were an acquired taste. And after that very strange conversation—for lack of a better word—with Helena at halftime, the Tanner boys seemed to place him somewhere on the spectrum between "friendly acquaintance" and "evil despoiler of virgins," treating him nicely enough and including him in conversations, but maintaining a protective, if less in-his-face, presence, hovering around Shelby like a menacing yet oddly friendly pack of guard dogs. Their message was clear.

Later, they—minus Helena, Adam, and the younger Tanners, but plus about a dozen of Shelby's friends—somehow ended up in the middle of nowhere around a makeshift bonfire, drinking something called Firefly Tea out of red plastic cups. Declan had no idea such things happened outside of 1980s teen rom-com movies. But Shelby sat next to him—not too close, but her thigh running alongside his, barely touching—and offered the occasional whispered piece of backstory to explain who people were or what they were talking about.

Someone named Justin, who Shelby explained was

a cousin of the Howie he'd met earlier, was complaining about a speed trap he'd been caught in in Mississippi last week. It was a dramatic telling—although Declan couldn't quite figure out *why*—full of big arm gestures and detailed descriptions of the blowhard deputy.

Shelby leaned over. "We can leave if you want." The firelight cast parts of her face into shadow, so it was hard to tell if *she* wanted to leave or was just giving him the out.

"No, it's fine. It's nice here by the fire. Do you all do this a lot?"

"Not a lot, but it's not unique or anything. We used to go down to the Shore after football games, but that's pretty much the turf of the high school kids and it makes me feel really old and a little creepy to do it now. What did you do on Friday nights in high school?"

"Studied." Shelby made a face that was somewhere between admiration and pity. "Yes, I was a big old nerd with few friends," he confessed, "so I read a lot."

Her eyebrows went up. "Poetry?"

"Sometimes." He leaned in a little closer. "Why? Do you want to hear more?"

Her lips twitched. "Maybe."

Touchdown scored for all lit nerds everywhere. Validation at last. "'*Shall I compare thee to a—*'"

"Right, Shelby?"

Shelby's head snapped around, and he looked up to see most of the circle around the fire looking at them both. He couldn't remember the name of the guy asking Shelby the question.

"What?" she replied.

"Back me up here. It was your idea to go to Biloxi that time and nearly got us all arrested, not mine, right?"

He heard her sigh. "Yes, it was my idea, but it was

your fault you were nearly arrested because you couldn't keep your big mouth shut."

"What was in Biloxi?" Declan asked.

"Casinos," Eli replied. "Shelby wanted to gamble."

He wouldn't have guessed that. "Are high schoolers even allowed in casinos?"

"No," Shelby said, "Hence the nearly getting arrested part because Kevin mouthed off."

"It sounds like you had an adventure, then."

"Yeah," Shelby muttered into her cup.

"Shelby always came up with the craziest ideas," Justin said.

"And the stupidest, most dangerous ones," Eli added.

"But they were always fun," Justin insisted. "Tell Declan about the time you got Charlotte to borrow her mom's truck—"

"Let's not," Charlotte interrupted.

Shelby nodded. "Really, let's not." Although she said it lightly enough, she was staring intently at her drink, and he could see the tension settle in her jaw.

"But that was the time that she—"

"Justin," Charlotte smoothly interrupted, "wasn't that the same time that you got pulled in for exposing yourself in Wilson Park?"

While the others laughed, Declan noticed the relief that spread across Shelby's face and the grateful look she sent Charlotte. "That's one of the bad things about living in a small town," she said quietly to Declan. "You never get to forget anything."

"And I'm a new audience for the stories?"

"That probably has something to do with it."

"I'm sure you have embarrassing stories you could tell about them."

"Of course. I just don't think it's fair to drag all that

out. And with you here, I'd just be begging for them to pull out the *really* embarrassing stuff to tell you just to make me squirm."

"But Shelby's the only person who's ever been banned from *church*." Declan didn't know who'd said that, but he heard Shelby's exasperated sigh before she responded.

"That's how you make sure you get a front row seat in hell." Dropping her voice while the others laughed, she turned to him. "Wanna go? It's about a half-hour walk back to the marina from here, but it's a nice night."

He was fine either way, but Shelby had gotten visibly uncomfortable. "Sure." He pushed to his feet and helped Shelby to hers. As she said her good-byes, he could see Eli giving them the hairy eyeball. Shelby noticed, too, and just smiled as she waved.

The evening had thrown some weird curves, and he felt like he was missing a pretty important piece of the puzzle. At the same time, *Shelby* wasn't acting strangely—just her family and friends—so maybe it wasn't actually that important. And he wasn't sure if he should ask about it—or even *how* he would, since he didn't know what it was he didn't know.

And was it even his place to say anything?

Shelby seemed perfectly fine as the light of the bonfire and the noise of the gathering disappeared into the shadows behind them. She even reached out and took his hand, twining her chilly fingers between his.

"So was that the most redneck thing you've ever experienced?"

"It was different. I don't know about redneck, necessarily. But it was fun." He squeezed her hand. "Thanks for including me."

"My pleasure." She moved a little closer, tucking her

other hand under his arm. "You can check that official small-town experience off your bucket list."

"I didn't even know it was on my bucket list."

She grinned up at him. "Now you do. Anything else you want to experience while you're here? Now that I've got you off that boat and out in public, there's a whole wide world—or small town, actually," she corrected with a giggle, "that I can show you."

He stopped, right where they were on the side of the road, and pulled her close, taking the kiss he'd been waiting for all evening but hadn't seemed appropriate in the middle of a crowd of people. She sighed into him and rose up on tiptoes, kissing him back with a passion that was dangerous when they were still a good twenty-minute walk from the marina. He broke it off with a groan and got a quick thrill when she echoed it. "I'm game for anything."

"Anything?" she asked. When he nodded, her eyebrows went up. "Ooh, I like the sound of that."

So did he.

Although Declan fell asleep Friday night with Shelby wrapped around him, she was gone Saturday morning when he woke up. Even though intellectually he knew the marina would be busier on weekends, he was a little disappointed to wake up alone, without even a note or a text from her. It also gave him no small helping of something akin to shame or guilt—he'd kept Shelby up late when she had to get up early and he could sleep in. And she was working while he had nothing better to do than laze around surfing the Internet. But what did one do in a small town on a Saturday afternoon?

Shelby's idea to get him out and do things had been a decent plan, but it had both worked and backfired.

He wanted to do something, but the one person he wanted to do something with was busy doing actual important stuff. He was no longer happy just doing nothing, but he didn't have much to do, either. So he was still doing nothing, but now he felt bad about it.

Shelby just laughed when he told her that.

The sting was less than it might have been, simply because Shelby was laughing while draped across him like a naked nymph, and he wasn't bored at all at the moment. "I can't entertain you twenty-four hours a day, but there are chores for everyone. I've got tanks that need cleaning."

He wasn't sure he'd felt that much shame yet. "Pass."

"Lazy bones."

"I've got to keep my strength up," he rebutted, pulling her up for another kiss, just as her phone went off again. "Do you want to get that?"

"Not really. That's Jamie's ringtone."

There had been other calls, each with its own ringtone. He'd bet those were all Tanners. "They don't like me at all, do they?"

Shelby snorted. "I hate to deflate your ego, but they honestly probably don't care that much about you either way. In fact, it might not have anything at all to do with you. I do talk to my brother on a regular basis about all kinds of things."

"Then why not answer it? It could be important."

"If there was something major going on, my phone would be blowing up with texts and calls from ten different family members, and there'd probably be someone banging on the door downstairs, too." Then she looked up at him and grinned. "But it is probably sort of about you, but not because they don't like you. They all just like to annoy me, and you're the weapon of the week."

"Last night at the football game, though—"

"Yeah, Helena told me how they ganged up on you. I'm sorry they're so obnoxious. I just try to remind myself that they love me and they mean well."

"I'm not worried about me. I recognize it for what it is, and I can handle it. You're a grown woman, though."

"They're overprotective." She said it with such a sigh that no matter how she tried to convince him—or herself—otherwise, he could tell it frustrated her.

"Just because you're a girl?" he teased.

"There's some of that, sure." She sounded uncomfortable. After the way both her family and her friends had acted last night, whatever the *rest* of it was would probably explain that strangeness.

"And?" he prompted when she didn't say more.

"I've always been flighty, disorganized, impulsive, and easily distracted. I've made a ton of bad decisions. Jamie and the others have spent a good portion of my life pulling me out of messes of my own making. I tell myself they're just trying to head trouble off at the pass to save themselves some work later on."

The Shelby he'd seen was confident and capable and fully able to run her own life. "No wonder they infuriate you so much."

"Yeah, but lifelong habits are hard to break."

"Not that. The fact they think you're flighty."

"I was. Still am, sometimes." She sounded disappointed in herself.

"No. I don't believe that for a second."

"I really was."

"Maybe, but now? No way. You're probably the most grounded and sensible person I've ever met."

"Thank you." She grinned at him and ran a hand

teasingly down his chest. "Flattery will get you everywhere."

"It's not flattery." Why he was so indignant on her behalf, he didn't know, but it was rather surprising she *wasn't*. If nothing else, being treated like that all the time, regardless of the reason or the fact they were family, had to be brutal on her ego. "I know what it's like to have people treat you like something you're not."

"You?"

"I was a shy, bookish kid from the wrong side of town on a scholarship to a good school. People thought that because I was poor, I was stupid."

"No one should be made to feel stupid when they're not." She said that very quietly yet very earnestly. "I'm so sorry."

"But I left all that—and all those people—behind. It sounds like you've got people treating you like a child, all day, every day."

"I'm used to it."

"You shouldn't be."

"Like I said, old habits are hard to break. What am I going to do? Stand in the middle of Front Street and shout about it until people change their minds?"

He remembered the rather patronizing tone Officer Rusty had taken that day. "Wait, you're telling me the whole *town* treats you like that?"

She was quiet for a moment. Then she sighed. "People don't take me seriously."

"Why not?"

"Well, I'm female in a primarily male occupation."

"This town may look stuck in the sixties, but you can't tell me the entire population is, too. Everyone knows you're good at what you do."

Shelby didn't say anything, which piqued his curiosity. There was definitely something else in play. And it suddenly seemed very important for him to figure out what that was. This was the piece of the puzzle he'd been looking for, the piece that would make this all make sense. "What's the deal? Tell me."

There was a very long pause. "People think I'm slow. Cute and sweet, but not too bright, ya know?"

"Because you're pretty, you can't be smart? Or because you're supposedly flighty and disorganized?"

"I *am* flighty and disorganized. That's my ADHD, but I'm now on good meds, and those have helped a lot. But in high school, when we were still trying to get the dosages and everything right, well, that was just one long string of bad choices and disasters."

His high school roommate had had ADHD, so he knew from experience what that was like for the bystanders. In that sense, he could relate to the Tanners' hovering, trying to prevent the possible catastrophes and protect her from her own mistakes.

Shelby's ADHD must be well controlled *now*, though, because he wouldn't have guessed. She didn't need hovering over, but the lifelong habit she had of *letting* them hover was probably equally hard to break, even if they annoyed her.

But there was something else. Something more to this story. He could feel the tension in her body, feel her jaw flex against his chest. Whatever it was she wasn't telling him, it was bad, but he couldn't for the life of him begin to guess what that might be. He could feel the change in her body when she decided to tell him, a subtle shifting of her muscles as she resigned herself to say it at the same time she was bracing for his reaction.

He concentrated on keeping *his* muscles relaxed, his face neutral. He just hoped he could appropriately handle whatever it was she was about to say.

"I'm also pretty severely dyslexic. The ADHD kept me from getting diagnosed earlier than I did. I struggled all the way through school, and barely graduated. I'm not dumb, or anything, it's just that I can't really read. I mean, I *can* read, just not well, and it takes forever and makes my head hurt to do it . . ."

Her words were tumbling over themselves at such a speed it took him a moment to sort them out enough to realize that this was, indeed, the deep, dark secret and shame she felt she had to confess like a sinner in a confessional.

It wasn't exactly a bombshell revelation—he'd been braced for something bad—but things snapped into focus for him nonetheless. The hovering of her family made even more sense now. The fact she tried so hard not to make him feel stupid when she taught him about boats—God, she'd probably dealt with that a lot, explaining her instant empathy for him being called stupid just because he was poor. Hell, even the fact that Shelby didn't have a single book or magazine lying around in her apartment now made sense.

It had to be a bitch of a thing to deal with—he couldn't even imagine—but she obviously had it figured out. She should be proud of all she'd overcome. But as she kept talking, he realized she was trying to convince *him* she wasn't dumb. He waited for her to trail off and take a breath. "And?"

Her head snapped up so quickly, it bumped his chin and rattled his teeth. "What do you mean, 'and'?"

"You've obviously figured out how to accommodate for it, so I'm not making the connection."

The look on her face now questioned *his* intelligence. "People assume I'm completely illiterate. Even in Alabama, that's a big deal. We do expect our kids to read and write. People may like me, but they still think I'm a little slow."

He couldn't believe how angry that made him. Both the attitude of the people who'd misjudged her intelligence, and Shelby's seemingly calm acceptance of that like it wasn't infuriatingly insane. "I find myself questioning the entire intelligence of this town because they're questioning yours," he said carefully.

That was obviously the right thing to say, because he felt her relax in his arms. Then she shrugged. "It's a small town. Everyone knows there's something going on in my head, but it's not like I'm going to run informational meetings to educate them on the ins and outs of dyslexia."

"Maybe you need to."

"Nah. I just still need to prove myself to them, I guess."

"If they haven't figured that out yet . . ." His indignation on her behalf finally boiled over. "You know what? Move. Pick a town—any town—and *go*."

That made Shelby laugh. "Nah. Believe it or not, I do like it here, even when I get frustrated with people. I grew up here, and I've got friends, family, a job I like, and hey, I already know what all the signs say."

"That doesn't mean you belong here. Or that you have to *stay* here."

She balanced her chin on her fist and looked at him closely. "Is that why you left Chicago? You didn't feel like you belonged there?"

The sudden one-eighty caught him off guard. He hadn't thought about it quite like that. "I thought we were talking about you."

"And now we're talking about you. It only seems fair."

"I left Chicago because I got offered a better job."

"Just because a better job comes along in a different city, that doesn't mean you belong in that city. Especially if you won't be happy there."

"I think I'll be very happy in Miami. Who wouldn't be?"

She snorted. "All the people who choose *not* to live in Miami."

"You've got a comeback for everything, don't you?"

She pushed up onto her elbow and gave him a pitying look. "Do you think you're the first tourist boy who's tried to convince me that Whatever Town is better than here for whatever reason? I'm not saying that Magnolia Beach is the bestest of all possible places on earth or that it's the right place for everyone. I'm just saying it's the right place for *me*, warts and all. You can live anywhere, but it seems hard for some people to find a place that's *home*. We get plenty of drifters through here, you know, and it makes me wonder if that's what they're looking for. A place that feels like home."

There was something very unnerving about the surety in Shelby's voice—the utter confidence behind the words and the implication that his decision to move to Miami might not be as uncomplicated as it seemed. He'd had a beautiful girlfriend, friends, a good job, a great apartment in Chicago . . . All in all, he'd built a nice little life for himself, and he'd ditched it all with hardly a second thought. "Are you saying I'm some kind of drifter?"

Shelby looked up at him. "Maybe a bit of a wanderer."

"'Not all those who wander are lost.'"

"But they are looking for *some*thing." She sat up and straddled him, rubbing her hands across his chest seductively. "What are you looking for, Mr. Hyde? Fame? Fortune? Adventure?"

His blood wasn't exactly rushing in the direction of his head at the moment, making a thoughtful answer to that question impossible. He ran his hands from her knees to her hips and up to her waist. "Nubile Southern belles with honeyed drawls."

Shelby batted her eyelashes at him. "Well, I do declare, sir," she said in an accent so thick it added extra syllables to every word, "you might be hard-pressed to find many Southern belles willing to be nubile in the company of a Damn Yankee."

"I'm not a Yankee," he insisted.

"To me you are." A tiny bit of pressure applied to her waist had her leaning down over him until the tips of her breasts tickled against his chest. She closed her eyes briefly, seeming to savor the sensation, then opened them to meet his evenly. "And I'm sorry to say I don't know a parasol from a pinafore. How do you feel about rednecks?"

He gathered her hair into a loose ponytail and pretended to inspect the back of her neck. It was tanned the same color as her arms and legs—a few shades darker than the skin of her breasts and belly. "It doesn't look very red to me."

"Hm. I promise I really *am* Southern," she murmured as he kissed the side of her neck and her collarbone. "Which is more than I can say for the ladies of Miami, by the way."

He flipped her to her back and settled between her legs. "Florida's a Southern state."

She snorted. "On a map, maybe."

He leaned down onto his elbows. "So I'm a Yankee even though I'm from the Midwest, but people in Miami aren't Southern even though they live in the southern-most part of the southernmost state?"

Grinning, she nodded. "Yep. The northern part of the state is Southern, though."

He couldn't help laughing. "Your logic is just twisted. So is your geography. Remind me not to let you draw me any maps."

She ran her toes over his calf and lifted her head to kiss him. Then she gave him the sultriest, sexiest look he'd ever seen. The hand absently caressing his lower back shifted course, skimming over his butt and upper thigh. He hissed. "I don't need a map," she challenged. "Do you?"

The South wasn't the only thing that wanted to rise again.

Chapter 11

Amazingly enough, things settled into a pretty good routine over the next week. Shelby couldn't complain, and in fact, she'd developed an embarrassing habit of humming or whistling to herself for no reason. Both her mother and her grandmother had called her on it last Sunday—random humming and whistling not being good manners—much to the amusement of the peanut gallery she was related to, but aside from some ribbing, the boys had been rather circumspect in their comments.

It was odd, but it was a blessing she wasn't going to question too closely.

Charlotte had been acting the strangest, making herself scarce unless Shelby tracked her down. "I'm always here. I'll always *be* here. Declan won't. Make the most of it, and tell me all the good stuff," she'd said by way of explanation when Shelby had finally asked why her best friend was suddenly avoiding her.

She had to love Charlotte.

And Declan was practically the perfect friend-with-benefits. Although he was on an extended vacation, he seemed to understand that she wasn't, and he didn't cling or expect to monopolize her time.

Her days were spent doing her usual, and Declan's days were spent doing . . . well, whatever it was he did with his days. Sometimes he'd go off on one of his day trips, and in the evenings he'd tell her, often in great detail, about the buildings he'd seen that day. It was like talking to a kid who wanted to be a vet after a trip to the zoo.

It was cute. Sweet, too.

But he was around a lot, and she'd catch glimpses of him as she went about her day. Lately, he seemed to have taken up the habit of sitting out on the deck of the *Lady Jane* in the late fall sunshine to read. She wasn't sure if Declan had always been that visible or whether she was just noticing him now.

Or maybe it was a little of both. Even with all the screaming, toe-curling, world-rocking orgasms Declan was providing her, her hormones seemed to be constantly on alert, seeking him out like a junkie needing a fix.

It didn't help that he was always happy to comply, which made staying focused on what she was doing at any given moment difficult at best. Daddy had been dropping hints she might need to check her meds, but it wasn't like she could flat out tell him *why* she was so distractible these days.

And Declan was definitely growing out of his hermit ways, too. For someone who said he didn't like people all that much, he was doing a good job of faking it, like today.

Not only was he helping assemble a dunking booth with Howie and Todd for the school's Halloween Carnival, he'd *volunteered* to do it when Todd had mentioned it the other day at the Bait Box.

When she'd been left gape-jawed at overhearing that, he'd laughed and claimed that since he was between jobs at the moment, he had more time than most. He hadn't realized that that statement was a beacon for every committee chair within the town limits in need of muscle-bound help, and he'd become very popular the past few days as everyone got ready for the carnival.

But she had to admit, not only was that the fanciest dunking booth Magnolia Beach had ever seen, it certainly seemed to be the sturdiest. Every year, Howie came up with a new design for the dunking booth, and every year, Howie's contraptions looked unstable, if not downright dangerous, and only the foolhardiest people could be talked into climbing onto the seat. It was practically one of those rites of passage for teenage boys looking to prove their manhood.

Usually Ryan and Howie would be locking horns about now, with Ryan mumbling about safety, and Howie insisting it was fine, but with Declan in the mix, Ryan had given it a nod of approval and gone off to do something else.

Maybe having a genuine architect around wasn't a bad thing.

"Shelby!"

Her head snapped up just as the balloon she was inflating popped in her hand. "Crap."

"That's the third one." Helena tsked and shook her head as she fitted another orange balloon over the nozzle of the helium tank. "You seem to lack focus on this super important project we've been assigned. Not that I blame you, though. He is *very* pretty to look at."

That was true. And Declan was proving quite the chameleon, too. From hippie to hipster to handyman in a snug T-shirt and work boots, he climbed ladders and pounded nails, flexing all those muscles in a way that had her mouth watering. "Yeah," she said, hating the sigh in her voice and the smirk that sigh put on Helena's face. But . . . "Hey, now, you're engaged to my cousin, remember?"

"Yes, but I'm not dead. I can still appreciate the man candy. I'm glad he's out and about more these days so we all can appreciate it often and fully."

"Yeah."

"It's just not healthy, either, spending that much time alone. I'm not exactly a social butterfly and even I know that's true. He was practically a step away from the beginning of a true crime show. You know, loner drifts into town, holes up off the grid until he snaps and bludgeons the townsfolk in their beds."

"I said almost exactly the same thing."

Helena laughed as she tied a ribbon to the balloon, then tied the other end to the weight behind them, where it joined the others in a black and orange pond. They probably still had at least fifty more to fill and not much time to do it. The carnival opened in three hours, and at this rate, she and Helena wouldn't be finished before Christmas. *Ugh.* "And how about the Terrible Tanner Trio? Are they leaving you alone?"

"Yes, thank God. And thank you, too. It's so annoying that you can scare them into behaving when I can't, though."

"At least my bad reputation is worth some good today. And anyway, as long as Jamie knows I still have copies of his foray into erotic fan fiction, he will never not be my bitch." She smirked. "And I will never not enjoy that, either."

"I so want to see that. Name your price."

"Nah. Blackmail loses its threat when too many people have the goods."

"You'd think, though, as family, I'd have more dirt on them to control them with."

"Honey, you'll never control them. And while I know it's annoying, just try to remember they mean well—

Damn it!" The balloon squirted off the end of the nozzle and flew into the other balloons with a *pbbbffft.*

"I know," Shelby said, handing her another. And here was her opening. While things had been in an uneasy, if superficially pleasant, truce between her and Helena, she needed—*wanted*—to make things right. "So did I, you know."

Helena's eyes snapped up.

"Last fall, with you and Ryan."

"I know you did. You were just trying to look out for him."

"But I crossed a line. I know that. And I'm sorry, really. I was completely wrong to try to break you up. You two are great together, and he's really happy. I'm glad I failed."

"Thank you for saying that." Helena's smile seemed genuine, so Shelby had hope she might actually be forgiven for her meddling. "I must admit that Tanner family dynamics often leave me scratching my head, but it's my first time being part of a big family, so it's interesting, too."

"Just try to remember we *all* mean well. But keep your powder dry," she advised. "You never know when you'll need to fire the shot."

"Who's in the line of fire?" Ryan asked as he snaked an arm around Helena's waist and hauled her up for a kiss. Declan was with him, and Shelby couldn't help noticing his greeting for her was far less enthusiastic—a little side hug that would be considered chaste at church camp. But as much as she'd *like* more, it was probably better not to cause talk.

"Now, if I told you, that would ruin the surprise, Mayor Tanner," Helena said sweetly.

"Be nice," he warned.

"The dunking booth looks good," Shelby told Declan.

"Well, it's not the Willis Tower, but I'm pleased with how it turned out."

"And it looks like less of a death trap, so I'm happy," Ryan added. "I won't have to sneak back in later while Howie's distracted and shore the thing up. Adam can't even look at Howie's contraptions. He says they're a lawsuit waiting to happen."

"Then why let him build them?" Declan asked.

"Because Howie's grandfather did it and so did Howie's father," Shelby explained. "It's a family tradition. Sadly, Howie lacks the skills his daddy and papaw had, but because traditions must be respected, we let Howie do it anyway."

Declan looked carefully at her project. "So you come from a long line of balloon inflators?"

Helena laughed. "The Tanners *are* a bunch of clowns."

"The boys maybe," Shelby corrected. "It's definitely a Y chromosome thing." She gave Helena a serious look. "If y'all procreate, hope for girls."

Crissy Cassidy, the president of the Magnolia Beach PTA, came by with her clipboard. "Ryan, Declan, I could use your help getting the supplies into the concession stand." Crissy frowned as she saw the condition of Shelby and Helena's project. "And maybe y'all should quit bothering the ladies so that they can finish up."

"We'll be over in a second," Ryan promised as Crissy left. Then he looked at Helena. "You slackers. Shame, shame."

"Be gone from my sight," Helena declared regally, but she lost the upper hand when Ryan hauled her up for another kiss.

Then Declan kissed her. It was quick and natural, and definitely not as chaste this time. She was left amused and a little giggly as Declan left with Ryan. Any talk would be worth it.

"Oh, my," she heard Helena say from beside her.

Oh, my indeed.

The Magnolia Beach Halloween Carnival had been an experience—that was for sure. The people went all out for it. Not that he had anything to compare it to, of course. His neighborhood school had ten-year-old textbooks barely holding together at their spines, so there hadn't been much of a budget for things like carnivals. His high school had done things like field trips to amusement parks that he couldn't afford and hadn't been included in his scholarship, so he'd stayed behind when the others went, claiming he didn't want to go anyway.

There hadn't been fancy rides or anything at this carnival, but the midway games and cake walks had been popular with both adults and kids alike. He'd eaten cotton candy and bobbed for apples, and no one had blinked twice at the sight of a thirty-two-year-old man in a bouncy castle.

That was a short-lived moment, though. He'd learned he was way too old for that—a lesson he was sure he was going to regret tomorrow. He was already sore.

And he'd gotten to soak young Kirby Peterson in the dunking booth—twice—to cheers from the assembled crowd. Even Kirby had seen the justice, however immature it might be.

Then, because he was an actual adult, he'd gotten to come back to the marina and have sugar-high-fueled sex with Shelby, who was now lying beside him bemoaning the three—or was it four?—cupcakes she'd had earlier.

"There's a reason women substitute sugar for sex.

Blech," Shelby said. "Back-to-back cupcakes *and* sex are just too much. Pity me."

"Poor baby. There, there." He patted her head. The orange jack-o'-lantern she'd had painted on her cheek was smeared. He wiped a hand across his face and checked his palm. No orange paint. "I heard Helena warn you about eating that last one, though."

"So I don't often take good advice when it's offered. Sue me."

"Stubborn girl." There was a scratching at the door. "Cupid wants in," he told her.

Draping an arm dramatically over her eyes, she asked, "Would you mind? I'm going to lie here and moan a bit more."

Rolling off the bed, he grabbed for his jeans, pausing and then grinning as he noticed an orange streak across his thigh. *Well, that explained that.* His jeans were inside out and half under the bed—how had that happened?—and they were hung on something, keeping him from extracting them. The scratching was becoming more insistent, though, so he left them there and went to let Cupid in.

Cupid ignored him completely and went directly to Shelby to determine she was okay—the dog did that every time they finished having sex. Shelby was noisy. Not that he really minded, but it *was* genuinely scaring the dog.

Crouching down, he gave his jeans a tug, and they slid out, pulling Shelby's sketchbook with them. The button was caught in the spiral binding. The book was folded back, open to a page, and while he wasn't being nosy, he couldn't help looking.

Especially when he realized it was a drawing of a building.

It wasn't what he'd expected to find in Shelby's

sketchbook—although he wouldn't have been able to say what he had expected—but it was definitely a building.

She didn't have the greatest artistic talent, but he could see what she was trying to achieve: a Mediterranean-style building with arches and wide breezeways.

Curious, he turned the page. That page was more like a scrapbook, with pictures of both Victorian and neo-Mediterranean buildings clipped from magazines and printed off the Internet glued side by side onto the paper, as if in comparison. Red circles called attention to some details; arrows with question marks at one end pointed to others. The third page was another sketch, this time an aerial view of buildings and a shaded area with wider lines extending out into it and little triangles attached to the lines . . . She was drawing a marina. *Designing* a marina.

Possibly the Bay Breeze Marina. He wasn't expert enough on the layout to know for sure, but it was a possibility.

"Shelby, what's this?"

Shelby had Cupid by the ears, nuzzling nose to nose and making kissy noises, but she rolled over at the sound of her name. When she saw him, she jumped up so quickly, Cupid barked in protest.

"That's private." She grabbed for the book, and he reflexively pulled it out of her reach. That earned him a killing look and a very serious "Give me that."

Reluctantly, he handed it over. Shelby flipped the book closed and slid it between the bed and the nightstand. Then she went back to petting the dog, obviously choosing to pretend he hadn't seen it at all.

But he was curious. "You're designing a marina, right?"

"It's nothing. Just doodles."

"It looks like it could be this marina."

She shrugged. Her cheeks were flushed pink from embarrassment.

"I think you've got some good ideas," he said carefully. "The neo-Mediterranean is a really good choice because it gives that instant 'welcome to your beach vacation' feel. And a red roof really pops against a blue sky." He tried to sound casual and professional, just like he would be when discussing a project with any other client, but she was shut down and stony-faced, so he knew he was going to have to coax information out of her. "There's so much Victorian already up on the beach, you'd stand out instead of blend in. And I think this place could really use the face-lift."

Her eyebrows pulled together. Crap, he shouldn't have insulted her marina. It might be ugly, but she loved it—and hell, she might love it just the way it was. But the fact she'd been collecting ideas, sketching them . . . She didn't love it exactly the way it was. He hurried on, trying to appeal to her business side. "You have a prime location here with a lot of potential. Improvements on the property would increase your traffic—bringing in more tourists, acting as a funnel into Magnolia Beach—"

"You think I don't know that?" she snapped.

"Obviously you do. That's why I think it's great you've got so many ideas already."

"They're just ideas, though."

"But you can turn them into—"

She held up a hand. "First off, I don't have that kind of money, and secondly, what am I supposed to do? Close the marina down for a year while we build a new one?"

"Honey, you are talking to the right guy. I love a challenge." He sat crossed-legged on the bed in front of her. "You just have to adjust your design around the structures you already have—then you build extensions, add false fronts, things like that to make the new design. It'll cost less than an all-new building and be less disruptive to business. You might even be able to stay in part of the building for most of the time, only going to a trailer, which could be brought on-site, when absolutely necessary."

"Whoa, there. Down, boy. You're getting carried away."

He was, but he wasn't sure why she *wasn't*. The marina had been in her family for at least three generations, so there was a good chance the land was paid off. That would be the guarantee for any loan she'd need to take out—it was valuable property, worth far more than a renovation on this place would cost. "It's totally doable, Shelby."

"And you're forgetting the biggest issue."

"And that is?"

"It's not my place to make changes," she said in the most resigned, yet reasonable, tone. "I don't own the marina. I just run it. I can't do anything like that, even if I wanted to."

"But you want to."

"Of course I do. If the Bay Breeze were mine, there are all kinds of changes I'd want to make. But this place still belongs to my parents, and they're happy with it just the way it is."

That just didn't make sense, not since updating the place would most likely increase their business and therefore their profit. No one could run a successful business for as long as the Tanners had with such a limited vision. "Is that what they said?"

Shelby's mouth twisted, but she didn't answer.

To clarify his suspicions, he asked, "You *have* talked to them about this, right?"

Shelby squirmed. "Not exactly."

"Why not? You're the one running this place. Part

of being a manager is managing things. Long-term planning and improvements are even more important when you're the one who will take over someday."

"I really don't need you to lecture me on how to do my job," she snapped.

"I'm not. I just want to know why you're not actually doing it."

"*Excuse* me?"

"You're paid to run the marina. Like I said, this would fall under your purview. It would be one thing if you'd pitched your ideas and been shot down, but you're saying you haven't even broached the topic."

"If they wanted to change this place, they would have already," she argued, definitely a little exasperated. "Therefore, I must assume they like it as it is. The marina turns a profit and serves its purpose as is, so who am I to go and tell my parents that what they've done isn't good enough? I'm supposed to tell them that I know better than they do? That I know better than my grandfather? It seems disrespectful."

"It's not an insult to be offered ways to improve and modernize your business."

"They're not going to want to fix something that isn't actually broken, and there's so much history here that I don't think 'modernization' is the magic word you think it is."

"Wait. Which is it?"

"Which is what?"

"Which one is the problem?" She gave him a confused look. "Is it the money? The fact it belongs to your parents? The fact it's 'not broken'? You've given me five different excuses, and I don't understand which one is the actual speed bump."

"That's because it's all one big problem. It's all

tangled up together. I can't just pull on one string and unravel it."

"How do you know?"

"I just do."

"So you haven't said anything at all. How do you know for sure that any of these so-called problems are actually barriers?"

"I know my family."

He would not claim to have encyclopedic knowledge of the Tanner family, but it was impossible to be in Magnolia Beach for *any* amount of time and not learn *some*thing about them. Even he knew the family was successful, owning several businesses around town and a swath of rental properties. There was at least one doctor, lawyer, and CPA; the current and a couple of former mayors were Tanners. The family as a whole was well liked and heavily involved in the community. He could attest firsthand to their tight-knit familial bonds. There was absolutely no evidence that they were not the almost perfect, disturbingly well-adjusted, and functional family they appeared to be.

And Shelby, by her own admission, was a bit of an outlier. The only girl in a generation of boys. The one people thought wasn't all that bright. The one who had a history of impulsiveness and disorganization.

Which meant when Shelby said she still needed to prove herself to people, "people" included—and might actually outright mean—"family."

"I think I understand."

"Good. Let's move on."

Granted, he didn't have a whole lot to go on, but he couldn't believe that her family *honestly* thought she was incompetent or silly. He had to be careful, though. He couldn't bad-mouth her family—no matter how irritated Shelby might be with them, he doubted *he'd* get away with insulting them. And he couldn't—in fairness, at least—stir up a bunch of shit she'd have to deal with long after he was gone.

At the same time, he couldn't say nothing at all.

He took hold of her hand. "I know you're more than capable. And believe it or not, I think your family knows that, too. Deep down, at least. They let you run this place, don't they? That means they have to have *some* faith in your abilities, even if, out of habit, they act like they don't. How are people supposed to know about the good ideas in your head if you don't tell them?" Risking her wrath, he reached beside her to fish the sketchbook back out. Her lips thinned out, but she didn't stop him, so he flipped through a few more pages. In addition to spiffing up the exterior, it looked like Shelby wanted to add a café of some sort with outdoor seating. There weren't any written notes outlining her ideas, which would have helped make sense of this, but then he wanted to smack himself; *of course* Shelby wouldn't jot down notes, but the pictures she drew were enough to give him the gist.

She had a great sense of space and ways to use it. He didn't necessarily know enough about the day-to-day business of the marina to know if it was the *best* use of the space, but it seemed well thought out, and he trusted her to know what she needed.

Function took priority over form, but her ideas were simple, clean, and attractive. Unless she was willing to raze the place, she couldn't implement them wholesale, but her plans could be tweaked to work with what already existed.

He didn't know how long they'd been sitting there, but he'd looked through almost all of Shelby's pages without a peep from her. He looked up to see that Shelby wasn't watching him, instead using the time to carefully inspect her cuticles. It wasn't until he closed the book that she finally looked up.

"You have great ideas."

When he saw the start of a smile, he realized how nervous she'd been to hear his opinion. "Really?"

"Definitely."

"Wow. I didn't know." A slow smile spread across her face. "I always figured I was sketching some kind of architectural unicorn."

"I'm not saying it could be exactly what you have here—there are space and budget restrictions no matter who you are—but you could have something close. Something you'd enjoy and be proud of."

"Thank you. Your opinion—especially considering what you do—means a lot to me."

"Did you and Jamie run the numbers already? Do you know . . ." He trailed off as Shelby shook her head.

"I haven't said anything to Jamie. Or anyone else, for that matter. Not even Charlotte." She half laughed softly. "You're the first to see any of this."

However accidentally or strong-armed it had been. He was still flattered, honored even, to be the first. "You should get some estimates, put your case together, and then start talking to your family. No matter how they act sometimes, facts and figures and a plan are the best way to sway people to your side."

"I don't know . . ."

"Well, you don't have anything to lose, do you? Worst-case scenario is that your parents will veto the idea outright. Then you'll just go back to what was obviously your Plan A—waiting until it's actually yours and doing it anyway."

"But Jamie—"

"You will not convince me that you'll be unable to

get Jamie on board. If facts and figures don't work, you'll annoy him until he agrees just to get you to shut up about it."

Shelby laughed. "True. Sad, but true."

"You say you need to prove yourself to people. Well, here's one way. Bring the Bay Breeze Marina into this century and make it a better, more profitable business."

She ran her hands over the sketchbook. "It won't be easy."

"Nothing ever is. But I'm sure you can do it." He leaned in and gave her a kiss. It was just intended to be a punctuation mark to his statement, but Shelby returned the kiss with an enthusiasm that obviously forgave him for his snooping and meddling.

When the kiss finally broke, she lifted an eyebrow at him. "I thought you were an architect, not a life coach."

"I'm multitalented, don't you know?" He attempted a leer, but realized it had failed when Shelby giggled. Fully intending to prove it to her, he crawled up beside her on the bed, only to be stopped short when Shelby dropped her sketchbook back into his lap and flipped open to the page that had the Victorian and neo-Mediterranean buildings side by side.

"I like the Mediterranean the best, too, but the cost of and upkeep of stucco scares me a little." Shelby seemed excited about the topic now, pretty much ignoring the hand he had caressing her knee. "And while you're right that there's a lot of Victorian on the beach already, maybe it would be more fitting to the overall 'look' if I went that way. Plus, the siding is much easier to keep up . . ."

He sighed, removing his hand from her knee, and resigned himself to the discussion. He'd started it, after all. He had no one to blame but himself.

* * *

More than anything, Shelby hated running errands. Running errands in the pouring rain was even worse. Dodging in and out of buildings, getting progressively wetter . . . her mood was pretty foul. But she'd put off so many things recently that her to-do list simply could not be ignored any longer. She blamed her hormones; they were definitely running the show. Instead of running errands yesterday while the sun was shining, she and Declan had taken the *Lady Jane* out again. Ostensibly for another "lesson" for Declan, but in reality . . . well, it hadn't been a very thorough lesson, unless showing Declan how to drop anchor in a secluded spot to have sex on the deck could be considered imparting important boating knowledge.

In her defense, though, the days were getting cooler, and pretty soon outdoor nakedness would be out of the question. Yesterday had been downright chilly, but they'd persevered. And since Mother Nature seemed to have been watching the calendar, sending the temperatures diving into the sixties as soon as the Halloween festivities were over, a girl had to take the opportunities that she could when they presented themselves.

Since she'd slacked off yesterday, she sucked it up today and dashed into the pharmacy to pick up her medications. She also needed condoms, but that errand had been given to Declan—with the instruction that he go outside the city limits, where no one knew who he was, in order to buy them. Neither one of them could purchase them in town without word spreading, and while she could deal with the speculative assumptions she probably was sleeping with him, there was no way she'd provide the confirmation, too.

In her Jeep, she had Siri read her the list. Her meds—check. Cupid's meds—check. Jamie's office—check.

Bank—check. Post office—check. Lunch with Gran—check. She still needed to go to the grocery store, but with all that productiveness under her belt already, she decided she'd earned a cup of coffee and a cake pop from Latte Dah.

Plus, the coffee would warm her up. *Hello, fall.*

Molly always ran a rainy day special at Latte Dah with games and such, and in the height of the season, the shop would be overrun right now with people. Today, though, it was active, but not too busy. Inside the door, Shelby wiped her feet and shook the worst of the rain off onto the mat with Latte Dah's logo. Molly, bless her forethought, had a stack of small hand towels on the table beside the door, and Shelby grabbed one to wipe the moisture off her arms and shoulders.

Molly was behind the counter rinsing out the metal pitchers she steamed milk in, but she smiled and waved Shelby in. "Hi, there! I'm surprised to see you out in this weather."

"So am I. But I had to run errands." She settled onto one of Molly's stools.

"Without a raincoat?" Molly scolded gently.

"You sound like my grandmother."

"Only because half the people in this town refuse to acknowledge the existence of rain and wander around in downpours like frogs in search of a pond."

"Rain, rain, go away," Shelby singsonged as Molly filled a mug and set it in front of her.

"So how are you? I haven't seen you around much lately."

"I'm good. I've just been busy."

Molly's lips twitched almost into a smile. "Really, now? Busy doing what?" It was so innocently said and

Molly looked like a sweet little angel, but the meaning was very clear.

"I am enjoying getting to know a new friend."

Molly grinned. "I'm glad to hear it. He seems nice. And he's really cute, too."

Molly was engaged to Tate Harris, the town vet and the brother of one of her employees. What *was* it with engaged women and their need to drool over Declan? "He is," she answered. "Both nice and very cute."

"I'm glad you're having fun, then. Excuse me a second," she said as another customer came up to the counter. Any conversation with Molly at Latte Dah had to be carried on in bits and pieces. Everyone was pretty much used to it, and Shelby was not one to stand between anyone and their caffeine fix. Hell, that's why she offered coffee to everyone who wandered into her office before noon.

Which brought her back to her daydreams about the marina. While neither she nor Declan had really brought it up much after the other night, it kept popping into her head—far more than it used to. Just hearing Declan say that her ideas weren't crazy—and were, in fact, even possible—had sparked something inside her. They might still just be pipe dreams, but they were now pipe dreams with the blessing of an actual architect.

And just telling Declan about them . . . well, that had been quite the experience. She'd been mortified that he found her book, but his enthusiasm about her ideas had been quite the ego boost. She'd never told anyone about them—not even Charlotte, who knew she wanted to make some changes, but not the extent or the fact that she had a scrapbooked obsession to rival some girls' Pinterest wedding boards.

And while he didn't sugarcoat the reality of her

ideas—the expense, the disruptions it would cause, the hassles it would create—he also provided great feedback and ideas of his own, allowing her to tweak and refine her ideas.

And never once did he try to dismiss the idea or treat her like she was crazy to even think about it. It gave her confidence in her ideas and something to look forward to.

Everyone had to start somewhere, right? Hell, Molly had moved here knowing no one, and started Latte Dah. At some point that had to have seemed like a crazy dream, too, but Latte Dah was awesome and successful.

"Did you want a snack, Shelby?" Molly was back, drying her hands on a towel.

She did, but not right at this second. "No thanks. Can I ask you a question, though?" She hurried ahead before she could chicken out.

"Of course." Molly leaned on her elbows.

"I was just wondering . . . How much did it cost you to open Latte Dah?"

Molly's eyebrows went up, and she blinked. "I wasn't expecting that question."

"I know that's a little nosy of me—"

"No, that's not it. I'd be happy to share numbers— even though I should warn you they might give you heart palpitations. I had seed money from my grandmother, and I *still* had to take out a loan from the SBA while scrounging every thrift shop and rummage sale in the county for furniture and coffee cups."

"That's what I was afraid of."

"I just had no idea you had any interest in a business outside the marina. Should I be worried about getting some competition?" she teased.

"No, not at all. I was just thinking that we might want to think about adding something like that at the marina.

For the folks that are on that side of town or at the marina already. Maybe offer some simple food . . ." Jeez, this idea was sounding lamer by the second.

"You know, I've been thinking the same thing. Opening up another place over near the beach for the tourists. The rent over there is just too god-awful expensive for me to even contemplate. And there's not a lot of open space anyway. I've looked. I'd have to open a shack directly on the beach."

"Yeah, it was just a thought."

"Well, let me know if that idea ever gains any traction. We could talk about maybe partnering up."

Shelby's heart skipped a beat. "Are you serious? You'd consider putting a Latte Dah outpost in at the marina?"

"Yeah. Totally. It's not right on the beach, but I know y'all get a ton of traffic through there during the season. And since it'll take me forever to save up the money to open something on my own, finding a partner—especially one with real estate already—would be a major plus."

Maybe it's not so crazy after all. "Like I said, it's just an idea, but I'll keep that in mind. Can I get a couple of cake pops and that coffee to go?"

"Sure thing. And tonight or tomorrow I'll e-mail you some numbers to look at. It'll give you an idea of what it takes."

"Thanks, Molly." More facts, more figures, more data. More bricks for the foundation of her plan. Well, it was still more of an idea than a plan, but that little residual thrill of "it's not a totally *crazy* idea" vibrated through her again.

Regardless of what Declan said, she wasn't ready to go running to her family with this scheme, but it was nice to roll it over in her head knowing that someone, other than herself, thought it had merit. Someone who didn't actively balk the second she mentioned anything.

Someone who thought she might have the ability to pull it off.

And Molly had just blown her mind. Maybe she should spend more time with people who *hadn't* known her for her entire life. Molly had only been in town for maybe three years, so she didn't have the same low expectations as other people—as clearly evidenced by her "sure, let's talk about a coffee shop" attitude. It wasn't a firm commitment or anything, of course, but still . . .

She might never really change people's minds or expectations of her, but folks who had no reason to question her brain or abilities? That was kind of cool.

No wonder Declan encouraged her to move.

Not that she ever would, but she could understand the appeal.

Her mood greatly improved—whether it was the coffee, the fact the rain was tapering off, or that little thrill, she didn't know—but grocery shopping was a quick and easy chore, and she was back at the marina just about the time the sun started to peek out from behind the clouds.

It wouldn't be enough to warm things up at all, but she'd take cool and sunny over cool and gray any day.

The puddles and bare spots in the parking lot reminded her that she still needed to order that load of gravel, and while her reasons for forgetting to do it last week were Declan-based distractions instead of just her usual disorganization, it underscored how off her game she was right now.

But while she might gently scold herself for it, she wasn't going to berate herself. She was having a good time. She wanted to enjoy it.

While she still could.

Chapter 12

Declan hadn't had much sleep in the last few days, because he hadn't been able to turn his brain off.

He was obsessed. It wasn't unusual for him to get this way about a new project—Suzanne used to get very annoyed about it—but this was a different kind of obsession.

Shelby's ideas for her marina had sparked something in him. This was a real challenge. Designing from scratch was fun, but this required him to be creative in different ways. There were cost considerations, of course, but every project had a budget. Modernizing, updating, and reinventing the Bay Breeze Marina within a proscribed set of parameters required new thinking.

What could be salvaged? What could be repurposed? How to turn a nondescript cinderblock building into an attractive neo-Mediterranean-inspired one without razing it to the ground? All the current usage of the property—the huge maintenance shed, the bathhouse, the boat ramps—had to remain, yet Shelby wanted to add amenities like a café, too. Extending the current building would be difficult simply due to its current positioning on the property, and building a new freestanding one would be an unnecessary expense—even if he could find a place to put it.

The Bay Breeze Marina was a family business and part of a larger community. It served a purpose in that community, one that couldn't be set aside or ignored. There had to be a way to make it all work, and he was determined to find it.

Every idea ran into a pothole. Every thought got countered with a "Yes, but . . ." Every easy and obvious solution came with a hefty price tag.

And he was loving every hair-pulling moment of it.

This wasn't an impersonal office building designed to impress both clients and competition, like the glass and metal monstrosities that filled the Chicago skyline. This was the kind of project where all those concepts like "New Urbanism" and "sustainable" and "vernacular" design he used to toss around in college actually came together to become a real thing.

He'd been obsessed with projects before, but this was the first time in a long time that he'd been excited about it as well.

He found himself walking the property, getting the feel of how it was currently laid out and how much he had to work with. It was an old-fashioned way to do it, as opposed to being given a list of specs and surveyor's measurements. It made him think differently, though, and he was consumed by the challenge.

The only weird part was that, in a way, he was doing this behind Shelby's back. He might have won her over enough for her to share some of her ideas and get his feedback on them, but when he'd brought it up the next day, she'd just shaken her head and said, "It's fun to play with the idea sometimes, but it's not in the cards right now. Thanks, but it's best to let it go. I'm just not ready yet."

And she'd put her sketchbook away. He hadn't exactly gone searching for it, but it certainly wasn't out in the open now.

Whatever had aligned on the night of the Halloween Carnival to open Shelby up on that topic had passed, and now she didn't want to discuss it. He didn't know why, and she wouldn't tell him.

But he couldn't let it go. When Shelby finally worked through whatever was holding her back and decided she *was* ready, he wanted to have something ready for her.

More important, he didn't *want* to let it go. Partly because he felt awake and energized for the first time in ages. He hadn't even seen the rut he was in, which was ironic for someone who'd spent his whole life working toward a goal, only to discover that goal had pretty much put him *in* that rut. This, he realized, was why he was so intrigued with the hurricane damage and recovery along the coast: those people were rebuilding their lives and homes, wanting to keep what they could of what they'd lost, which was far more interesting for him than a new office block that looked just different enough from the one next to it to be considered "progressively modern."

The constraints on those projects went beyond financial and environmental or even aesthetic—these were lives and histories and communities being rebuilt, and those reasons were equally weighty, but hard to capture and respect.

Shelby's marina had been through rebuilding before—there were pictures in the office of hurricane damage—but they'd recovered and continued on. There was a history and resilience here that had to be admired, and understanding that—*respecting* that—was as much a part of the challenge as the layout of the property and the financial constraints.

Juggling all those pieces was keeping him up at night—well, not literally—but it was definitely filling up a lot of his free time, decreasing his Netflix habit significantly. He wanted to figure this out—partly because it was a challenge, and now also because his pride and ego were committed to getting it done.

But mostly he wanted to figure it out for Shelby.

And for no real reason beyond it was something she wanted, so he wanted to get it for her. If not literally, at least give her the answers and plans she needed to face down her family and get it done after he left.

Why that was so important to him was a question he wasn't willing to examine too closely.

So he focused on the marina instead.

"Hello, the boat!"

Damn it, he'd lost all track of time.

Other than that first night they'd been together, Shelby never boarded the *Lady Jane* unannounced. She said it was something about modeling correct protocols for him, but since all of his notes about her marina were spread out over the table at the moment, the warning was much appreciated. Of course, it would be hard to tell exactly what he was doing at a casual glance, but Shelby was sharp and he never knew what might catch her eye. He scooted the papers into a messy stack, then closed his laptop and set it on top.

"Declan?"

Opening the cabin door, he saw Shelby on the dock in jeans and a jacket, the collar turned up against the wind.

It was all he could do not to laugh. Even when the sun went down, the temperatures were only dropping into the fifties, yet Shelby acted like the ice age had returned. *Southerners.* "Hey."

An eyebrow went up. "You don't look ready to go. I know the Bait Box is casual, but even they require shoes. And even if they didn't, I'd recommend them. That floor is nasty."

"I just lost track of time. Come on in."

She took the hand he offered—even though he knew she didn't need it—to help her aboard.

Shelby dropped onto the couch and propped her feet up while he went to grab a clean shirt and some shoes. "What were you working on?"

"Nothing. I was just surfing the Internet and got sucked in." He didn't like hiding the truth, but he wasn't ready to bring that topic up yet. "What did you do today?" he asked to change the subject.

"Ordered gravel for the parking lot. You'll have to park somewhere else next Tuesday. Then I scheduled the inspection for the gas tanks, set up a deep-sea fishing trip for a senior citizens' group, helped Harvey with a repair on the *Three Brothers*, renewed my subscription to *Playgirl* . . ."

He paused, only one arm through his shirt properly, and stuck his head back into the main cabin. "*What?*"

Shelby grinned. "Just seeing if you were really listening."

"Funny."

She looked him up and down carefully. "Hummina, hummina. Who needs *Playgirl*? That's a very good look for you."

He struck a silly pose, but in all truthfulness, there was something almost erotic about the simple, honest assessment. *Playgirl* jokes aside, she'd made it very clear she liked what he had and wasn't at all coy or afraid to show or tell her appreciation.

But that was just how Shelby was. She was clear and upfront, no games or empty flattery. It just wasn't in her nature. Everything was given and taken at face value, which, while it could sometimes be jarring, also made being with her easy.

He'd done some casual no-strings-attached relationships before with women he'd called friends, but in hindsight, they'd been more acquaintances than actual friends. He might have been primarily driven by lust at the beginning, but he actually liked Shelby as a person, too. An actual friend-with-benefits.

Shelby leaned back, extending her arms along the back of the couch. "Well, if you're not going to put that all the way on, why don't you take it the rest of the way off instead?"

"If the Bait Box requires shoes, I assume they require shirts as well."

"Such a pity. It's their loss." She smiled as he shrugged his arm out of the shirt. "Truly, such a loss."

"Your turn," he challenged.

Although he'd said it, he was surprised when Shelby stood and stripped out of her jacket and shirt with a speed that left him blinking. A snap and a flick, and her bra landed on the couch.

He was across the room in two quick steps, moving her hair back over her shoulders and angling her face up to his. "I thought we were in a hurry."

Shelby's arms wrapped around his waist, pressing her skin against his. "Nah."

"Aren't your friends waiting for us?"

"Charlotte will understand. I'm easily distracted, remember?" Her hands were sliding inside the waistband of his jeans. Rising up on her tiptoes, she nipped at his chin. "And this won't take me long anyway."

She was wrong on both counts.

They were nearly forty-five minutes late, and Charlotte began blowing up Shelby's phone with calls and texts when they were just twenty minutes late. She'd had her phone read her the texts aloud where he could hear them until Charlotte's messages got racier and racier as she speculated—quite accurately, actually—why Shelby was late. When they finally arrived at the Bait Box, nearly half the bar cheered their entrance.

Shelby greeted Charlotte with, "I'm going to kill you."

"Then don't be late next time," Charlotte replied pertly.

"A least *I'm* getting known for something other than getting stranded on my boat," Declan observed. "It's a pleasant change." When Shelby frowned at him, he merely shrugged. "I'm just looking at the bright side."

"Remind me of that bright side when my family ships me off to a nunnery and my cousins kick your butt," she muttered under her breath.

He got a slap on the back that wasn't really that friendly. "Careful, dude, you're gonna find yourself hauled up in front of one of Shelby's uncles."

That was Shelby's friend Mikey—or maybe his name was Mickey; Shelby had introduced him to so many people, he couldn't keep them all straight now—who'd definitely started his night early and was already slurring his words.

"Oh, hush," Charlotte scolded, but Mickey-Mikey just grinned. "You'll scare Declan."

Why they thought he'd be cowed by middle-aged men, he wasn't sure.

"You're such a sore loser, Mickey," Shelby said. "It's just another reason you never had a chance with me."

An *oooh* rippled over the group, and Mickey obviously felt the burn.

Shelby took off her jacket and tossed it onto a bar stool, then grabbed Declan's arm. "Let's go get a drink."

Since it was Friday, the place was busy, causing them to have to wind through the crowd to get to the bar—which took forever as Shelby spoke to pretty much everyone on the way. A three-piece band set up over in the corner kicked into a decent version of "Twist and Shout," the music just loud enough to make conversation difficult, but not impossible. When they got to the bar, he leaned in close to Shelby's ear. "So Mickey's a jilted ex?"

"Not even that. He's been hitting on me for about fifteen years now. I don't think he'd know what to do if I ever actually said yes."

"Then why—"

"It's the principle of it now. Seeing who can out-stubborn who."

"No one could out-stubborn you. It's simply not possible."

She grinned at him. "I've told you that flattery will get you everywhere."

Hooking a finger in her belt loop, he tugged her a little closer. "I can do a lot better than that," he promised.

"Geez, don't do it here. I might swoon, and I've given this crowd enough entertainment for the evening already."

Oddly, he was a little disappointed. He tamped that down and said, "So then tell me why I'm supposed to be afraid of your uncles."

The bartender set drinks in front of them. He'd gone

to the same bars in Chicago for five years and the bartender never remembered his order, yet after just a couple of weeks here, he was already a regular, it seemed.

Shelby handed him his and took a long drink of her own. "One's a justice of the peace and the other is an ordained minister."

He nearly spit his beer at her. She merely laughed. "Don't worry. Magnolia Beach may feel like a time warp to the 1950s, but my family's not into shotgun weddings."

He coughed. "Good to know."

"Come on. I can't promise that group will behave, but I need to be back over there to keep them from getting any worse."

"Nice group of friends you've got there."

She shrugged. "It's a small town. You have to pick from what's available."

"Well, that lowers the bar."

"Maybe. But it also makes you look for the best in everyone." She looked at him evenly. "It also makes you more forgiving of the little stuff."

Damn, that's deep. "I guess if you're going to live in the same town with people all your life, you do have to put up with a certain amount, but I think the annoyance of Mickey hitting on you for fifteen years would cross the line."

"I was out fishing with friends when my dad had his heart attack. The whole family went to the hospital, of course, but Mickey waited for me at the marina until I got back and drove me to the hospital in Mobile," she said simply. "He's good people. He might annoy me sometimes, but that's just the price of admission to the fair." Then she grinned. "And we're also like fifth cousins or something."

"Ew."

"Welcome to Alabama," she teased.

While the plan, as explained to him earlier, had been to meet up with a few friends, play a little pool, and have a few drinks, it wasn't exactly a clearly demarcated group—unless by a "few friends," Shelby had meant "the entirety of everyone at the Bait Box." And although it still shocked him a bit, everyone seemed very accepting of his presence and went out of their way to include him in conversations—something he wouldn't have expected. They'd all known each other for years, at the very least—some of them for all their lives—and he'd expected more cliquishness from them. And while he couldn't discuss the intricacies of Alabama and Auburn football—which was a very popular topic—he found himself in enough other conversations about everything from gas prices to the band to keep himself busy.

The small dance floor was also busy, and he looked up to see Shelby dancing with some friends—including Mickey, who lacked rhythm and jumped around with more enthusiasm than style. But Shelby was flushed and laughing.

"Don't be jealous," Charlotte said from beside him. "They're harmless. Even Mickey."

"I'm not jealous." At Charlotte's expertly arched eyebrow, he added, "I'm not. Why would I be? They're friends."

"Glad to hear it. Jealousy isn't pretty."

"And it's not like any of them are actively hitting on her."

"No, and they won't, either. They can be patient."

"Excuse me?"

Charlotte kept her eyes on the dance floor. "Why get all bowed up and stir up trouble when the issue will resolve itself soon enough? They know they'll still be here long after you're gone. And they know Shelby knows that, too. So all they have to do is be patient and hope they'll be the rebound guy."

Someone called Charlotte's name, and she gave him a shrug and a knowing look before she walked away.

That was both cold and true, and it grated across both his conscience and his nerves. And he had a feeling Charlotte had planned for it to do exactly that. He just wished he knew why. Yes, this was temporary, but it wasn't like he was actively counting down. Or that he'd even started it simply *because* it was temporary or because he had nothing else to do. He wasn't stringing Shelby along on any kind of pretense or false promises.

There was no reason to romanticize what they were doing, but it wasn't calculated, either. This was . . . They were . . . It . . .

It was *this*. No more, no less, and it was pretty damn good.

The music ended on a crash, and after a brief round of applause, restarted—this time just one guy and an acoustic guitar. There was a bit of an exodus from the dance floor, then the remaining crowd merged into couples. He saw Mickey extending a hand to Shelby, and his feet were moving before his brain fully processed it. He slid between them—he knew it was rude and probably reeked of jealousy and insecurity, with a whiff of caveman to boot, but he didn't care.

He heard Mickey's "Hey, now, that's not cool," but Shelby gave Mickey a look over his shoulder that seemed to defuse him, and she stepped into Declan's arms. Her heartbeat was up and her breath was a little short from the up-tempo dancing, and the heat of her skin released the light fragrance of the soap she used into the air around her.

She eased into him, swaying gently with the music, a folksy song about rivers and wiregrass and white sands that Shelby seemed to know. He could feel her mouth moving against his chest and the light breaths that proved she was singing softly along.

"Should I apologize to you—or Mickey, for that matter—for cutting in?"

He felt her shake her head. "No."

"Good." *Because I wasn't going to. Mickey could just go perfect his patience.* "I guess I should have warned you that I'm not really a dancer."

Shelby lifted her head and smiled at him. "I think you're doing fine."

Happy, he folded their hands against his chest as the chords changed into the chorus.

Oh my love, I've found you a thousand times,
And I let this weary world take from me everything
*   that's kind,*
Oh my love, you hold heaven in your hand,
My heart's down in Dixie, but my soul's in
*   Alabama.*

Shelby wasn't the only one singing along, and the whole bar seemed to be swaying, like this was some local version of the national anthem—which was kind of weird, but Shelby felt warm and right snuggled against him.

And because it felt good, he didn't question it too much.

Shelby felt like the worst best friend alive.

The other night, when Charlotte's hot post-doc from the lab had shown up at the Bait Box and Shelby had

had absolutely no idea Charlotte was even seeing him, much less who he was, she'd felt like she deserved to lose her Best Friend Merit Badge.

Charlotte hadn't been mad, and she'd given Shelby her permission at the beginning to be all but ignored while things with Declan were so hot and exciting, but that didn't alleviate Shelby's guilt. Guys might come and go, but BFFs were too important to take for granted.

So to salve her conscience, she needed to make an offering.

Which was why she was at her parents' house baking cookies. Her one go-to recipe was snickerdoodles and was therefore the currency of all her apologies and over-tures. She already had a dozen cooling on the table to drop by Charlotte's this afternoon. While she was at it, she'd baked two dozen for Harvey to thank him for picking up her slack at the marina recently, and another dozen for her dad, just because he liked them.

And then she made a dozen for Declan, too. Just because.

After all, he was in the same position she was: lack of access to a proper kitchen. The *Lady Jane* had a basic galley, and she had a tiny kitchenette, and neither of them was good for serious cooking. Hell, at least she could come by here and scrounge a free home-cooked meal on occasion. She had no idea what Declan was eating when they weren't together. Some home-baked cookies would be a nice change for him. Probably. Hopefully.

When she heard the back door open, she looked up at the clock. Four o'clock exactly. Her mother was a creature of habit. "Hey, Mom."

Her mom hung her coat and purse on the hook behind the door and sniffed the air. "Oh, Shelby, honey, what did you do now?"

"What do you mean?"

"Snickerdoodles? You only make those when you're in trouble. Or when you're sucking up to someone." After a long look around the kitchen—Shelby wasn't exactly a *tidy* cook—she added, "And you will clean this up, whether or not you leave cookies for your father."

"Yes, ma'am."

Mom picked up a cookie and took a bite. "Hm . . . extra cinnamon? Definitely apology cookies. Who's mad at you?"

"They're for Charlotte." At her mother's surprised look, she quickly added, "She's not mad at me or anything. We just haven't gotten to spend much time together recently, and that's what I'm sorry about."

"That's a lot of cookies for such a small transgression."

"There's some there for other people, too."

"The other people you're not spending as much time with as you probably should? Or someone you're spending a lot of time with?"

Well, I did set myself up for that. "Mom . . ."

"Please don't take that tone, Shelby. I'm not criticizing you. But you are spending a lot of time with this Declan—whom I have not met, by the way."

"Er . . . um . . ." Thankfully, the timer dinged and she was able to busy herself with taking one sheet of cookies out of the oven and putting in the next.

But Mom was just warming up. She came to stand next to the stove. "From what I hear from Jamie and the others, he seems like a decent enough young man, well educated even if he is currently on a rather extended vacation, and definitely a step above some of the other boys you've dated."

"We're not really dating, Mom. We're just . . . um . . ."
Oh, God, there is no way to finish that sentence.

"I think everyone is quite aware of what you're doing."

The spatula slid out of her hand and clattered to the floor. Whether it was her mother's words—which were enough to make her want to slide under the stove—or the completely conversational no-big-deal tone they were in, Shelby was completely stunned. The snort that followed those words, however, nearly did her in for real. "*Mom!*"

"You're an adult. I can't really sit here and lecture you on the choices you make."

Since when? she thought, but wisely kept the words behind her teeth.

"But," she continued, "I *can* encourage you to be very careful."

Please don't make this be a sex talk. She chose her words carefully in hopes she'd shut that down. "As you said, I am an adult"—hopefully that would be all she'd have to say about *that*—"and I realize I could have tried to be a little more discreet, but in all fairness, that's not exactly easy to do here. Especially in the off-season."

"If you have nothing to be ashamed of . . ."

"I'm not ashamed of myself. I may not have taken out an ad in the *Clarion*, but I wasn't sneaking about, either. I just lived my life. And you're right. Declan *is* a nice guy. I like spending time with him."

"But to the exclusion of everyone else? Including Charlotte?"

Mom may have said "Charlotte" but she meant "the family." "It's not like we've been shacked up on his boat this whole time." Her mother's lips thinned in disapproval.

Crap. Way to go, Shelby. Tell Mom more about your sex life. "We go places and do things—football games, the Bait Box . . . If you hadn't skipped the Halloween Carnival again"—Mom hated the Halloween Carnival—"you'd have met him there. Anyway, he'll be gone after the New Year." *Ouch.* "Everything will go back to normal."

"Well, I'll be glad to see more of you when it does. Until then . . ." Mom leveled a look at her. "Be careful."

"Yes, ma'am."

"Is Declan going home for Thanksgiving? Do you know?"

As far as she could tell, Declan didn't have a "home" to go to. He wasn't close to his sister, so she doubted he'd go all the way to Colorado for the holiday. And while he had friends in Chicago, she didn't know if he'd go to one of them or not. He hadn't mentioned any plans, though, so she could honestly say, "I don't know what his plans are."

"Well, I hate to think of anyone being alone on Thanksgiving just because they're far from home. There's always room for one more at your grandmother's. He's welcome to join us."

"Always room for one more" was debatable. They were bursting at the seams already. And *jeez*, was that the kind of thing she could invite Declan to? Would he want to come? Did she want him to come?

Thankfully, Mom didn't seem to want an immediate answer, as she grabbed another cookie. "And seriously, clean up this kitchen before you leave."

"Yes, ma'am."

Once the kitchen was clean, she left a plate of cookies covered in plastic wrap on the table for Daddy, then boxed up the others. She drove by Charlotte's, let herself in, and put the box on the kitchen table. Charlotte wouldn't need an explanation.

She'd give Harvey his cookies tomorrow, but she could deliver Declan's now. They hadn't made any plans or anything, but Declan's car was in the parking lot, and she could see lights on in the *Lady Jane*. He'd been almost as reclusive recently as he'd been in the beginning. She didn't know what he was doing, but if it was something he didn't want disturbed, she'd just drop off the cookies and leave.

Wasn't that supposed to be the beauty of a friends-with-benefits thing? No expectations, no demands, the freedom to do your own thing?

Cupid's nose went crazy over the scent of the cookies, so Shelby had to put Harvey's box on top of a filing cabinet out of paw's reach.

Cupid followed her part of the way down to the docks, only to lose interest and go back up to the building. She was getting older and didn't seem to be handling the cold weather as well as she used to. If last year was any indication, Cupid was going to spend all winter curled up on her doggy bed in front of the space heater in the downstairs office.

"Declan?" She tried to give him space, always asking for permission to come aboard, but Declan seemed to be taking longer and longer to answer her hails these days. When he finally opened the door, he looked a little frazzled, his hair all messy and looking like he hadn't shaved. Was that the same shirt he'd been wearing yesterday?

"Are you okay?"

"Of course," he answered. "Come on in."

"I was at my mom's and made cookies. I brought you some." The cabin of the *Lady Jane* was . . . well, not a mess, necessarily, but very untidy, which was odd for Declan.

"That's sweet, Shelby. Thanks."

"Are you sure you're okay?"

"Yeah. I just got caught up in something and well . . ." He ran a hand over his face. His eyes looked bloodshot, and tired lines were etched into his face as if he hadn't slept since yesterday, either. It was worrisome, to say the least. "I'm starved, though. You want to go to the diner and get something to eat?"

"Sure. I guess." That stack of papers with the laptop on top had been a staple of Declan's table for a while now, but it had grown since the last time she was in here. He'd found something to occupy him beyond bingeing on old TV shows—which she would normally consider a good thing, except whatever this project he was working on was, he was crossing a line into unhealthy.

"Let me go wash my face real quick, and we'll go."

I should not snoop. A legal pad stuck out from the stack. It was a bulleted list of some sort, she could see that much, but Declan's handwriting was too much of a disaster for her to even attempt to decipher it.

This was the kind of thing that made her feel dumb. The answer was probably right here in front of her, spelled out and everything, and yet it might as well not be. People didn't need to hide information from her— all they had to do was write in cursive and it might as well be Japanese.

But something in the corner caught her eye. A doodle, retraced over and over again, like he'd been bored. It took a second longer than necessary for her to recognize it as the logo for the marina, simply because it was such an odd thing for him to be doodling.

What the . . .

Declan was still in the head, water splashing, and while her conscience told her to sit down and keep her hands to herself, her curiosity was not to be denied. She opened the laptop, bringing the screen back to life. The screen hadn't locked yet, and Declan's project popped back up.

At first glance, the design plan on the screen didn't make sense.

But on second glance, it did. Because if there was anything she knew, it was the Bay Breeze Marina—in any incarnation.

"You weren't supposed to see that yet."

Declan, shirtless and holding a towel, stood in the doorway, a worried half smile on his face.

"What is this?"

He cleared his throat, then wrapped the towel around his neck to catch the drips off his hair. "Plans for rehabbing your marina."

She started to say something, but he held up a hand.

"I know you said to let it go, that now wasn't the time, but I wanted to do it. I wanted to show you what was possible and give you an idea of what it would take. You don't have to do anything with the information if you don't want to, but I wanted you to at least have it. For when you are ready."

Declan's enthusiasm for her ideas had warmed her and encouraged her, but it had still been a dream. She still had a lot to untangle—and not just whether her ideas were good. He wasn't able to see the depth of the issue, because to him, the Bay Breeze Marina was just a business. Just a bunch of buildings. Intellectually, she knew that as well, but she still had all the emotional stuff and dealing with her family to sort out.

She knew his time and expertise were truly a gift.

She couldn't justify the expense of even meeting with a designer at this point, but having Declan actually work on it meant that her vague dreams *could* become reality. Here was an actual step in the direction of that reality, ready for her when she decided it was time.

It was proof that his earlier statements hadn't just been pillow talk or empty flattery. This wasn't just encouragement; it was *validation*. Declan really believed in it.

In her.

Something squeezed her heart and her eyes burned. "Thank you."

"You're not mad?"

"What? *No*." She launched herself at him, wrapping her legs around his waist and hauling herself up for a kiss. "Thank you, thank you, thank you."

Declan grunted as he caught her. "No one has ever been quite so pleased with my work before. I'm usually lucky to get a firm handshake. And maybe a fruit basket, if they're really happy with the project."

"Oh, I can do a *lot* better than a fruit basket," she promised.

Because she didn't know how else to show him how much this meant to her.

Chapter 13

Shelby had claimed to be related to half of Mobile County. Declan hadn't doubted her claim, but he'd naively assumed all of them would not try to fit into her grandmother's house for Thanksgiving dinner.

It seemed he was very wrong about that.

He still wasn't entirely sure how many Tanners were packed into this place, and he'd quit trying to count. Aside from the fact there were a lot of them and they kept moving around, they all favored each other quite heavily, which made accuracy an issue. There was no way he could remember names—and Shelby had laughed at his wish for name tags—so he stuck with Mr. or Mrs. Tanner for anyone older than him and a friendly "Hey, pal" for the younger ones. So far that had worked.

When he was growing up, his mother had tried to make Thanksgiving something nicer than usual for their small family, but he'd never dealt with the abundance of food and family like this. In college, he'd always volunteered to work Thanksgiving Day, guaranteeing himself a little extra cash and brownie points with the folks who wanted or needed off. And while he'd gone with Suzanne to her family's dinner for many years while they were dating, it was always a formal affair, catered and choreographed from the pre-dinner cocktails to the coffee served exactly two and a half hours later. He hadn't experienced anything remotely close to the ideal family Thanksgiving picture he'd had in his head.

The Tanner family Thanksgiving didn't match up, either, actually, but it was still fun. He'd never seen so much food in his life: multiple turkeys, hams, casseroles of every kind, and a sideboard groaning under the weight of enough desserts to throw most of the town into a diabetic coma.

It was loud and crazy, with a game of touch football going on in the yard accompanied by all the family dogs—including Shelby's Cupid, who had shown more energy in the last hour than he'd seen from her in the entirety of his residency at the marina—and people in huddles surreptitiously checking game scores on their phones while others tried to figure out where to put one last table and chairs to meet the need.

It was simply a madhouse.

And it was awesome. Jamie, Adam, and Eli had dropped their Guardian of the Maiden posturing, and none of the Mrs. Tanners had any problem assigning him chores with the others. One of Shelby's uncles even taught him how to deep-fry a turkey. He felt like a part of it, not really a guest, which was a nice feeling—and a nice surprise.

One of many.

First had been the invitation itself. It had been a sim-ple, almost offhand offer—"If you don't have plans for Thanksgiving, you'd be welcome at ours"—that caught him off guard. Somehow it seemed like an important milestone, regardless of how informal the invitation had been. It was nice of her—and nice of her family—to think to include him, but meeting the family—not just the ones in her generation, but parents, grandparents, aunts, and uncles, too—rather *implied* certain things—at least to other people.

Didn't it?

That concern must have shown on his face because Shelby had burst out laughing at him. "Don't look for the trap because there isn't one. It's totally safe and it's totally worth coming for the food alone if you think you can deal with my family *en masse*. But there is a dress code, and my grandmother takes it seriously. Do you have a tie?"

He didn't, but Shelby had asked Jamie to bring an extra. And because it seemed no one in the Tanner family was able to pass up the opportunity to annoy another, Jamie had *un*surprisingly handed over the ugliest tie ever made—too wide, too bright, and completely awful. Shelby's cousins had found this hysterical, but Jamie got scolded by the older generation every time one of them saw the tie, so Declan wore it with glee all day.

But the biggest surprise of the day? Shelby in a dress.

Specifically, Shelby in a moss green sweater dress of lightweight cashmere that skimmed down her body, highlighting, but without overly hugging, her curves.

She'd done something different to her hair, too, giving it soft curls that floated around her face and shoulders.

And she was wearing lipstick.

He'd been struck nearly mute at the sight of her carefully making her way down the steps in heeled boots from her apartment earlier, managing only to get out a few indistinct and very inarticulate noises.

"Not a single word," she warned. "I told you there

was a dress code. If I want to be fed at Gran's, I have to wear a dress."

"Uh . . . I . . . um . . ." While she looked like a different person, her words and her tone were one hundred percent Shelby, which helped him regain his ability to speak. Kind of. But the light scent of perfume that floated off her as she got close shut him right back down.

Not that there was anything *wrong* with the way Shelby normally dressed—practical around the marina, and nicer, but comfortable for dinner or outings—but *this*.

Damn. He wanted to pet her, tangle his hands in those curls, and smear her lipstick.

He gave himself a strong shake. "You're beautiful."

He hadn't meant to sound like such a panting puppy, but the light flush and small smile he got in return were well worth the ding on his pride.

"Thanks."

"I mean . . . *Damn*, Shelby."

The flush deepened, turning her cheeks bright pink, but the smile told him she was flattered, regardless of how she waved away his compliment with, "Let's not get carried away. It's just a dress."

The woman seriously did not know how good she looked—and the compliments of her family didn't seem to convince her, either—and even two hours later, he couldn't stop staring at her.

"Dude." Jamie waved a hand in front of his face to get his attention. "Do you really have to drool over my sister?"

He pretended to consider it before finally nodding. "Yeah, I kinda do."

"Could you not be so obvious about it, then?"

"I'll try." He glanced over at Shelby, who was in an

animated discussion with her mother and her aunt, gesturing toward the tables. Someone was probably going to have to move them again. Possibly even him.

"Try harder," Jamie warned, following Declan's gaze. Then he sighed. "Good Lord, not the damn tables again. We're never going to get to eat at this rate. I think next year I'll suggest renting out the Fellowship Hall at First Methodist. It'll be easier to fit us all in. I swear, this family is becoming a logistical nightmare."

Sure enough, a second later, he and Jamie and two of the younger Tanner cousins were being summoned over. Mrs. Tanner was walking away with a "And tell Eli to get off his phone," leaving just Shelby to deliver her edict.

Jamie opened with a preemptive strike. "I'm not moving the tables, Shel. Seriously, this is getting ridiculous."

"Then you'll be taking your plate outside and eating in the yard. Aunt Claire miscounted and we're three chairs short. If you'll pull those two tables"—she pointed at her choices—"as far as you can toward the wall, I can put another chair at each end of that one, and just squeeze another setting in at the big table."

"There won't be room for anyone to actually sit."

Shelby looked Jamie up and down like she was measuring him up. "You're pretty scrawny. I think you'll fit. You and the younger ones."

"I'm not sitting with the Brat Pack."

"We don't want you anyway," one of the brats in question protested. Declan still didn't quite know who was who.

"Why don't we pull that table over there," Jamie said, "and—"

"Because no one will be able to walk through." Shelby

sighed. "Could you not fight me on this, Jamie, and just do it, please."

"Shelby's right," Declan said, drawing the attention of all four Tanners. "There's not enough room to do it your way. Shelby's solution is the better one, space and usage-wise."

"I rest my case." She inclined her head toward the younger two. "Joe, Mason, go grab that table. Jamie will help and Declan can get the extra folding chairs from the back porch." There were grumbles, but the Tanners dispersed as instructed. "Thanks," Shelby whispered, giving his hand a squeeze before she walked away.

It was a small thing, backing Shelby's call, but he was getting damned tired of watching Shelby let her family roll right over her. With the ease they'd backed down, though, he had to wonder if her family even knew they were doing it.

He grabbed the chairs and set them where Shelby directed, then watched her as she handed off plates and silverware to one of her cousins to set the places before she went back into the kitchen. The heels on her boots gave a sway to her walk that wasn't normally there, and it hypnotized him. Jaime threw an elbow into his ribs. "Seriously, man. Knock it off."

But Declan couldn't help it.

Maybe wearing a dress hadn't been a bad thing today. Beyond the fact that not doing so would have caused a headache she didn't need, the lack of a waistband was a good thing considering how much she'd eaten.

Declan's loss of speech had just been a bonus and a boost to her ego. Dresses weren't her favorite things to wear—though it wasn't a hardship, either—but this one was her favorite of the bunch. And the way Declan *kept* staring at her . . . She felt very much the femme fatale today.

It probably wasn't an appropriate feeling for a family gathering, but it was so new and unique, she wasn't going to let an inappropriate time and place smack it down.

Helena was helping her cover leftover desserts as the boys broke down the tables and chairs, and the moms tidied in the kitchen. It wasn't a sexist division of work, but a practical one: the kitchen simply wasn't big enough for too many people to help at one time. The moms did the first round of cleanup, and the dads went in for the second set of dishes and pans. Shelby was perfectly happy with her job assignment—even if it did put temptation right in front of her for a nibble here and a nibble there, which her waist really didn't need and she would definitely regret later when she was physically ill from sugar overload.

"So Molly says you're thinking about opening up a coffee shop at the marina and maybe partnering with her?"

Shelby nearly dropped the pie she was holding. *Damn it.* She should have known Molly would mention that to Helena. She looked around to see if anyone had overheard. "Maybe, but you haven't said anything to Ryan about this yet, have you?"

Helena looked a little surprised. "No, why?"

"Because it's just an idea and there's no need to get everyone all worked up over an idea."

"I think it's a great idea."

"Really?"

"Yes. Absolutely. No offense, but the whole place needs a face-lift and a welcome into this century. And a coffee shop is a great idea. Do you think your dad will go for it?"

"That's the thing. I don't really know. He's not real big on making changes he doesn't have to. He usually defaults to an 'if it ain't broke . . .' mentality."

"But you're in charge now."

"Supposedly," she muttered. At Helena's sharp look, she added, "He said he was going to retire, yet he's there almost every day. So no, I'm not really in charge."

Helena shook her head. "This whole family is stubborn."

"Tell me about it."

"Well, honey, you're the worst of the lot." Helena grinned and patted her on the shoulder. "Just out-stubborn them."

Declan had said almost the same thing. She was beginning to wonder if it really was a compliment. "I wish it could be that easy."

"Oh?"

"I've been thinking about it for a while now. It's not just a matter of convincing them that it needs to be done. There's family history there. And lots of family memories. It feels almost disrespectful to tear up and redo the place."

"I promise you, your grandfather will not haunt you for improving his business. Now, maybe if you tore the place down and built a brothel on the site—"

"That would kill my grandmother," Shelby finished for her with a laugh, and Helena laughed with her. "And it just feels impertinent."

"*Impertinent?* How?"

"Who am I to step in and tell my father, who's been running not only the marina but also other businesses for longer than I've been alive, that what he's built isn't good enough? That I somehow know more than he does?"

"You're not telling him it's not good enough. You're telling him how it could be better. There's a difference." Helena sounded so reasonable. And while Declan had said something similar, Helena knew her family, so her opinion carried a little more weight there. "If you're going to be the future of the Tanner marina, you need to start visualizing that future."

"That's what Declan said."

"Well, listen to him if you won't listen to me. That kind of stuff is right in his wheelhouse."

She wanted to. "Maybe. Just don't say anything to Ryan about this, okay? It's hard enough figuring out how to broach this with Dad. I really don't want to fight him and the others just yet."

Helena blinked. "Fight them?"

"Well, listen to them argue with me about it."

Helena took the pie out of Shelby's hands and led her over to the settee. "I may be stepping way out of line here—though honestly, it wouldn't be the first time—but why on earth would you think Ryan or the others would have anything against this idea? Not a one of them has anything to do with that place beyond taking a boat out every now and then."

"Jamie has a stake in it."

Helena waved that away. "Jamie's a number cruncher. Do the numbers crunch?"

"Yeah. They're a little scary, but they will crunch."

"Then that's all that matters, really. He'll be easy enough to win over as long as the money's right. And Ryan . . . Good Lord, that man will take on anything that will improve Magnolia Beach. A nice marina is a selling point, a boon to tourism. Hell, I'm actually surprised he hasn't been lobbying for that for years already. As for the other boys . . . they can just butt right the hell out."

That was easy for Helena to say. She wasn't in the bloodline, and they were all still kind of scared of her. "None of them have the time or inclination to get involved with a project like this."

"Who's asking them to?"

"Well . . . they won't trust me to do it." The admission stung to say out loud. "You've seen how they hover and—"

"You really need to break them of that habit. You're dyslexic. Not twelve."

Damn. Helena did *not* pull her punches. "But they've spent their lives either hovering over me or bailing me out of whatever mess I've gotten myself into. Every now and then I run an idea up the flagpole and none of them salute it. In fact, they shut it down. You were there last time I tried. When I pitched us taking on more live-aboards," she reminded her. "You heard them."

Helena seemed to think about it. Then she rolled her eyes and sighed. "I had no idea. I thought that was just Tanner smack talk. And honestly, I doubt any of them even realized you were serious."

"Because they don't take me seriously."

"And they never will unless you make them." Helena sighed. "Just for the record, I think it's a great idea. I will back your play. And if you and Molly can partner up, that's all the better. I won't say anything to Ryan, but I think you should. Get him in your corner first, if that makes you feel better, before you go to your dad. Even the legendary stubbornness of the Tanner family has to buckle under the weight of a sound business plan."

A little spark of confidence lit up in her chest. "Declan said something similar, you know."

"Then he's a smart guy. I like him."

"I do, too."

Helena blinked, then her face softened into something on the edge of sadness. "Oh."

"Helena? What's wrong?"

She shook her head. "Nothing."

"Well, it's obviously *some*thing." Helena seemed very unsure, even unwilling, to speak, which was so completely un-Helena-like that Shelby started to worry. "What?"

"It's just that I get it now. Why you tried to break me and Ryan up."

She wanted to be past this. "I don't know how I can apologize . . ."

Helena held up a hand. "That's not it. I've accepted your apology. We're good, and I'm over it. I just didn't really *get* it until now."

"Get what?"

"The why." Helena sighed. "You said you were worried that after I left, Ryan would have a hard time finding a local girl who'd measure up."

"Yeah. But he didn't have to. It worked out fine."

"But what are you going to do?"

Helena said the words quietly, gently even, but they felt like a bucket of cold water dumped over her head. More than anything, that surprised her. She'd known, intellectually, at least, that Declan was leaving in another month. It was just another adjective describing him—brown hair, green eyes, architect, about to move to Miami. And while she'd had the occasional pang about that, it seemed perfectly natural. People who left would always be missed by the ones who didn't.

But now . . . suddenly it was real.

And it put an empty feeling in her chest.

Uh-oh.

"I'm going to miss him a lot," Shelby finally said. "But I knew it was only temporary going in."

"Uh-huh."

It wasn't like Declan was the only person she'd ever known who'd ever moved away. Lots of people did—for love, for money, or just for excitement. Magnolia Beach wasn't for everyone.

"I thought the same thing," Helena added. "So did Ryan, for that matter."

But Helena was from here; moving back simply meant coming home, even if it had been fraught with its own difficulties. And she—but not the rest of the family—knew that Ryan had considered a move to Atlanta. But Ryan's job was completely portable, and he'd fit in anywhere he wanted.

That was not the case with Declan. Or her.

For many reasons.

Reasons she really didn't want to think about. Not now, and certainly not in front of Helena.

So she shrugged it off, and put a big smile on her face. "It'll be fine."

Helena nodded. "I'm sure it will." But there was something in her voice that clearly said she wasn't convinced.

And Shelby suddenly needed a lot more pie.

Chapter 14

Shelby had been oddly quiet, even distracted, after leaving her grandmother's on Thursday, but whatever had been bothering her seemed to pass overnight, because she woke the next morning full of nearly manic Christmas spirit. Declan spent most of the day stringing Christmas lights with Shelby around the marina and dragging a much-larger-than-she-needed tree into her apartment. The tree he could understand, but things were so slow around the marina, he wasn't sure who exactly the lights were meant to impress.

But he had to admit they looked nice and added an air of festivity. He even hung a few on the *Lady Jane*. He drew the line at a tree, though. There wasn't nearly enough room in the cabin, even if Shelby didn't see a problem with losing a good portion of her own living space to a tree.

And while he could appreciate the control of the citizens of Magnolia Beach not to rush the Christmas season too early, they certainly embraced it in all its glory before the Thanksgiving leftovers were fully cold.

There might not be a single flake of real snow and some days were still warm enough not to require a jacket, but that didn't stop Magnolia Beach from turning itself into an outpost of the North Pole, with enough Christmas lights to make the place visible from the space station, random acts of caroling, and candy canes being handed out by everyone—and that was just by Saturday. By Sunday, the two main churches had competing crèches on their lawns, Santa had a massive chair set up at the post office for pictures, and everyone seemed to be awash in so much peace, love, and joy that he felt like he'd stepped into a greeting card.

And then on Monday, Shelby was out servicing boats wearing a Santa hat on her head.

"Really?" he asked.

"Yes, indeed," she answered without even a hint of self-consciousness. "I also have an elf hat and reindeer antlers. 'Tis the season, you know."

Later that afternoon, he found a brand-new Santa hat hanging off the door to the *Lady Jane*'s cabin. To his very great surprise—and a little bit of ironic shame—he put it on and wore it to the Shop-n-Save that afternoon, where he received many seemingly sincere compliments from the other shoppers.

You kinda had to love this place.

But then the cashier gave him a knowing smile as she rang up the steaks and sides and the bottle of wine that was obviously going to become a nice dinner for two and then winked as she told him to have a good evening.

That part was still a little unsettling and something he just couldn't get used to. *Especially* when she added, "Say hi to Shelby for me," like that wasn't weird. He had no idea who that person was—or that she'd know who he was, either. No wonder Shelby had sent him out of town to buy condoms.

He was pulling back into the parking lot at the marina

when his phone rang. That happened so rarely these days that it jarred him, and the number on the screen was unfamiliar—and not the South Alabama area code.

"Mr. Hyde? This is Leslie from the leasing office at Curran Towers. I have good news for you."

Curran Towers had been his first choice of places to live in Miami. A set of older buildings that dated back to the fifties, meticulously renovated and restored to feel both modern and retro. It was close to the office, convenient to everything, and perfect. It also had a waiting list of over two years, minimum. He'd put his name on the list simply as a laugh and put down a deposit at another apartment building that had been able to guarantee him a unit in January. "You do?"

"We have had a unit suddenly become available. You could take possession as early as December first and be all settled in before the holidays."

"December first?" he echoed. "That's next week."

"I understand it's very short notice, but you implied you were very flexible in your current living situation and could take possession quickly if we had an opening. I'm sorry if I misunderstood."

He was having a hard time catching up to this conversation, and Leslie's tone was turning testy. "No, no, you didn't misunderstand. I'm just thinking of the logistics . . ."

"We do have other people on the waiting list—"

"I realize that. You just caught me off guard. Of course I'll take it."

"Wonderful! Is the e-mail address we have on file for you still good?"

"Yes." He couldn't believe his luck, like the planets had suddenly aligned in his favor.

"Great. I'm sending the paperwork, tenancy

agreements, and all that to you right now. It will include the instructions on how and where to send all your deposits. We will need to receive those within forty-eight hours in order to hold the unit for you. There's also a schedule of available days for move-in. With everything going on with the holidays, there are blackout dates, so take a look and let me know what day or days are good for you. Welcome to Curran Towers."

"Thanks." He was left holding a dead phone, still processing what had just happened. That apartment had been a long shot at best. Having it fall into his lap like this seemed to be a good omen. People normally didn't move right before Christmas. But now, he'd have plenty of time to settle in, learn his way around, even get his office set up first instead of hitting the ground running while still living out of boxes.

He should probably e-mail Charlie tonight, letting him know the new arrival date. He might be able to start a little earlier than planned, maybe even catch the office Christmas party.

He'd lost some of his enthusiasm for the move and the future under the inertia of his stay in Magnolia Beach, but now that it was imminent, all the excitement came rushing back. *This was finally happening.*

But damn, that suddenly gave him a hell of a lot to do. He could easily set up an online transfer to make the deposits to the leasing company. He'd need to call the other apartment people and tell them he wasn't coming. Even though the deposit he'd given them might be nonrefundable, he'd take that hit. It wasn't a huge amount of money, and Curran Towers was a much better place. Granted, he was losing a bit of money on the slip rental, too, by leaving ahead of schedule, but it wasn't that much in the grand scheme of things.

It might not be too late tonight to get in touch with the movers and his storage facility in Chicago to get that scheduled, but if it was, that would have to be the very first thing on his to-do list tomorrow.

Packing up the *Lady Jane* would be easy enough—he didn't have that much stuff—but he needed to let Thomas's family know that they could arrange for the boat to be picked up whenever. Maybe Shelby could help—

Shelby.

That brought his spinning brain to a screeching halt. A feeling of dread settled around him at the thought.

It didn't make a lot of sense. It's not like Shelby didn't *know* he was going to Miami—even if she did think that would be another month from now. He wasn't breaking her heart or a promise. They were never supposed to be anything more than exactly what they were, and they'd never even pretended that they were more than that. This had had an expiration date right from the very beginning. The timetable might be accelerated, but the situation hadn't changed.

Then why the dread?

It wasn't that he dreaded telling her because he was worried about what she might say or how she might react.

He just didn't want to tell her. To *have* to tell her.

It wasn't that he didn't want to go. He just didn't want to say good-bye, either. At least not now. Knowing the day was coming was one thing; he was supposed to have another few weeks to ease into it—a natural progression to the inevitable end.

Since it was an inevitable, already-planned-for end, why did the timetable matter?

Maybe it was just because he was having a good time. Enjoying himself. Had he not gotten involved with Shelby, he'd be *ecstatic* that his time in exile had come to an end. This was his ticket out of here, a free pass out of this limbo and into the rest of his life. No more waiting.

And yet he was kind of sad, too. He'd miss it—all of it. Not just Shelby, but Magnolia Beach, the people he'd met and even sort of befriended . . .

Good Lord, this must be what Stockholm syndrome felt like.

But he still dreaded telling Shelby.

He grabbed his groceries and climbed out of the car. Shelby's Jeep wasn't in the parking lot—he hadn't planned to run and tell her this second or anything, but it still felt like a reprieve.

And speaking of Shelby and the marina . . . On top of everything else, he needed to finish up with that, too. He couldn't create full-scale plans or anything for her, but he did want to make sure she had a strong presentation to take to her family and, when she was ready, to a draftsman who could work with her.

It wasn't entirely for Shelby, either. He wanted to see this work out. It was a small thing, a project of little importance beyond the boundaries of Magnolia Beach, but it was important to Shelby and her family, and he wanted it to work. He wanted it to happen, even if he wouldn't be here to see it. It was proof his time here hadn't been wasted, a chance to leave his own little mark on the place.

But most importantly, Shelby wanted it, and for that reason alone, he wanted her to have it.

So he had a hell of a lot to do in a very short amount of time. But right now, he'd promised to cook for Shelby tonight, so that had to come first.

While the galley and gear on the *Lady Jane* were limited in both size and scope, he was able to put together a salad and potatoes and set a decent-looking table. He was no Martha Stewart, but he could cook a meal and serve it on something better than paper plates. He wasn't completely hopeless.

Shortly after the meat hit the grill, Shelby appeared, casually dressed in jeans and a sweatshirt and wearing her elf hat over hair that was still a little damp from the shower. "Oh, that smells *so* good," she said by way of greeting. "I'm starving."

He felt a small twinge of guilt when she rose up on her tiptoes to give him a quick kiss, even though he really didn't have a reason to be. "Nice hat, by the way," she added.

He had forgotten he was wearing it. "Thank you. And these steaks won't take long. Why don't you go in and open the wine."

"Will do."

When he came in with the steaks a few minutes later, he found Shelby on the couch, eyeing the table. "This is very fancy. Cloth napkins and everything. I feel a little underdressed."

"You seem surprised that I can set a table."

"Not surprised. Impressed. What's the occasion?"

He couldn't ask for a cleaner opening. "Honestly, when I told you yesterday that I'd cook tonight, there was no occasion."

"But there is now? Are we celebrating something?"

He set her plate in front of her. "In a way. I got some good news today."

Her face lit up. "I like good news." Even with the opening right there, Declan still hesitated at the moment of truth. "Well?" she prodded with a laugh. "Are you going to tell me, or will I have to guess?"

"There was an apartment in Miami that I was really

interested in. Just a great building, great space, really convenient to everything—perfect for me. But a lot of people want to live there, and they keep a waiting list. Today, they called and offered me an apartment."

She seemed genuinely pleased. "That's excellent. Definitely a cause for celebration."

"Yeah. But . . ."

Shelby's nose crinkled up. "There's a 'but'? Yikes. I hate the 'but.'"

That's what worries me. "I guess it's not really a 'but.' It's more of an 'and.'"

"Okay . . ." She sat up a little straighter. "And?"

He took a deep breath. "It's available December first. I mean, I can take possession as early as the first."

"The *first*? That's next week." She seemed surprised, but that was all. Just a blink of surprise, but nothing else—and he was watching pretty closely.

"I know that's almost a full month earlier than I planned . . ."

Finally, her eyes showed concern—but it seemed it wasn't for the reason he thought. "Is that a problem?"

I guess not. He'd braced himself for nothing. "Logistically, it can be done. It's a lot that has to happen in a short amount of time, though. I thought I'd have a couple more weeks, not days . . ."

"But that's *great* news," she insisted. "You'll be able to get all settled in before the holidays—ooh, I bet their New Year's Eve celebrations are epic."

"Probably very epic." He should be pleased by her enthusiasm, but it was jarring, especially after all the angst and dread of the last couple of hours . . . "I don't *have* to take possession right on the first, but they only allow people to move in on certain dates in December because they don't want the tenants disturbed during holiday parties and such, but I'll need to do it early in the month . . ."

"Of course. Plus, it will be good to have some time to learn your way around and find your footing before you have to start work."

"Yeah."

"Well," she said, lifting her wineglass. "Here's to your fresh start and new life in Miami. I know it will be awesome for you."

She is taking this well. But what had he really expected? They had an understanding, and this was part of it. Shelby was holding up her end perfectly, so any disappointment on his part was out of line. He'd thought she cared, at least a little bit, but he'd obviously invested more than she had. That was his bad. "Thank you."

"And let me know what I can do to help. Don't worry about the *Lady Jane.* Just tell the owners to let me know when they want to pick it up, and I'll make sure it's ready to go. I even know a girl in town who'd give it a good deep clean, if you want, before you return it."

"That'd be great, thanks." As odd as it was—as *self-ish* and wrong as it was—he was starting to get a little annoyed that Shelby was cheerleading this so hard. Hell, she seemed one second away from grabbing a box and starting to pack for him. That kind of hurt. But what *did* he want? Her tears? He wasn't that much of a jerk.

"I will be sad to see you go, though," she admitted, playing with her wineglass. "I know Magnolia Beach isn't really your kind of town, and I know you're probably really ready to leave, but I'm glad you came through here."

Maybe that was the best he could hope for. "Me, too. We should eat before it gets cold."

Shelby dug in with gusto, complimenting his cooking as she ate, acting as though nothing had changed.

But even though it irked him, he had to admit that nothing actually had changed. And maybe that was why it bothered him so much. Nothing *had* changed, really. The temporary layover was done, and he was moving on.

Except now he was going to miss her when he did.

Shelby waited until Declan's slow, even breaths told her he was asleep. Carefully untangling herself so as not to wake him, she eased off the bed and dressed. Tiptoeing out, she walked quickly back to the main building and took the back stairs two at a time into her apartment.

And only then did she let the knot in her stomach pull tight and take her breath away. She sagged against the door, then slid down it to the floor when her knees gave way.

Four years in the Magnolia Beach High School Drama Club and a lifetime of Southern repression had served her well the last couple of hours. She'd had no idea she was such a good actress. She'd kept her surprise and hurt to herself and been as perky and supportive as she possibly could. It had nearly killed her.

Get a hold of yourself.

She had no right or reason to react like this. She'd known since day one that Declan was leaving, she reminded herself. This wasn't exactly a surprise or anything, even if it was sooner than expected.

But that rationale didn't loosen the knot in her stomach at all. If anything, it pulled tighter.

I will not cry. She swiped at the dampness around her eyes and took a deep breath. She wasn't some weak female who shed tears over a man leaving her. Screw that.

Plus, that would just be stupid. Declan was just a guy, just a fling. It wasn't like he'd made her some kind of promise or led her on. In fact, he'd explicitly told her from the very start that he wasn't offering her anything but a good time. A *temporary* good time. If her feelings were hurt now, it was just her own damn fault.

They'd had some fun and now it was over. Life would go on, just as it had been before he came.

The problem was, she liked her life kind of like it was now. It was better somehow.

Maybe that was just the hormones and hurt talking; there hadn't been anything wrong with her life before he woke her up in the middle of the night six weeks ago. She'd been happy, perfectly fine, and satisfied.

But it still hurt.

Cupid padded over to her, nuzzling the side of her face in concern. She wrapped her arms around Cupid's neck and took a deep breath.

Six days, give or take. Maybe even a week, and then Declan would be gone. She could keep up the happy face that long. She certainly wasn't going to be some kind of weepy weakling, acting like there was something more than what there really was.

She had her pride, if nothing else.

Six days, though. Part of her believed it would be so much easier if he'd just leave now. Rip the Band-Aid off quick and fast rather than drag this out for nearly an entire week. But she did still want those six days to enjoy what she could—even if she would be internally divided the entire time, therefore keeping her from *fully* enjoying them. Of course, he could have just packed up and left next week without giving her any warning at all, which would solve the Band-Aid issue, but moving up his departure date without telling her would have hurt her feelings, too.

Damn it. There just wasn't anything easy about this. No way to split it where it didn't suck.

She took a deep breath. This wasn't supposed to suck. This was supposed to be like any other tourist boy she'd ever gotten involved with—brief, intense, and done.

Maybe the problem was that this hadn't been brief *enough*. You could get to know someone only so well when they were around for just a week or so. The time-line on this was just too long going in, and it had given her too much time to get invested.

So yeah, this was probably for the best. If it hurt this much now, another month in his company would be a real recipe for heartbreak.

But how she was going to smile and act normal for the next six days . . .

That she didn't know.

Chapter 15

"**Y**ou cut your hair." It wasn't much of a greeting and Shelby didn't like the accusatory tone in her own voice, but damn, she almost didn't recognize him when he appeared at her door, ready for their last trip to the Bait Box.

"Yeah," Declan said, running his fingers through what was left. "I was long overdue."

"I like it," Shelby lied. The short cut threw his cheekbones into sharp relief, and it looked good, but there was a knot in her chest. Although he was still casually dressed, Declan no longer looked like himself—or at least, the Declan she knew. This look was very much Big City Professional, upwardly mobile and ready to master the universe. It was too easy now to picture him in a coat and tie, and that just drew a stark line under the truth: Declan didn't belong here, not in Magnolia Beach, and so he was leaving, going back to where he *did* belong.

But she wanted to weep for the soft, silky locks she'd loved to weave between her fingers.

It was silly, and she forced the emotion back into the box. For once in her life, she was keeping everything under strict control, watching her words and expressions, carefully making sure no one—especially Declan—had any clue she wasn't happy, supportive, and perfectly freakin' *fine*. There would be no gloomy countdown dramatics from her.

She was determined to make the most out of the time they did have left. Life was too short and unpredictable not to make the most of good things. And Declan, as much as this was hurting her, was a good thing.

It wasn't much of a going-away party, but it was the best she'd been able to put together on such short notice, just a bunch of people at the Bait Box. Which, she realized as she surveyed the place, was not that much different than any other night they'd come here. There just wasn't a lot of variety to be had in Magnolia Beach, and she felt bad she couldn't do something more.

But Declan seemed to be having a good time. Even Jamie and Adam were being friendly—she couldn't hear their conversation, but it seemed appropriately manly and such with the posturing and backslapping that kind of thing entailed. Even Eli had been participatory, challenging Declan to a game of pool and losing before wandering off to a corner with his phone again. The boy had recently taken up texting like it was a second job. She should probably find out what was so—

"Oh my God. He cut his hair." Charlotte sounded heartbroken as she came up beside Shelby.

She pulled her attention away from Eli and joined Charlotte in a sigh. "I know."

"Colette told me he'd been in, but she didn't tell me she'd scalped the poor boy. That's . . . that's . . . What do you call hairdresser malpractice?"

"I think it's what he wanted."

"And you didn't try to talk him out of it?"

"It's not really my place, now is it? You gotta admit, though. He looks good with short hair."

"But he looked better with it longer. It was so pretty."

"But not really appropriate for an office job."

"I thought architects were creative types where dress codes were more lax."

"Honestly, I don't know, but he's been talking more about the job these last couple of days, and I think he's going to be the boss of a bunch of other people, so . . ."

Charlotte looked impressed. "Well, that kind of puts a different light on the whole 'in between jobs' thing."

"Yeah."

"How are you holding up?"

"Fine." Charlotte gave her a knowing look. "Really, I am. I'm going to miss him like crazy, but what else can I do?"

"I don't know. Have you asked him?"

"Asked him what?"

"What else you can do. Plans can change—"

"Be serious."

"I am. Maybe he might *want* to stay. You should ask."

Charlotte, bless her, could be an even bigger romantic than Shelby sometimes. At least *she'd* seen the light and taken off the blinders. "He's been waiting months to take this job. It's the job he's been working toward his whole life. He's not going to give that up. And I wouldn't ask him to, either."

"I think he cares about you. And I know you care about him. That can change people's wants."

"We've known each other for less than two months. That's not a relationship *anyone* should make major life changes for." And, Shelby reminded herself, Declan had left his girlfriend of five *years* for this job. He wanted it. And there was nothing wrong with that. It was *good* to have goals and plans. She had her own, and she wouldn't give those up for anyone, so it wasn't remotely fair to expect differently. "I'm going to go dance with Declan. Here, hold my drink."

Charlotte's eyes narrowed. She hated being cut off like that, and Shelby knew it. But being reasonable and mature was like balancing on a Windsurfer. If she broke that concentration, even for a second, she'd lose control and end up dunked.

Declan was touched, really, by the turnout at his going-away party. It seemed odd to have one here, in Magnolia Beach, when he'd left Chicago almost like a thief in the night. Part of that had been the situation—going from Suzanne's apartment to friends' houses like a lost nomad before coming up with a better plan—but he'd also lost a lot of friends in the breakup. He didn't blame them. Most of his friends had been Suzanne's friends first, and they'd been put in an awkward position, to say the least. While he had work acquaintances, the way he'd left his job had been a bit of a mess, too, so a trip to happy hour had been more than enough for them to see him off.

And while he was in the position again where most everyone here was actually Shelby's friend, not his, they'd made his time here enjoyable and seemed, if not sad, at least unhappy to see him go. That, at least, was something.

Shelby appeared at his elbow. "Wanna dance?"

There was no live band tonight, just the jukebox, and the dance floor was not nearly as crowded as it was on the weekends. While being one of the few couples on the dance floor would put them in everyone's sight, it was, at least, a chance to be somewhat alone in the middle of the bar. He was enjoying the party, but he hadn't had two words alone with Shelby all evening.

Shelby sighed as she relaxed into him, swaying easily to the music. "Thanks for the party," he said into her hair.

"My pleasure. I wish it could've been something a bit more than this, but I was under a gun to organize it so quickly."

"It's great, Shelby. Seriously." He pulled her a little closer. "I'm going to miss this," he said carefully.

"Me, too."

The confession shocked him. Shelby had been her usual perky self, helping him get things done in her usual no-nonsense way. She seemed neither personally happy nor sad to see him go, acting exactly as she had all along. It was driving him insane.

She might have said she was going to miss *him*, but it sure didn't seem like it was really bothering her. He didn't want her to mourn him after he left, for God's sake, but he'd like to think she'd at least notice when he was gone. He wanted to think he'd meant *something* to her, that he was someone she wouldn't later just shrug off as just another "tourist boy."

But she probably would, because that's what he was—another tourist drifting through Magnolia Beach—and she'd learned not to invest in them. Maybe he shouldn't take that lack of investment in *him* so personally.

But he couldn't help it.

It made him glad to be leaving. Staying longer would have only made this worse—if not for Shelby, definitely for him. He'd gotten used to her and would need time to detox—not more time to strengthen the habit.

The one thing he'd learned early on with Shelby, though, was that her enthusiasm alone was enough to buoy almost anything, and her enthusiasm for his move, for his grand plan finally coming together, bordered on manic. *She* was so excited for him that it felt wrong not to *appreciate* that excitement.

It was tangled and complicated, completely unlike

his move from Chicago—which while messy in some ways, still managed to be a clean, regret-free break. It was easier to just not think about it. To just roll along with the master plan.

Then Shelby squeezed his fingers and rubbed her cheek against his chest.

This was messy, but at least it would end well.

He'd have to settle for that.

Declan left on December third, right around three o'clock in the morning, so that he would arrive in Miami before the end of the business day. It was pitch black and overcast as she helped him load the last few things into his car, and the wind coming in off the water was damp and chilly.

All that worked to Shelby's favor, though—no one could look happy under those circumstances, so she didn't have to fake it anymore. She deserved a freakin' Oscar for her work this week keeping everything light and friendly and exactly the same as it had been. She was proud of herself.

"You didn't have to see me off. After all," he said with a smirk, "I did promise to never wake you up at three a.m. again."

That made her smile a little. They'd gone to bed early, really early, last night, to give them a couple of hours to *not* sleep before Declan had to. She'd been sated and floating in the afterglow, only for the alarm and now this chill to drive all of that out of her and leave her oddly empty. "Drive carefully," she said. "And obey the speed limits through those little towns across the Panhandle. They're serious about it."

He smiled and nodded. "It's been fun."

"Yeah. It has."

"Take care and feel free to call me if you have any questions about the plans I gave you."

All her dreams for her marina were on a thumb drive on her nightstand. She hadn't had a chance to really look at them, but Declan said it would get her started. But she couldn't think about that right now. "You, too, and I will." *But I probably won't.* The only thing making this bearable was the fact he wasn't saying something trite like "Let's keep in touch" when they both knew they wouldn't. There was no reason to.

Declan hugged her then, the warmth of his body taking the chill off hers as it blocked the wind, and she inhaled deeply, memorizing the scent of him. It was stupid and silly, but she couldn't help it.

After kissing her forehead, he lifted her face up to his. "I'm going to miss you, Shelby Tanner."

"You'll forget about me soon enough." She tried to sound flippant and teasing, but it didn't come out right. "But I'll miss you, too. I'm glad you ended up in Magnolia Beach."

"Me, too. And if you're ever in Miami, look me up."

"Will do." And that was the closest they could get to a future.

Declan opened his mouth to say something, then changed his mind and sighed deeply instead. "Bye, Shelby."

"Bye, Declan."

His engine seemed a little too loud in the silence of the darkness, and Cupid came to sit at her feet as he pulled out of the parking lot. Shelby patted the dog absently as she watched Declan's taillights until they were gone in the distance. Then she looked down at Cupid. "Well, I guess that's it."

Cupid cocked her head and whined low in her throat.

"Yeah. Me, too." She looked up at the dark sky and sighed. She'd done such a good job pretending she was fine the last couple of days, she was beginning to think she actually was. "Fake it until you make it" might be an actual thing.

Habit had her scanning the marina, checking for anything out of the ordinary before she went in, but nothing really was. Every boat was dark, including for the first time, the *Lady Jane*.

"It's just you and me again, puppy."

Cupid followed her in and up the stairs to her little apartment, which felt emptier than usual now. The bed was still rumpled from where she and Declan had been just a little while ago, and she rather worried that it would still be warm. It probably smelled like him, too, so while she should go back to bed and get some more sleep, she couldn't quite bring herself to do it.

There were limits to how okay she was. Or how okay she wanted to pretend to be. She might have come to the end of her ability to fake anything. At least she was alone now, with no reason to keep that up.

She curled up on the couch instead and pulled an afghan over her. Cupid jumped up to join her, shoving Shelby around until she was snuggled up against Shelby's chest.

She hadn't lied to Declan—or herself, really. It *had* been fun, she *would* miss him, and she was *glad* he'd come here. She had no regrets.

Well, just the one.

The one that made the fact he probably *would* forget her quickly enough sit heavily and painfully in her chest.

And while Shelby had never cried over a man before and had absolutely no desire to start now, at least Cupid would keep her secret.

Because she hadn't intended to fall for Declan Hyde, either.

And it sucked.

Chapter 16

Far more than simple distance separated Miami from Chicago. And Magnolia Beach might as well exist on a different planet.

Miami was warm and colorful, even in the dead of winter. The beaches were beautiful, the people even more so, and the whole place had a vibrancy that he could feel pulsing under the surface of daily life.

Not that he'd gotten to experience much of it. Aside from one walk on the beach the first day to celebrate just being here, his toes hadn't gotten near sand since then. There just hadn't been time. It hadn't taken that long to unpack the necessities—he didn't own that much stuff— but he hadn't been able to explore his new hometown much. Charlie had been more than happy to bring him in just days after he arrived, loading work on him to the point where he hadn't seen much of Miami beyond what was on his commute to and from work.

At least his new office had a decent view. That was a mark of success, right? The window office with the view of all the *other* buildings? After months in Magnolia Beach, all those buildings felt a little claustrophobic at first, and the city itself seemed too noisy and dense. And those big windows didn't even open to allow a breeze in, leaving him breathing stale, recirculated air as he sorted out the messes left for him by his predecessor—who officially didn't retire until January tenth, but seemed to have mentally retired months ago.

His new assistant had greeted him with a look of great relief and enough work to keep *him* busy until retirement.

It was nice to be needed, to feel valued and necessary at a job, but *damn*. Maybe he'd just gotten lazy during his stay in Magnolia Beach. Not just from his own untethered schedule of doing whatever, whenever, either; the whole town really did have that general ease of pace he'd seen on TV. He just hadn't realized he'd gotten used to it.

Jumping right back into real life had been a bit jarring.

But he'd adjust. This was what he'd been working toward his entire life. It had finally been handed to him—on a fifty-to-sixty-hour-a-week platter, granted—but he could honestly say he'd made it. That all the work had finally paid off. He'd achieved what he'd set his sights on, even when everyone had told him it would be damn near impossible.

He'd proved them all wrong. *Victory.*

Which he celebrated by collapsing on his couch every night, too tired and brain dead to do much beyond channel surf. He couldn't even enjoy the amenities of his apartment.

Supposedly the pool was very nice. Rumor had it there was a hot tub, too.

Declan stretched and leaned back in his office chair, propping his feet up on his desk and rubbing his eyes. On the wall across from him hung a horrible piece of "art"—one that he'd eventually replace with something else, but for now it added a bit of color to his otherwise drab office—of sailboats lined up at docks. It was very modern, with too-harsh colors and stylized lines, probably supposed to capture the vibrancy of Miami or some such tripe, but it made him think of the Bay Breeze Marina instead.

Not that he was sure why—nothing on earth, much less anything in Magnolia Beach, looked like that. But it made him wonder what, if anything, Shelby was doing with the marina. Had she shoved the thumb drive and all his notes in a drawer somewhere? Or had she gotten up the nerve to actually present the possibilities to her family? He wouldn't consider it a waste of time either way, but he hated to think of Shelby doing nothing with it, just continuing along in a place she *wanted* to love even more.

It wasn't like every idea he'd ever had or even every project he'd ever worked on came to fruition, but the marina was different somehow. It was more immediate; it carried a weight—an importance he'd actually felt. It meant something.

Very few projects actually meant something. He wanted that satisfaction, and he doubted he'd find it anytime soon.

And if nothing else, Shelby might think about him every now and then.

It was a little twisted. He admitted that much. But he couldn't help thinking of her. Her smile. Her sass.

He missed her. A lot.

Damn it, he wasn't supposed to be thinking about her, dragging out the whole "moving on" thing.

It was hard to fight the urge to call, just to chat and see how she was, but that would only drag the detox process out. Keeping one toe in Magnolia Beach was not healthy for him and would only make his transition to his new life in Miami longer and harder. It was better this way—it had to be.

His e-mail pinged, jerking him back to the present and Miami and the backlog of work on his desk. *Ugh*. He was three weeks into a new job, and he already needed a vacation.

I'll adjust. He'd settle in. He was just a little overwhelmed—it was hard to go from months of nothing to full-time. Zero to sixty in nothing flat. Once he got things here under control, he'd be able to have a life again, meet some people.

Then he wouldn't miss her anymore.

Shelby might publicly grump about being "volunteered" by her mother to help with the church Nativity play, but in reality, she loved it. She liked kids—in controlled doses—and she loved their excitement for the event. She wasn't the most faithful of church attendees throughout the year, but it just wasn't Christmas for her without the Nativity play.

And First Methodist put on one heck of a show every year, pulling out all the stops. Every few years, someone would get the great idea that live animals should be included in the play—really giving it that extra something—but Pastor Evans had placed a complete and final moratorium on that after the great sheep calamity the year Shelby was seven. She'd been one of the shepherds, dressed in a bathrobe with one of Gran's good napkins on her head, but it wasn't like she'd gotten any actual shepherding *training* before they'd set the sheep loose in the sanctuary.

It hadn't been her fault or anything.

But the edict had come down, with Pastor Evans

declaring there could be children *or* animals, but not both, and since then, the annual service called Holy Commotion had been human-only.

And all the Tanners were involved. None of her first cousins were still young enough to have parts, but when warm bodies were needed for grunt work, there was always a mom or an aunt ready to send one of them in.

The rehearsal was almost as good as the show itself. Lucy Evans, the pastor's daughter, was leading the kindergarten Sunday school class in an exuberant rendition of "Go Tell It on the Mountain"—complete with percussion instruments. Mrs. Evans and Aunt Claire were rehearsing Mary and Joseph, but the plastic Baby Jesus's head kept falling off and rolling out of the stable, causing the Star of Bethlehem to burst into traumatized tears. Helena, surprisingly, had stepped in to calm her down. Eli, Adam, Joe, and Graham were futzing with the lights, Jamie and Ryan had the younger boys and Todd West assembling risers around the altar for the angel choir, while her father, Uncle Dave, and Pastor Evans helpfully directed traffic. The adult choir was practicing up in the loft while the ladies of the altar guild were moving things to safety and out of reach of bored children. It was a zoo—minus the animals, of course.

Shelby was on costume duty, making sure the sheep and camels and donkey had all the proper tails and ears laid out on the pews where the kids could find them easily. She still had all the programs to fold, Wise Men gifts to make, and tables to set up in the Fellowship Hall for the after-play cocoa-and-cookie reception for the congregation. It was a lot to do, but she grabbed every task she could.

She needed the distraction. Badly. If she stopped moving or took her mind off her work even for a minute, she'd think about Declan, and she was determined *not* to think about Declan. She'd had one text from him, later the same day he left, letting her know he'd arrived in Miami safely, but her plan to put him out of mind, to quit him cold turkey, was not working.

She had to stay busy or she'd miss him so badly, it would hurt. She had to work until she was so tired each day that she fell asleep the second her head hit the pillow or else she'd lie there, staring at the ceiling. But Declan was even haunting her dreams, which meant she was always tired and grumpy and on edge. Even Charlotte had called her on it—kindly, and couched in concern and love, but still . . .

She was in bad shape, but the only way out was through.

She recruited Adam and Eli to go get the tables out of the storage closet and drag them into the Fellowship Hall, where Jamie and Aunt Mary were organizing the presents for the Toys for Tots pickup.

Helena came in, carrying a still-sniffling Star, who seemed to be nodding off against her shoulder. "Need some help?"

"I left the tablecloths in the nursery. Could you get them?"

"Will do. I can drop this one off for a nap while I'm in there."

Jamie waited until Helena walked away to come over. "She better be careful walking around with a baby on her hip. Aunt Mary will get all kinds of ideas."

"My mother already has all kinds of ideas. Trust me on that," Ryan said, joining them. He held a clipboard. "Do you know where your mother is?"

"If she's not in the sanctuary, no."

Jamie looked around and shrugged unhelpfully.

"I need a copy of the script so Joe and Graham can

mark the lighting cues. They don't want to screw it up their first year on the job."

"You're going to trust them to do that?" Shelby asked.

"I'm just glad I'm not going to have to do it. But no one seems to have an extra script."

"I have one," Shelby said. "I left it with the box of programs—which are still in my Jeep. I'll get my keys."

"Where do you want these, Shelby?" Eli gave an overdramatic groan as he set down another table.

"Anywhere for right now. I've got to go get something for Ryan."

She'd gone only about two steps when she heard, "Typical Shelby. Taking off in the middle, leaving us to finish up," followed by laughter.

It was an average, even expected, offhand remark and not even said with much snark, but it was the last freaking straw. She didn't even care which one of them actually said it. "Oh, shut up," she snapped, whirling around. "Just. Shut. Up. I'm sick of it, and I'm sure as hell sick of y'all."

Amazingly, all four of them did as she said, staring at her in varying stages of surprise. While everyone outside of their immediate circle continued on unaware, it felt very still and quiet where she was. "I'm not an idiot, and I'm not a child. I'm certainly not the dipshit you all seem to think I am." Her mother would kill her for cussing in church, but she'd worry about that later. "Maybe I *was*, but I was also younger, and people do stupid shit when they're young."

Jamie opened his mouth like he was going to say something, but she held up a hand. "Just hush. *You* caused the entire school to be evacuated because you were dicking around in chemistry and nearly poisoned your entire class. You"—she turned to Eli—"set a dog-house on fire, nearly burning down Granddad's shed in the process, just so you could practice putting it out with a garden hose. Ryan managed to drive a parade float into the damn *bay*. Don't even talk to me about my dumbass stuff when you've all got your own. At least *I* can say I was unmedicated at the time. What's your excuse?"

"Shelby . . ." Adam put his hand on her arm.

She shrugged it off and turned on him. "Halloween, 2008. Do I need to say more?"

Adam's lips thinned. "Actually, I'll pay you not to."

"It's not like the dog was actually *in* the doghouse at the time," Eli muttered.

"I'm not even sure how I got pulled into this," Ryan added.

Jamie gave her a look. "Jeez, Shel, we're just teasing you."

"I said *shut up*. I'm an adult, and I expect y'all to treat me as such. And until you can, I'll thank you to *keep* your goddamned mouths shut."

They were gaping at her like a school of fish, but she just turned on her heel and strode away, the anger buoying her all the way into the church's kitchen, where she leaned against the sink and took deep breaths.

"Nice shootin', Tex. Four bull's-eyes, and you didn't even need to reload." Shelby looked up to see Helena in the doorway, a big grin on her face.

Helena was still holding the tablecloths she'd been sent to get. She could only wonder who else had heard her explosion. "Yeah, well, maybe I . . ."

"Oh, honey, don't backtrack now. They're out there right now arguing about who's been the bigger asshole and why. I had to leave before I laughed in their faces, but I think you made your point."

"Ah, it's a Christmas miracle, then."

"And it's about damn time." She came to lean next to Shelby and patted her on the back. "Are you okay?"

She was angry. She was frustrated. She was a little ashamed of losing her temper like that, and upset that it had taken her so long to do so.

But she felt *great*.

Declan spent New Year's Eve at the beach, even though it was sort of drizzly. It was the principle of the thing. He had to get out of his apartment and office and breathe fresh air before he lost his mind. Not quite the "epic" New Year's celebration he'd been promised, but it capped off a really strange year in an oddly fitting way.

And now that it was a new year, he should probably start it off right. He wasn't the type of person who did the whole resolutions thing, but he was in a new place, with a new job, and it seemed important and also fitting to start the year off properly.

Which included finally unpacking so he wasn't still living like a college nomad.

He hung pictures on the walls, put books on the bookshelves and organized them, and rearranged the furniture.

By that evening, he had only two boxes left. They'd been the least important, just the odds and ends he'd collected over the fall, but they made him smile as he took them out of the boxes: a couple of new books he'd found in a bookstore in Mobile, some artsy tchotchkes he'd found in New Orleans that he'd liked, his water safety certificate that Shelby had framed for him in a tacky "Good Times in Magnolia Beach" picture frame as a joke.

That day on the boat seemed a long time ago. Shelby had been so earnest in teaching him enough so she'd feel comfortable with him living on the *Lady Jane.* He remembered her stretching out on the seat, enjoying the sunshine and telling him—with just a hint of exasperation—that "This is what you *do* on a boat. You relax." She'd said something about finding his Zen. It had been a new idea for him because Suzanne had been very into finding the Zen, too, only she'd made it sound a lot more complicated . . .

Damn, that had been the last time he'd actually talked to Suzanne. It was certainly the last day he'd thought about her for longer than a second or two, and he hadn't thought of her at all in the last month. He didn't feel bad about that, though. *She'd* been the one saying how he couldn't be happy, implied that he was some kind of failure for leaving Chicago.

How wrong she was.

Well, mostly wrong. He certainly didn't regret leaving Chicago, and even if he wasn't completely thrilled with Miami just yet, he was still settling in.

Shaking his head to clear it, he went back into the box. There was the T-shirt he'd been looking for and the extra power cord to his phone. He obviously hadn't been paying much attention while packing . . .

As if to prove that exact thought, tucked in the bottom of the box was a small, brightly wrapped box with a bow and a "Merry Christmas" gift tag signed only with an oddly shaped *S*.

He sat back hard. It was an unexpected gift, but even more unexpected was the wave of longing that crashed into him at just the sight of Shelby's handwriting. He tried not to think about her, really he did, and when he did think about her, he tried to distance himself from it, either by thinking about the marina or Magnolia Beach as a whole. That way he could miss her in the same way he missed Magnolia Beach—with fond nostalgia, as a pleasant interlude in his life. Nothing more.

It wasn't working.

There was no note attached to the gift; not that he expected one and not that it needed one. It was a gift, pure and simple. Shelby wouldn't attach strings to it, and though he felt bad now that he hadn't given her anything for Christmas—he hadn't been planning that far ahead in November—he doubted her feelings were hurt or that she'd even expected one.

If she had, she wouldn't have stuffed this in a box without comment.

Shelby loved Christmas, that much he knew, and she wanted him to have a Christmas present. Simple and honest. Quintessentially Shelby. Christmas itself had been just a day off for him. He hadn't put up a tree or anything, and being new in town, he didn't have a place to go. Oh, he'd had invites from coworkers, but he hadn't accepted any of them—spending the holiday with strangers somehow seemed worse than spending the holiday alone.

His sister had sent him a sweater that didn't fit and wasn't appropriate for Miami's balmy weather, and he'd exchanged e-cards with some friends back in Chicago. While he'd never been fully comfortable with the excesses of Suzanne's holiday celebrations, he wasn't unaware of the pitiful nature of this one.

But he hadn't been bothered by it—at least not much—until now, holding Shelby's package in his hands. Having witnessed Thanksgiving with the Tanners, he had to wonder what Christmas would be like . . .

Pulling off the paper, he found a CD—the semiprofessional kind, a step above one burned on a computer but not mainstream, mass-produced either. It was Chapman James, the folksy-rock band that played at the Bait Box occasionally. Now suddenly nostalgic, he popped it into his laptop and hit Play.

Who'd have thought that a born-and-bred Midwest city boy would ever miss a tiny little place like Magnolia Beach, Alabama? Closing his eyes, he settled back against the couch cushions and let his mind drift.

Magnolia Beach didn't have Miami's mix of culture and history, but it had its own unique kind, nonetheless. He'd gotten used to it. Six months ago, he'd have dismissed a small town as boring just out of hand, but now he couldn't. He could see the appeal.

Of course, a lot of that appeal was probably Shelby. He couldn't really separate the two. Magnolia Beach was her home. It was where she *wanted* to be, and she wasn't interested in hearing why someplace else might be better. She was happy right where she was.

That knowledge, plus her clear-eyed understanding of—and even enthusiasm for—his temporary state, had, in retrospect, been a great blessing. Otherwise, he might have made an ass of himself, trying to convince her to stay in touch, come for a visit, or even move with him.

That wouldn't have gone over well. He sighed.

Shelby's roots ran deep in Magnolia Beach. And while she'd never said it, he knew that her dyslexia was one of the reasons she felt she belonged there. She'd spent her whole life creating coping strategies in that place—she wasn't about to set off for strange new lands that lacked the people and places and situations she could handle easily and comfortably.

But that aside, Shelby really did belong there. She

was a piece of the place, and it was a piece of her, kind of a symbiotic relationship. It was part of what made her special, part of what he loved about her.

That was why he couldn't have her. He couldn't ask her to give that up.

At that point, a bright light finally went off: Shelby was honest to a fault, and that would give her a solid sense of fair play. She wouldn't ask him to do anything she wasn't willing to do herself. Since she would never give up her home, her dreams, or her happiness, she would never ask anyone else to do it, either.

Even if she wanted him to. He couldn't take the fact that she hadn't asked him to stay as any kind of statement of how she felt about him. That made him feel a little better.

She'd mentioned the drifters that came through Magnolia Beach, wondering if they were looking for a place that felt like home. He remembered now the odd tone of her voice—a mix of surety of her place and sadness for those who didn't have that.

And she'd asked him what he was looking for . . .

The band's cover of a John Prine classic ended, and he recognized the opening notes of the song he'd danced to with Shelby. The praise of Alabama's geographic diversity no longer seemed silly, and he found himself wishing for bay breezes and white sands. It was a pretty song, and he could remember the way Shelby fit perfectly against him, swaying gently in that moment.

Too late, though, he remembered the chorus, and it slammed into him before he could hit Pause.

Oh my love, you hold heaven in your hand,
My heart's down in Dixie, but my soul's in
    Alabama.

That's what that constant echoing emptiness in his chest was.

Hell, even Suzanne, who was not exactly known for her keen insight, had seen it. She'd told him point blank that he didn't know what he was looking for. That he didn't know what would make him happy.

And he'd been too focused on what he *thought* would make him happy to recognize happiness when it had dropped into his lap.

After all this time, he'd finally felt like he'd found "home."

And it was Shelby.

Shelby finished her speech and waited for Ryan to say something. He'd been a bit hesitant and amused at the beginning—she'd made an official appointment with Mayor Tanner through his secretary, trying to guarantee both his undivided attention and his serious consideration of what she was going to say.

It was a sly trick, she knew that, but an appointment on his schedule at least brought him into this meeting with the understanding this wasn't just some easily brushed aside cousin crap. Granted, having the mayor in her corner would help, regardless of his kinship, but more importantly, she needed her cousin on her side. Her forward-thinking town mayor and general contractor cousin. An ally that covered multiple bases.

If she could get him on her side. She'd spent two weeks pulling together the information and putting together—with some help from a very excited Charlotte—a presentation complete enough to win pretty much anyone over. Her fit in the Fellowship Hall had made Christmas a little uncomfortable, but it had given her the final kick and confidence to just do it, and she'd made the appointment to meet with Mayor Tanner as soon as the office reopened after the holidays. As far as she could tell, she was Ryan's first official appointment of the year. She wanted that to be portentous.

She needed to do this—and not just for the obvious reason of "it needs to be done." She needed something to consume her focus and give her something to do other than mope.

Because she certainly wasn't getting over Declan. Hell, she almost felt like she was getting worse, sliding deeper into the misery.

So now was an excellent time to try.

"I assume you have a plan to finance this?" Ryan asked. He'd been polite and attentive during her speech, and this was the first comment he'd made.

She nodded. It required a loan and possibly her firstborn child, but the money was there. "It's explained on slides seven and eight."

Ryan glanced over the presentation she'd printed out, then leaned back in his chair. "Seems like a good idea to me."

Shelby felt her jaw drop.

"Your budget needs to be redone, though. These estimates here"—he grabbed a highlighter and marked them—"are a little high. This is Magnolia Beach, not Miami Beach," he scolded. "And if you hire me to do these jobs"—he grabbed a different pen and circled a few things—"I can give you a good deal on labor that will save you some money. I'll write up a bid for you tonight, so you'll have better numbers to pitch to the bean counter."

She was still trying to get her mouth closed. "Really? You are on board for this?"

Ryan raised an eyebrow. "As mayor—which is why I assume we're having this conversation here—of course

I am. The marina is important to the overall economy and health of the town. Improvements to the property will benefit everyone."

"And as my cousin?" she asked carefully.

"It's going to tie up a lot of money and put the marina back in debt for a while, but that's just the cost of doing business. No one is going to starve or anything because of it, and the place could really use a face-lift. It's a smart idea, and your plan seems solid."

It was a good thing she was sitting down. "So you really do support me—it," she corrected.

Ryan frowned. "I'm not sure what you mean, Shelby."

"You don't think it's crazy or that I don't know what I'm doing?"

Ryan blinked. "No and no. Why?"

"Because I've brought stuff like this up before and everyone just blows me off like it's crazy talk."

"It's one thing to throw out ideas. Anyone can have an idea. But an idea with a plan and a budget and a fourteen-slide PowerPoint presentation can't be considered just crazy talk."

"And you don't think I'll flake on it? Screw it up somehow?"

He laughed. "I don't know. Are you still on your meds?" He held up his hands in surrender at the killing look she sent him. As a whole, the boys were doing better, but some things just never changed, it seemed. *Family. Ugh.* "I'm kidding. No one knows that marina better than you do. And no one loves it more than you do, either. I can't imagine you wouldn't ride herd hard on every detail."

She didn't know what to say. "Wow. Thanks."

"Did Uncle Mike say something to you to make you . . ." He trailed off and gave her a scolding look.

"You haven't even talked to him about this yet, have you?"

She shook her head.

"I see." He sighed. "You wanted me in your corner before you brought it up."

"Aside from the fact you're my *favorite* cousin and by far the *smartest* of the entire lot of Tanner boys—not to mention the best-looking, too—I wanted to run it all by you to make sure it was even feasible first."

"Fine. I've got your back."

She grinned at him. "And that's why you're my favorite."

"The competition isn't exactly stiff. When are you going to pitch this to your dad?"

"Today. While I'm feeling it. Any advice?"

Ryan blinked. "He's *your* dad."

"I know. But I don't want to come across as the young upstart, out to change everything . . ."

"But you are."

"But I don't want to imply that I think he's not running his own business properly. That it's not enough somehow."

"If you were talking about Uncle Dave, I might worry, but Uncle Mike's not like that. He's ridiculously proud of the way you run that place."

"Really?"

Ryan rolled his eyes. "Disgustingly so. To hear him tell it down at the diner, you're the love child of Neptune and Sam Walton, Queen of the Bay Breeze, and a better sailor, fisherman, and captain than any of the old guys running boats out of there."

It was a little hard to believe, but there was truth in the resigned and disgusted tone of Ryan's voice—this was something he'd both been forced to listen to and probably been compared against, too. Oh, that gave her a happy little giggle. Pride expanded in her chest. Daddy might not have said it to her, but he'd said it behind her back, and that was even better.

She'd been worrying herself for nothing. Trying to prove herself to someone who already believed in her.

Everyone else could go suck it.

"Whose handwriting is this?"

That jerked her back to the moment. He was looking at a page of notes that wasn't even supposed to be in there. Since her handwriting looked like the scratching of a stoned chicken and Ryan knew that, there was no sense trying to claim otherwise. "Declan's."

She wanted—and tried—to sound casual, offhand even, but she wasn't quite there yet. It caught up with her at the oddest, most unexpected, moments, wrapping steel bands around her chest. It was enough to almost make her wish Declan had never come to Magnolia Beach at all.

At least the owners of the *Lady Jane* had arranged for pickup pretty quickly. Seeing it there all day, every day, had done bad things to her emotions—even once she got past that point where she forgot he was gone and tried to visit.

But the hole it left in the neat lines of boats was appropriate, echoing the hole in her. She'd cried hard that day, scaring the dog.

And while making plans for the marina kept Declan close in mind, she'd learned to separate herself from it—some. She got to indulge her need to think about him, but in a way that kept her at a distance, too. It wasn't a big distance, but it was something, at least.

Either that, or she was just some kind of glutton for punishment.

Ryan nodded. "I figured he was involved in this somehow. You probably saved a ton of money getting this much done for free. Not that a draftsman will be cheap, but this is a big start. That's one good reason to hook up with an architect when he passes through town."

There was an ugly undertone to that Shelby didn't like, as if she'd traded favors. "I didn't ask him to, you know. He did it on his own," she snapped.

"Whoa, there. I never said you did. I just think it was nice of him."

"Well, he had some spare time on his hands."

"I liked him."

So did I. "Yeah."

Ryan looked at her evenly. "You miss him, don't you?"

"Of course." She went for an easy and light tone. She was getting better at it. "He's a good guy. And we had a good time."

"Did you fall for him?"

"What? No." *Well, that was a little too adamant.*

Ryan seemed to agree. "Helena seems to think so."

"I like Helena, and I know you think she hung the moon and the stars, but she's not infallible." *And she needs to keep her opinions to herself.*

"But she does know how she felt after she left, and I know how I felt after she left, and I hate to think of you feeling like that at all."

That was sweet. "Thank you for worrying, but don't. It doesn't matter."

"It doesn't?"

"No. You and Helena are an anomaly. The stuff of movies and love songs."

Ryan looked a little sheepish and proud at the same time.

"Declan is in Miami," she continued, "and I'm here. He's not coming back and I'm not going there."

Ryan started to speak, but she held up a hand. She didn't need people throwing false hope at her, regardless of their good intentions. "I don't regret the time we had together, but I knew going in that it was only temporary. I'll be fine."

If she kept saying that, eventually it had to be true.

"So instead, you're going to rebound by building a giant freakin' marina."

"Actually, my plan is a little smaller and simpler than that. That was an opening gambit," she confessed, "so I could negotiate down to what I really wanted."

Ryan nodded, impressed. "You frighten me, Shelby Tanner. You really do."

"Good." She stood and stuck out her hand. "I thank you for your time, Mayor Tanner."

Ryan returned the handshake professionally. "My pleasure, Miss Tanner. Good luck with your project. The citizens of Magnolia Beach appreciate your desire to improve our town and the benefits it will offer both the tourists and the people who live here."

"I'll see you at Gran's on Sunday." On impulse, she grabbed him into a quick hug. "And thank you," she whispered, "for supporting me."

"Always."

Chapter 17

"If you ask me, you should go to Miami."

Shelby had asked Charlotte nothing of the sort. "Do you want another drink?" wasn't even in the same ballpark as *any* question that might be answered with, "I think you should go to Miami."

"There is plenty of beer right here. If not behind the bar, someplace in Magnolia Beach—or at least someplace in Mobile County—will have more beer. There's no need to make a beer run to Miami."

"That's not what I meant."

Shelby lined up her shot. "Three ball, left corner pocket."

"I mean, really, Shelby, why not?"

"I do not want to go to Miami, I have not been invited to visit Miami, and I haven't even spoken to Declan since he left."

"Have you tried?"

"No." The three rolled in and she lined up the six, hoping Charlotte would take the hint.

"I broke up with Jacques, you know."

Shelby delayed her shot. "I'm sorry, honey."

"He's going back to LSU."

Shelby gave her an innocent smile. "Maybe you should go to Baton Rouge with him."

"Good Lord, no. It's too humid in Baton Rouge. And he was allergic to Chester anyway."

"Then I rest my case."

"But it's different," Charlotte insisted.

"How? If you're dating a guy who's only in town temporarily, you don't get to follow him home when he goes. You're not some kind of lost puppy."

"I was just a pleasant diversion for Jacques. I knew that."

"Ditto."

"Nah. You can try to lie to anyone else in this town, Shelby Tanner, but don't you dare try to lie to me. I know you. It was more than a fling."

"Not to him." Charlotte knew she was hurting; there was no sense trying to hide it from her.

"I'm not so sure about that. I saw how he looked at you. The boy was crazy about you. Probably still is."

"Regardless, he is currently about eight hundred miles away. It puts a real damper on the romance. And no, long-distance is not an option."

"Miami is not a bad place."

"For other people."

"I'm sure you'd adjust."

"Need I remind you that I wasn't invited to go to Miami. I'm not some stalker to follow him to a different city."

"Well, did you *ask*?"

"What? No!"

Charlotte sighed. "Then how do you know—"

"Look, it goes both ways. Declan could have said something about staying here, but he didn't."

"And again, I must say, 'Did *you*?'"

"He was a little too busy actually leaving, you know. The closest thing to anything was a 'look me up if you're ever in Miami.'"

"Maybe he's shy and needed you to make the first move. Guys like Declan don't just wander into Magnolia Beach every day. You got lucky on that. You can't expect God to send you a great guy who's *also* a mind reader."

Argh. "New topic," she declared. "I'm done with that and am not going to talk about it any longer. Or ever," she stressed when Charlotte opened her mouth to argue. "It's over. It's done. Now, six ball, side pocket."

She hit the ball a little harder than necessary, but it made a satisfying sound as it slammed into the pocket.

"Yeah. Over and done," Charlotte muttered. "I can tell."

Shelby felt a little bad about snapping at Charlotte like that, so she missed the next shot and left a duck for her to take. Charlotte meant well, Shelby knew that, but that kind of talk just wasn't helpful. Maybe she should have spoken up, been honest with Declan about how she felt, but aside from the obvious ground rules of any no-strings-attached affair, she'd been broadsided by Declan's gleeful willingness to get the hell out of Dodge the moment the opportunity presented itself. Confessing some deeper emotion would have been outside of the rules and unfair to him—not to mention potentially traumatizing to her.

And what could she have possibly hoped to gain? Declan sweeping her off to Miami to the orchestral strains of big-budget movie soundtracks where she'd know no one and have to build a life from scratch? Had Charlotte, lost in her wild romantic notions, not realized that she just couldn't do that?

At best, a declaration from her would have led to awkwardness and a lack of direct eye contact for the entirety of the short time it would take for her to die of shame.

No, it was brutal and heartbreaking, but it was the right way for things to be, all things considered. She'd be just fine, damn it.

Charlotte sank the easy shot then, high on her own success, tried for a harder one—and nearly made it. "Can I have a do over?" she asked.

"Of course," Shelby answered, resetting the balls. "This time think about trying to make the cue ball just barely kiss the fourteen right..." She trailed off because Charlotte looked pale. "Are you okay?"

"Yeah. Look, honey, don't yell at me, and I promise I'll never broach this topic again, but I just want to make sure I'm really clear on one thing."

Shelby prayed for patience. "Okay, what?"

Charlotte laid her stick on the table and walked to Shelby's side, grasping her arms and making Shelby stare her directly in the eye. "You're *positive* Declan didn't have feelings for you? And you're sure he didn't know how you felt about him?"

Boy, the knife just didn't get any duller no matter how many times it stabbed into her heart. "Yes, and yes."

"Then why is he here?"

That simply wasn't possible. "W-w-what?"

Charlotte tightened her grip on Shelby's arms, making it impossible for her to move. "Look at me. Don't look over there yet. Just look at me for a second. Tell me if this is a good thing or not."

Caught in surprise, shock, and wonder, she couldn't quite form a thought, much less a sentence. "I ... I don't ... I guess. Maybe?"

"If you don't want to see him or talk to him, you don't have to."

That brought her right back into focus. "Why? Does he look angry or something?"

Charlotte shook her head. "No." A little smile quirked her mouth. "I just want to make sure you want to open this up again."

Shelby took a deep breath. "He came all the way here from Miami. I think I should at least find out why."

"I think you know why."

A girl could dream. And on the really slim, off chance that Declan was about to offer her that impossible dream of a happily-ever-after on the beaches of Miami, at least she'd have the one really nice, really romantic moment when he asked to remember for the rest of her life. She nodded.

Charlotte turned her around, and she saw Declan. Her first silly thought was, *It's January, why is he not wearing a jacket?* but that was quickly replaced by the easier to process, but much more fraught, *I've missed him so much.*

He looked tired, with a two-day stubble and a wrinkled, untucked shirt. He also seemed very hesitant, hanging next to the door in a very un-Declan-like manner, as if he wasn't sure whether to approach her. He gave a small wave when he caught her eye, but he still hung back.

He came all the way from Miami. I could at least cross the Bait Box.

While things seemed to be continuing on around them as normal, Shelby couldn't help noticing the subtle staring of people trying to hide behind normal-looking conversations. Everyone was watching, even as they pretended they weren't—well, except for Charlotte, who was flat-out staring—and Shelby hadn't felt this conspicuous since . . . well, *ever.* Then Declan smiled at her and her heart flipped over almost painfully. She'd only thought she was getting better about this.

Guess not.

And, damn it, now she was standing right in front of him and she didn't know what to do. A hug? A handshake? What the sweet hell was she supposed to say?

She ended up hugging her own arms and settling for a lame, "Hey."

"Hey."

"I'm surprised to see you here."

"Yeah." He took a breath like he was going to say something, then stopped and shook his head slightly. Finally, he said, "I wanted to thank you for the Christmas present."

That was unexpected. *And a little disappointing.* "You're very welcome. But you didn't have to come all this way for that." She tried to break the tension. "A phone call or even an e-mail would have worked just fine."

He didn't laugh at her joke. "Can we talk for a second?" He looked around at the small crowd in the bar, many of whom had given up even attempting to be sly and were now openly staring. "Privately?"

"Um, sure. I guess outside will do. Let me grab my sweatshirt."

She started back toward the table, but Charlotte met her halfway, practically throwing the hoodie at her. *Yeah, this wasn't embarrassing and awkward at all.*

The Bait Box had a few outside tables and chairs for when the weather was nice, and Shelby let Declan lead her over to one of them as she zipped up against the chilly night air. Before she could sit, though, Declan grabbed her hand. He pulled her close and held their clasped hands against his chest. His other hand came up to stroke her cheek. "God, I've missed you."

The longing in his voice choked her. "I missed you, too."

The smile she got in return nearly broke her heart. "Really?"

"Of course." And this was the now one perfect moment where Declan stared deep into her eyes, and she felt the subtle change in his body that meant he was going to kiss her . . .

Shelby knew then that she'd made the biggest mistake of her life. *Again*. This was going to break her heart for sure, and she wouldn't survive it.

She took a step back, seeing the flash of disappointment in his eyes, but forcing herself not to soothe it. She released his hand and shoved both of hers deep into the pockets of the hoodie, restraining them from the temptation of reaching for him. Sitting in one of the chairs and feeling the cold seep through her jeans, she tried to put an emotionally neutral yet interested smile on her face and strove for a normal tone. "So how's Miami?"

"I hate it."

She blinked. "You *hate* it?"

He dragged his hands through his hair. "I hate my job, I hate the people I work with, I hate the noise and the traffic . . ."

"But you've got a great apartment, right?" she teased, still trying to break the tension.

"Well, I kind of hate my apartment, too."

"Why?"

He took a deep breath. "Because you're not in it."

How was it possible to have one sentence fill her heart

with joy and smash it at the same time? She allowed herself to wallow in the joy for just a brief second before getting real again. "Declan, don't."

"Don't what?"

"Don't say anything else." She took a deep breath, hating the fact she was going to be the one to have to actually say it. It would be totally real then, and she wouldn't be able to take it back. "You and I are just not meant to be. We had our thing, but now it's done. I don't regret anything, but it's best that we both just make a clean break and move on."

Shelby's words hit hard, and if not for the tension he could see in her jaw and the pained look in her eyes, the blow probably would've been fatal.

"Shelby—"

She held up a hand. "Declan, please. I can't choose between you and the entirety of my life, so please don't ask me to. Just go back to Miami. It'll be better that way. Easier."

He understood. She just didn't know that yet. "I'm not asking you to choose, Shelby."

She blinked. "Pardon me?"

He grabbed a chair and dragged it over, sitting knee to knee with her. Her hands were deep in the pockets of her hoodie, so he placed his hands on her knees instead. "All I want to know is, do you love me?"

Shelby's eyes widened in surprise at the bald question, then she quickly dropped her gaze to her lap. He nearly laughed. Shelby, who lacked a filter and had no problem asking personal, prying questions, had been made uncomfortable by his bluntness.

"You came all this way just to ask me that?" she finally said, still not making eye contact.

"Yeah." She'd avoided answering, sending the ball back into his court instead. He had nothing to lose except his pride, and he was willing to risk that rather than risk losing out by playing it safe. This was new territory for him, but he knew he was doing the right thing. He just hoped the gamble would pay off. "Because I'm in love with you."

That got her attention. Shelby's head snapped up like it was attached to a bungee cord.

"It took me longer than it should have to figure that out, but once I did, I had to come tell you. I had to find out if you felt the same way."

She swallowed, hard, as tears welled in her eyes. "I do. It nearly killed me to let you leave."

Relief poured into him. The possibility that he'd been reading this wrong, letting his hope attach a feeling to Shelby that she didn't actually have, had nagged at him the whole trip up here.

"But—"

He knew where that "but" was heading and cut her off. "Do you remember telling me about the drifters that come through Magnolia Beach?"

Her eyebrows knitted together as she thought. "Um, not really."

"You wondered if they were looking for a place that felt like home. Well, *this* feels like home to me."

"You can't mean Magnolia Beach."

"Did you not hear the part about how much I hate Miami? Me, a city boy, can't stand the city and wants to move back to Magnolia Beach. I miss this place, and the people and . . . *you*. This place feels like home because you're here. And so I want to come home." Her eyes were wide, but he couldn't tell if that was a good thing or not. "If that's okay with you," he said, giving her an out while praying she wouldn't take it.

Shelby launched herself at him with a force that rocked his chair back on its hind legs and nearly caused them to overbalance. Catching her, he shifted his weight forward to keep himself from falling and cracking his head open on the concrete, then settled her in his lap, her thighs on either side of his.

Shelby cupped his cheeks in her hands and lowered her mouth to his. It was the sweetest, most important, most memorable kiss he'd ever participated in, and he didn't want it to end. But it eventually did, and Shelby was grinning at him. "I take that as a yes."

"Yes. I love you, and yes, I want you in Magnolia Beach." Shelby punctuated each "yes" with a quick kiss. "I missed you so much it hurt, and I wasn't sure it would ever stop hurting."

He slid his hand into the warm, soft hair at the nape of her neck and pulled her in for another kiss. A split second before his lips touched hers, though, she pulled back, her eyebrows furrowing. "What are you going to do, though? You just moved to Miami. And what are you going to do for a job? We don't build a lot of new buildings here."

"I'll pack it all back up and come back. As for the job, Mobile's not that far, and I'm sure they have a need for architects. But I'm not worried. I'll figure something out, even if I have to design fancy doghouses and sell the plans on the Internet."

She looked at him strangely. "That's oddly specific."

He shrugged. "I had a two-hour delay at the Miami Airport, a four-hour trip, and an hour-and-a-half drive from Pensacola today. I've had a bit of time to think about things. The point is, I'll make it work. I've spent my whole life working towards a goal, and I only just now figured out I really didn't want it. What I *want*, what I've been *looking* for, is *you*. Everything else, all the other pieces . . . they'll all fall into place."

"You really mean that, don't you?"

"I do. And trust me, that surprises me a hell of a lot more than it surprises you."

"Thank you," she said seriously.

"For what?"

"For not making me choose. I would've been miserable no matter what."

"Well, I can't have that. My main job now is to make you happy. Any and every way I can."

She smiled and traced a finger along his jaw. "You can start by taking me home."

"That would be my pleasure."

Epilogue

Shelby stuck her arm through her shirtsleeve and banged her funny bone against the cabinet. The long string of curse words that erupted from her mouth were partly from the pain in her elbow, but were also fueled by the frustration of living on a stupid boat that was so damn small she could barely turn around without running into herself.

Declan grinned at her as he shoved his shaving kit into that same cabinet and closed the door. The facilities on the *Castaway* were very basic, so they used the marina's bathhouse for showering and such. They'd never be able to both get ready in the mornings otherwise. Getting dressed at the same time was difficult enough. "You like boats, remember?" he teased.

"I do like boats," she said, rubbing her elbow and looking for her shoes. "I also like having a little bit of space to breathe. And I know," she said, forestalling what she knew Declan was going to say, "it's only temporary."

The problem was that *everything* was temporary right now. The small trailer serving as the Bay Breeze office was temporary, too, and she wasn't dealing well with that, either. On the one hand, she was completely thrilled that the work had begun, that the marina was on its way to bigger and better things, but the first step had forced her out of the main building as it was gutted and the third story—which would be her new living space, as she still wasn't willing to move off-property—added on.

The *Castaway* was smaller than the *Lady Jane*, but it beat the other option, which was moving back into her old room at her parents' house. And although Mom and Dad would tolerate, if not ever condone, Shelby living with Declan in her apartment at the marina, they would not allow Declan to move into Shelby's room with her. So she'd borrowed a boat. Declan had managed to live just fine on a boat for several months, and he'd practically never even been on one before.

Admitting she was not loving this was simply not an option.

Whenever she felt like she was going to lose it and start screaming, she'd go sit on the bench up by the trailer and make note of how things were coming along and dream about how wonderful it would be once it was finished. It was going to be slow going, as things were planned in specific stages on a careful timeline to keep the marina open and functioning during the busiest parts of the year, but it was happening, and she could take pleasure in that.

Today, though, she didn't have time to sit and breathe calmly in the midst of her construction site. In fact, she wondered if she'd ever have time to sit and do nothing ever again.

Be careful what you wish for.

To her drop-jawed surprise, Daddy had been on board for this idea practically before she'd finished making her opening statement. *He'd* wanted to make changes, but didn't know if Shelby wanted to, and since he was soon to be retired, he didn't feel it would be right to make them since he wouldn't be dealing with it after. Then to top it all off, Daddy had been more than happy to retire completely, becoming simply a silent partner, leaving the Bay Breeze entirely in Shelby's hands. He'd have done so sooner, he said, but he didn't want to overwhelm her if she hadn't wanted to take it on—especially since Jamie was hands off, and she'd be running it alone.

And it had been a bit overwhelming at first. Extremely validating and good for her ego, but still overwhelming and quite a pain in the ass.

"I'm probably going to be late getting home tonight," Declan said, draping a tie around his neck and letting it hang. But he'd let his hair grow back out a bit, offsetting the stuffiness of his work wardrobe. "I've got a late meeting. I'll just meet you at the Bait Box."

Although Shelby had been worried that Declan wouldn't be able to find a job he liked and that, without one, he'd begin to resent her for it, he'd surprisingly found work in Mobile pretty easily. It seemed like a bit of a commute to her, but Declan was used to big-city traffic dragging out his commute anyway, and he insisted it wasn't that much of a difference, timewise and far less maddening than inching through bumper-to-bumper traffic.

But he had, during the weeks it had taken him to find a job, designed and built a pretty amazing doghouse for Cupid—who far preferred it to joining them on the *Castaway*.

During those first few weeks, Shelby had been on edge, worried that Declan would wake up and realize he didn't want to live in Magnolia Beach and just move on. All of his stuff was in storage, so it wasn't like it would have been difficult for him to beat feet quick out of town.

But he hadn't.

It took a little longer for her to accept that he wouldn't tire of her, either, or regret his choice, but she figured if the last four weeks on this tiny, silly boat hadn't pushed him over the edge and out of town, he might just be here for the long run.

While they might be all in each other's pockets and tripping over each other, the last four months had been incredible. And living on this boat might suck, but she wouldn't trade it for anything.

That didn't mean she wouldn't be glad to move off the boat and back into her building, though. Hopefully very soon.

Shelby dropped her brush and it skittered under the small table. On her knees, she crawled after it, bumping her head hard as she did. She lifted her hand to rub the sore spot, and the back of her hand brushed against something soft. She jumped at the strange and unexpected sensation, then tried to see what it was.

A felt bag had been duct-taped to the underside of the table. *What the* . . .

"What are you doing?" Declan dropped to a crouch next to her.

"There's something under here," she replied, picking the tape loose with her fingernails.

"Don't! Do . . . that," he finished with a sigh. They were both under the table now, and Declan looked extremely uncomfortable—but not because of the tight squeeze. He took the bag out of her hands.

"What is that?" she asked carefully. Taping it up under the table seemed to be something to do with drugs or guns or other illegal things, but she couldn't imagine Declan involved with anything like that.

"Well, it was supposed to be a surprise."

"For me?"

"Yes, for you. I assumed you wouldn't find it under here." He opened the bag and took out a small box. As he started to open it, Shelby recognized the logo from a jewelry store in Mobile, and her heart began to pound hard in her chest. "I was going to wait until we got moved back into the building, but . . ."

He put the ring in his palm, and held it out to her. It was lovely, almost delicate, a simple band with inset gems all the way around catching the light.

"I picked this so that you might actually be able to wear it. I know a solitaire is more traditional, but it would get caught on everything. This should be small and smooth enough not to get in your way while you work." He smiled self-consciously. "Do you like it?"

"It's . . ." Her throat was tight, so she swallowed and tried again. "It's beautiful."

Declan slid the ring on her finger. It was a good fit. When he didn't say anything else, she finally asked, "Does this mean you want to get married?"

"More than anything. Tomorrow even, if you want."

She tried to hug him, but the space was too small to maneuver, and she bumped her head again. Laughing, Declan scooted out and helped her to her feet when she followed him out, then met her halfway for a kiss.

"Will you marry me, Shelby?"

"Yes." She kissed him again. "But not tomorrow. And probably not until the fall when things calm down some. Is that okay?"

"That's fine." He kissed her nose and shrugged. "It's

not like I'm going anywhere." Then he cursed. "Except to work, and now I'm going to be late. This is so *not* how I planned this."

"Things don't always go as planned."

Declan took a long look around the tiny boat and laughed. "Tell me about it."

Shelby smacked his arm. "Hey, now—"

He pulled her in close. "I certainly never planned on you," he said quietly before kissing her one more time— a kiss that was equal parts love and lust, want and need, that left her legs shaking and her heart beating triple-time.

Who said nothing exciting ever happened in Magnolia Beach?